UPROOTING

SUZIE CARR

For anyone struggling to find their way home...

ACKNOWLEDGMENTS

I have many people to thank for their guidance with this book. Two of them had a direct impact on the story's initial spark, Ash Harris (a.k.a. AcousticAsh) and Michelle Barrow. AcousticAsh, an amazingly talented musician, joined me on my Curves Welcome podcast last year and composed a song, "Anxiety," half an hour before the podcast began. AcousticAsh performed it live, and I was moved to tears. The lyrics became the inspiration behind Harper Ray's character, and with AcousticAsh's generous permission, those soulful lyrics are shared in this story. Michelle Barrow, a former colleague of mine at UMBC, one day came into my office and planted a seed by encouraging me to create a character who is a green witch. Ivy Homestead's character sprang to life in the moments that followed our rich conversation. Michelle shared her insights into the amazing world of witchery with me, and the spells, teas, and rituals that appear in this story were all gifts from her. Michelle, I am grateful for your insights, as well as your guidance as a beta reader. To my other beta readers, Jennifer Morris, Ted Beveridge, and Dana Holmes, I remain incredibly grateful for your honesty and time. You helped me turn this story from its infantile, confusing state to one that is complex and well-grounded. I also have Jennifer to thank for being my sounding board for the blurb writing and cover design sessions. To my editor, JoAnn Collins, thank you for the gift of your eagle eyes! To Amelia Berger, I'm grateful for the feedback you provided me in the initial ARC release. You helped me get a very important part of this story correct, and I'm forever thankful to you for that. To McGee Mathews, I'm truly thankful for you taking the time to read Uprooting and offer your guidance in so many of the areas, especially the musical parts! To Joanna Darrell, for your generous support and continued faith in my ability to create work that matters in this world. And finally, to my readers, I am humbled and thankful for your continued support.

1

SHOW UP. STAY IN FLIGHT

HARPER

arper Ray first met Barry and Nancy when they found her and her family huddled together in a park after the sun had settled into the summer evening horizon. Harper and her little sister, Tess, had arrived home from school that day to find their door boarded up. Their parents were both high in the stairwell on the opposite side of the dilapidated building they lived in.

Red-eyed and stupefied, they would've ended up sleeping in that stairwell had Harper, in all of her nine years, not had the good and sober sense to lead them across the street to her favorite tree in the city park.

They lost everything that night, their home, their clothes, her notebook with her songs in it, the necklace her best friend gave to her for her birthday three weeks before.

Everything.

Her parents were out cold, sleeping off their drug-induced highs, when Barry and Nancy sashayed toward them holding hands.

"Are you okay?" Nancy lowered herself and showered Harper and Tess with the first of many kind, loving smiles.

"We're fine. Just enjoying the nice summer breeze." Harper had been programmed since her parents first started abusing drugs to never complain or else end up with a painful pinch on her forearm. That's what a daughter did when she had caused the car accident that served as the catalyst for an opioid drug habit. The ill-timed outburst of laughter that she had in the backseat that day would haunt her, and the rest of them, forever. She learned that day to never startle a driver while maneuvering on a snowy road.

Barry remained stoic in what Harper would soon recognize as his typical protective stance. He surveyed her sleeping parents. "Storms are moving in soon. Let's wake your parents."

Harper put up her hand. "No."

He eyed her hand.

"They're tired. They worked fifteen hours today."

He studied her. "Are you hungry?"

"Yes," Tess said, quietly.

"No, we're not," Harper corrected over the low and constant growl in her tummy.

Her father stirred awake. He sat up and wiped drool from his lips, shaking Harper's mother. "You can move along now," he said to them. "We were napping."

Harper would later learn that Barry and Nancy navigated the ornery sides of drug addicts often by keeping a subtle and gentle tone. That's what happened when you ran a community center. "Your daughter told us about how much she enjoys the summer breeze," Barry said.

Harper's father grabbed her wrist and squeezed it. "She's always been a fan of summer."

Her mother still had not woken. Harper shook her, and finally she groaned.

The man who Harper would soon trust more than any other adult spoke to her with his eyes and told her everything would be okay. Even back then, she and Barry had a connection.

Barry and Nancy wouldn't have them sleeping on the ground. With their gentle tones, they managed to talk her father into following them to the Life Bridge Community Center, a place where families could stay until they found residence.

As they walked and Barry talked about innocent things like the weather and the smells of the city, Nancy removed her sweater and wrapped it around Tess's shivering skinny body. Harper and Nancy shared a knowing smile. Seven-year-old Tess needed protecting more so than Harper.

For the following several weeks, her family stayed at Life Bridge. During that time, she and Tess met a boy named Andrew. He spent his spare time there when not in school. Harper and Andrew bonded as *The Flintstones* played on the big television in the rec room each afternoon. They'd share snacks and tell each other their dreams for the future. Andrew wanted to grow up and become a kind man like Barry, and Harper wanted to grow up and be free like a butterfly.

Thank goodness for Life Bridge. Four years later, long after their mother had overdosed and shortly after their father killed a pedestrian while drunk driving, Life Bridge connected her and Tess with Andrew again.

They even ended up living in the same foster home.

That only lasted a year, though, because Andrew was kicked out of their shared home when he told their foster parents that he liked both boys and girls after they caught him kissing a boy. Their foster parents left him out like a dog in the wild, and Nancy and Barry swooped in to his rescue. They welcomed him into their family like one of their own children.

Harper wished the terrible foster parents would've kicked her and Tess out, too, and that they would've ended up in that family who loved deeply. Although, with her and Tess being a package deal, and Nancy's elderly mother suffering with Alzheimer's, they didn't have the capacity to care for them, too. They did continue to bring Harper and Tess along on their family outings to the beach and to their favorite snowball stand on hot summer days, which strengthened their familial bonds.

Harper cherished those moments. They helped her get through the rough times in her cold, hardened foster home where no one smiled, laughed, or paid her and Tess any attention.

It didn't take long for Harper to decide that if life couldn't change for her, she'd change for life. If butterflies could change, then she could, too. They transformed from terrestrial crawlers to gorgeous majestic beings, traveling over fields sprinkled in sunshine and rainbow colors.

Andrew caught a majestic flight. Maybe Harper and Tess could, too.

From that day forth, Harper never stopped living by her new motto — Show up. Stay in flight.

2

ADULTING

Harper tucked her ponytail into the loop of her Red Sox baseball cap, put on an oversized set of sunglasses, and strolled through the parking lot of the grocery store.

The sun shone high in the sky and the air smelled like a freshly cut watermelon. She was free of her ex-girlfriend, Kate, and her cheating ways. And, she was happier for it.

She'd find a way to survive on her own, even if that meant tabling her music career for a little longer. Kate always overshadowed her in that department with her endless trail of fans and full-gig calendar for the next century. Now that she didn't have to compete with her, she might catch some success for herself.

Free of her presence and the distraction it placed in her life, Harper glided through the parking lot. Life had begun to balance itself out. She was set to begin her new job cleaning hotel rooms. If she played her cards right and could prove herself during the open mic nights in the hotel bar, maybe she could land her own gig without Kate's help.

As she entered the store to grab a few things for dinner, her cell dinged. She glanced at it. A message in all caps from her sister Tess, CALL ME.

After she grabbed a shopping cart and stood off to the side, she called her back. "Hey, Sis. How are you?"

A man coughed and cleared his throat. "Harper?"

Her father.

She exhaled sharply. "Where's Tess?"

Cough.

Sigh.

Cough.

"Sorry about that. I caught a little cold."

Harper didn't give a rat's ass if he had blood squirting out of his carotid artery. He surrendered his privilege of having a daughter who gave a fuck many years earlier. "Why are you using Tess's cell?"

"How else would I get you to call me back?"

"Again, Harold, where's Tess?"

"Ah, yes, we're still playing the first name game. Okay, that's fine. Have it your way. She ran to the store to get milk."

"You have her phone?"

"I swiped it from her pocketbook before she left."

Harper sighed loud enough that the vibration could've caused the oranges to fall from their balanced position had she been a few inches closer to them. "Does not surprise me."

"I didn't steal it maliciously. I had a good reason." A kindness Harper didn't recognize washed over his words. No slurred speech. No angst. No defensiveness. No attitude. Just concern coupled with an ill-fitted compassionate tone.

"Tess is going to flip out when she realizes you stole her phone."

"It's a risk I'm willing to take." He coughed again.

Her father spent his life taking stupid risks.

"Get to the point, please." Harper said, digging into her pocket-book for ibuprofen. Not even thirty seconds into the conversation and her temples throbbed. That kind of pain could shove her into a dark room for days to come.

"Have you talked to your sister lately?"

She hadn't talked with her since her birthday five months earlier. "Sure, we talk all the time."

"Then you already know?"

"Know what?"

A long paused ensued. He coughed again, cleared his throat. "She hasn't talked to you about anything serious lately?"

"Serious? How serious?"

"I had hoped she told you."

Harper rubbed one of her temples with her free hand. "You're talking in circles. Tell me what you have to tell me."

"Oh, right." His voice dripped with familiar sarcasm. "Sorry, I forgot how important you are. I shouldn't keep you too long."

She ground her teeth, seeking a patience that never came easy. Harper pulled her lips in tightly and scooted to the side of the green beans and avocados, letting an elderly couple pass by en route to the turnips. "I'm going to hang up if you don't speak."

"Something's happening to Tess, and we need to be here for her."

He tossed the word *we* around like they were a close-knit family who ate dinner together on Sunday afternoons while cheering for a shared favorite football team.

Her father would never be there for anyone, unless someone offered him whiskey. Conversing with him was like digging through hardened cement. Torture. "If something were wrong with Tess, she'd tell me. She wouldn't tell you first."

"She doesn't know that I know."

"Oh for goodness' sake. If you know something, spill it."

"I was fixing her boyfriend's leaky roof yesterday and had to access the attic through their bedroom. I found something on her dresser."

Harper leveraged another breath. "Okay, and?"

"It was a lab report. I didn't mean to read it. But my eyes couldn't stop once I spotted the word."

A buzz filled Harper's head, numbing the throb of her headache. "What word?"

"It sat right there for me to see. She wanted me to see it because why else would she leave it there on her dresser in plain sight?"

"What did it say?"

"I'm afraid to say the word out loud. It turns it more real that way. Do you suppose that's why she hasn't told us? She's afraid it'll be more real?"

"You're scaring me now. Tell me what it said."

He sniffed and let out a gush of air, which fell into another round of spasmodic coughing.

"Dad?"

"Breast mass," he whispered.

"Breast mass?" Her voice pushed to new levels.

"She won't ask for help, Harper. But if this mass is anything like the one they cut out of my lung last year, she's going to need it."

"You had a tumor cut out of your lung?"

"I'm fine. Now we need to focus on Tess."

Tess had a mass.

Harper steadied her hand over her heart, eyeing an over-ripened avocado and focusing on its grooves to keep her heart from beating right out of her chest.

"Did you hear me?" Her father's gruff voice knocked Harper out of her stupor.

"I'm in the middle of a grocery store and you're telling me Tess may have cancer. So forgive me for being a little flighty."

"Will you call your sister and ask her what's going on? Don't tell her I snooped. Just ask her if everything's okay."

As a good sister, Harper agreed.

When she hung up, she pushed the cart aimlessly up the aisles. If Tess did have a cancerous mass, Harper would be spending time back in Maryland. She dreaded going back there, to that place she had tried to avoid ever since her foster father slammed her against a wall because she forgot to dry the dishes in the strainer.

Two terrible ideas inflamed her headache into full swing. One, Tess might have cancer. And two, Harper would have a hell of a time trying to avoid their father if she did have it.

Should she call her right then? Or visit?

The kind of crucial conversation they needed to have as sisters couldn't be done over a phone call, especially since too many months had been wedged in between their last one. She couldn't ask about the weather and then spring, "Oh hey, how's your recovery from your party days going? Oh, and by the way, I hear you have a mass growing in you. Is it true?"

Harper took a different approach.

The next day, she packed a suitcase and her guitar and hopped a bus from Rhode Island back to Maryland, back to where she started out in life. She asked for a two-week delayed start to her new job and asked her landlord to water her plants.

She called Tess to alert her she was coming to town.

When she arrived, Tess fell into her arms and remained there for long enough to show Harper how much she'd been missed since she last ventured to Maryland years before.

A day into their visit, long after they reminisced about old times and shared a few giggles over their woes of finding gray streaks in their hair and a few lines around their eyes, Harper wanted to get to the point of her visit.

She entered Tess's living room, carrying two teacups, and sneezed five times in a row. "Allergies are tough."

"Ah yes, it's the good old Baltimore City mold settling into your lungs. Good thing Andrew has an extra bedroom that you're able to stay in."

Tess and her boyfriend rented an old bungalow house in the not-so-safe part of Baltimore. "I can stay here if you prefer."

"And wake me up every time you sneeze or sniffle? No, thank you!"

Harper laughed, and managed to set the teacups down on a tray table next to Tess on the couch.

She walked past Tess to the other side of the couch, deciding how best to ask her what she came to ask her. She chose a straight-forward approach. "I need to ask you something."

"The answer is yes."

Harper tripped over a basket of dirty laundry. "Yes?"

"Yes, Dad was here. Yes, I asked him to fix my roof."

Harper opened her eyes wide.

"I saw the call history between you two on my phone." Tess patted Harper's arm.

The two of them had enacted a pact to stay clear of their father. Shortly after getting out of jail, he had accidentally set Tess's couch on fire when he fell asleep with a cigarette dangling from his calloused fingertips. The man was a disaster, and didn't apologize for it.

"I was surprised to hear his voice."

"Andrew said you'd be pissed. But, I needed help with my roof, and Dad knows a thing or two about roofs. So, I asked him to help."

"So Andrew knew Dad helped you," Harper stated matter-of-factly.

"Of course. I tell Andrew everything."

"Of course." A dull thud knocked against her chest. Did Andrew know about Tess's mass too?

"Andrew and I have been roller blading. Oh, and get this, we have this contest going to see who can last the longest without eating a burrito. You know how we all love burritos? You do still love them, right?"

Harper enjoyed the light-hearted side of her younger sister. "I miss that rambling mouth of yours."

Tess giggled that time. "It's been on full-time rambling mode lately."

Harper swung the intangible door wide open. "Oh?"

"With Dad showing up sober to losing my job at the diner because they're slow, my head is spinning. I don't know up from down."

Harper had the sinking feeling, she wouldn't anytime soon either. "Yeah, I haven't been balanced in some time either."

"I've never known balance," Tess said. "So what did you want to ask me?"

Her matter-of-fact question smashed against Harper's chest. Time to cut to the chase. "Is it true? You have a mass?"

Her little sister's chin quivered. Her long, mousy-colored, stringy hair hung depressingly over her scrawny shoulders. "It is."

Harper cradled her arm. "It's going to be all right."

She closed her watery blue eyes. "I'm so scared, Harper." A big tear rolled down one of her cheeks. "I'm really glad you're here."

Harper's heart broke over the sight of that tear staining her cheek as it had so many times when they were little and frightened of the big, scary unknown world.

Harper had gotten used to living in chaos, always in a state of surprise at what the next second would bring. Tess had turned to alcohol or drugs to help her face the monster behind the broken walls of their once stable family life.

Harper wiped away the tears with the back of her hand and tucked her sister's hair behind her tiny ear. "I'm not going anywhere. We'll get through this together."

FOR THE TWO weeks that Harper had been in town awaiting the biopsy results, she and Tess earned extra cash by helping a friend of Barry and Nancy's clean out their junk-filled garage. That helped her to keep up with her living expenses in Rhode Island during her extended visit.

She hoped her new job would understand and be willing to keep her on staff once she returned.

Keeping busy helped them both get through the stress of wondering what the biopsy results would bring. During that time, they shared more giggles and bonded over pizzas, lemonades, and singing songs in harmony like they used to as kids.

On a sunny morning, as she and Tess sipped freshly-brewed coffee, the phone rang.

Harper paced frantically as Tess answered and proceeded to say an outrageous number of yeses, I understands, sures, and okays. By the time Tess hung up and raised her bowed head, Harper could no longer feel her extremities or keep balance in the shrinking space of her sister's living room.

"Well?" Harper asked.

Tess placed her hands on Harper's shoulders and squeezed them. "She said I don't have cancer."

The room stopped spinning and a stillness blanketed them. "You don't have cancer?"

A smile creeped onto Tess's face. "I don't have cancer."

Joy took over, and Harper picked Tess up and swung her. "You don't have cancer!"

Tess filled the room with a laughter that woke Harper back up to life.

They leaped around the room like a couple of sugar-crazed kids, bouncing on the natural high of the good news. After Tess texted her father to tell him the good news, they spent the next few hours singing and laughing, carrying on like young children on the brink of Christmas Eve.

Life had finally offered them a brief break from stress, and they rode that freedom straight to Andrew's for a celebration feast cooked up by his wife, Catalina. Barry and Nancy joined them, and together they chimed like a well-nourished family should.

Harper could get back to her life with a lighter heart, knowing everything would be okay. They survived, and even thrived on the other side of that scare.

The next day, as Harper packed her bags, Tess arrived at Andrew's.

"I was going to stop by your place to say goodbye," Harper said. "Looks like you saved me the time. Thanks!"

Tess's face drooped.

"What's wrong?"

"My boyfriend kicked me out. He said I'm too much to handle."

Her boyfriend, from what Harper had heard of him from Andrew, was a verbally abusive asshole. Catalina said that a saint would be too much for him to handle.

Andrew came into the room. "Well, you'll stay with us then."

Harper dropped her bag to the floor and pulled her sister into a hug. "Everything will be fine. You're better off without him."

"Yeah," she muttered into Harper's shoulder. She pulled out of the embrace. "I'm exhausted. I'm going to lie down for a while. Will you still be here when I wake up in a little while?"

Harper nodded instinctively. "Of course."

Andrew and Harper watched her walk away and down the hall to the guest room.

"I might stick around for another day." Harper looked to the couch and back at Andrew. "If that's okay?"

"I hoped you'd say that."

Later on, with Tess still napping, Harper, Andrew, and Catalina gathered in the living room.

Andrew turned to Harper and whispered. "How long can you feasibly stay? We all need you." He tilted his head toward the spare bedroom. "She really enjoys when you're around."

Harper enjoyed being close to Tess, too. If only life didn't get in the way.

"I've got to get back or else I risk losing my job and my rented room."

"You really want to go back to Rhode Island?"

Rhode Island suddenly felt like a stranger she'd barely shared a smile with over the years. Rhode Island only made sense with Kate in her life. She had no allegiance to the state anymore. She could always clean hotel rooms in Maryland and find someone willing to rent her a room. Tess did need her. And she needed Tess on some level, too.

"I suppose I could stay a little longer. I'll lose my new job and rented room, but there are always more of those to go around wherever I am. Maybe I'll have better luck finding gigs here being out of Kate's networked grip in Rhode Island."

He smiled. "I bet you will. And, I'll help you out. I'll even take a road trip to Rhode Island with you to get your stuff."

"I have very little stuff. I'll ask my landlord to ship it and I'll send her a check for her troubles."

"Sounds like a solid plan." He tapped his chin with his finger.

"You know, I recently met the manager of a new music store in Catonsville. I'll give him a call. And I'm sure Barry can hook you up with something else in the meantime. It'll all work out."

Harper hoped so.

3

FINDING NEW LOVE

Harper Ray never walked away from a good opportunity. She'd spent her life running toward them. That's what a survivor did. She feasted when times were good and buckled down when things were, well, less than optimal.

Ever since arriving back home in Maryland from Rhode Island eight months earlier, things veered more toward the lesser side of optimal.

On that particular morning, she arrived at the Music and Arts store to give a seven a.m. guitar lesson to a fifteen year-old boy.

Well, he didn't show. Harper's car had burned through fifteen minutes worth of gasoline for nothing. So what to do but lace up her sneakers, strap on her Fitbit, a gift from her brother Andrew, and power through a brisk walk.

Airing her frustration did her some good. Forty minutes into her assertive pace around the town of Catonsville, a pretty community on the outskirts of Baltimore City, and she had burned three hundred calories. Yahoo.

At that rate, she'd be able to add a spoonful of Parmesan cheese to her garden salad later on and not worry about the button of her jeans popping off. Hey, a win was a win. And at that point in life,

Harper would accept all that life wanted to gift her. After all, she understood that things rarely fell down from the heavens by wishful thinking alone. Sometimes, not even by hard effort, in her case.

In her experience, the more she forced, the less she gained.

She'd forced her demo tapes into the hands of most every pub in town, and not a single callback.

Her bank account sure suffered as a result. It sat in the negative as of six a.m. that day. So until she could figure a way to be discovered, she'd have to continue to tinker with odd jobs like teaching kids how to play the guitar, waiting tables, and cleaning houses.

She pumped her arms extra hard.

As she walked, she passed one of her favorite spots along the main road: an architectural oddity with its sharply pitched roof and adorable window arches. A *For Lease* sign hung from her favorite wide window. In her dreams, she'd buy the place and turn it into a café where she'd serve delicious coffees, teas, fruit drinks, yummy desserts, and a few delectable appetizers. Each table would be a checker board, and shelves would house her favorite childhood board games. She'd perform with her acoustic guitar on the café's stage when not on tour.

She wanted what her ex, Kate, had. Financial stability. Creative freedom. A place to call home while doing what she loved. She'd yet to find that.

Harper tore through her workout, fueled by the fumes of stress and envy. She turned the corner to an idyllic street lined with trees and houses with bright red doors adorned with wreaths. She inhaled a strong whiff of cherry blossoms.

The sun shone brightly in the deep blue spring sky and the wind tickled her face, yet familiar bitterness scratched the back of her throat.

She needed a lucky break. That's it. Just one to be able to get on a track that mattered. Her big break would come one day, according to Andrew. *Stay with it. Keep pushing. The universe will eventually respond.*

Andrew and she had far different views on the way the whole life thing worked. "Ask and you shall receive," he'd say.

Thankfully, he ended up with luck on his side. His life turned into a blissful Norman Rockwell scene, thanks to Barry and Nancy.

Harper couldn't have been happier for him.

Good people deserved good things.

Pump.

Sway.

Pump.

Harper continued down the pretty street, forcing her lips into an upward curve. "Smile and the world will smile back on you," Andrew would tell her each night when she first moved back to Maryland. He'd sit with her on his pullout couch and sprinkle her with nonsensical mumbo-jumbo like that. "It's universal law," he'd say before kissing her forehead and bidding her goodnight.

She needed that upward curve to her spirit after losing her one and only acoustic gig—and a repeat gig, at that—at T-Rex Pub the week before. They closed their doors for good. "Your music helped keep those doors open longer," Andrew said. "A tasteless burger can only go so far. Catalina and I will keep an eye out for more opportunities."

Catalina and Andrew were a power couple who lived to help others.

Andrew, the person who started out unwanted and discarded in life, understood the value of his existence. Just because his biological parents didn't want him didn't mean he didn't deserve to be alive and fruitful.

"All of us foster kids have value," he always reminded Harper. "Our lives matter. We're not our parents. They don't determine who we turn out to be. We can choose who we want to be. We have as much value as those who were lucky enough to be born wanted. Even more."

Talks like that and witnessing how Andrew turned his life into one of impact kept Harper going. Not only did Andrew voluntarily serve on the board of directors for Life Bridge Community Center, but he also ran a women's shelter.

He made something of his life. She would, too.

Harper swung her arms wider and opened her stride.

In the distance, she spotted some kids gathering around a bush.

As she neared them, she glanced at a boy kneeling in front of the bush. He extended his hand toward it, whistling. Harper peeked into the fluffy, pokey branches, and there sat a small dog with scraggly hair who couldn't have weighed more than ten pounds. It trembled and eyed her as if begging her to save it. Harper was a sucker for animals. She involuntarily cooed when she bent to say hello.

"Is this your dog?" the boy asked.

Harper's chest tightened. "No. It's not yours?"

"No. It's been sitting here scared. It won't come near me. Every time I move closer, it whines and backs away."

The poor dog stared up at Harper with fright.

A car sped by and the little dog jumped backward, deeper into the pokey branches of the bush. Harper knelt down and spoke calmly to it. "It's okay, little one." She extended her hand, and the dog stretched its neck in her direction. The dog inched toward her slightly.

"Come here." Harper extended her hand more. The dog stared wide-eyed at her, crawling low toward her hand.

"You have tags, I see."

The dog's wet nose touched her knuckle.

Harper tapped her knee with her free hand, encouraging the dog to come to her lap. A second later, the dog curled up in front of her, shivering. Harper slowly placed her hand on the dog's back to win trust. It responded with another touch of its nose to her hand.

Another car sped by, and Harper grew concerned the dog would skitter away and get hit. So she scooped it up and learned the dog was a male. A timid, scared male in need of some love. "Oh, little guy, don't worry. I'll take care of you and help you find your way home."

Harper snuggled him tighter to her chest to stop his shivering. She stood, holding him like a baby, cooing him to relax.

"What are you going to do with him?" the boy asked.

"I'm going to somehow find out where he lives." She rocked him in her arms and searched the surrounding houses. Not a soul glanced out a window or called for him. If she had lost her dog, she'd be running up and down the streets screaming. She pressed him against her chest, and he squirmed.

"No, little guy, you can't wiggle too much. We have to get you home safely."

He wiggled even more.

She feared he'd jump out of her arms and dart into the street. At least he had a dog tag on his collar.

"I'm going to take him back to my work and call animal control," she said to the boy.

"I hope he'll be okay."

"I'll make sure he is." She smiled at him, then carried the dog down the street, hoping someone would recognize him, stop their car, and wail for joy at their reunion. But no one did.

When she unlocked the music store's door, the little guy dashed through it like he owned the place. He scurried down each aisle, sniffing, snorting, and whining with glee. Then he lifted his leg and peed.

"No, none of that," Harper yelled out. "No peeing!"

He sprinted away from her and toward the pianos, lifting his leg again.

Harper ran toward him.

He bolted down the hall lined with lesson rooms, wagging his tail. Then he headed back her way and sat, staring at her.

She laughed at his cuteness, then gathered supplies to clean up the pee spills.

As she swiped the spills with a wad of paper towels, the dog remained still, staring at her.

The situation was too much to keep to herself. She needed to tell someone, and that someone always happened to be Andrew. She lowered herself to the floor and called him.

"I found a dog on my walk this morning."

"I can't find my hat, and you found a dog."

She laughed at the humor in that. Of all things to find, she found a dog. She couldn't find a bag of money? A new gig? A better place to live? A stable paycheck?

"Animal control doesn't open up for another half hour. He's got a dog tag, so hopefully everything will work out."

"What if his family doesn't claim him? Will you keep him?"

"No."

"No?"

"No, Andrew." She never should've called Andrew. He had a way of talking her into things before she could counter them. Like the time he talked her into jogging with him and Catalina at five a.m. around Lake Elkhorn. She wanted to say no, but there she ran at five a.m. panting alongside Mr. and Mrs. Fitbit anyway. Now she turned into her own version of Ms. Fitbit after they gave her one for Christmas.

The dog walked over to her and curled up into her lap.

"So what's the plan? Will animal control come and then toss him into one of those scary, lonely echoing cages at the pound?" he asked.

Harper petted the dog's tiny head, and he stretched his neck back to stare deeply into her eyes. "That's what's done, right?"

"I've never found a dog before. I imagine animal control would rather have someone foster him until they find the family. No?"

Harper didn't have time or money to foster. She wouldn't tell Andrew. He'd offer to hand over money that his women's shelter could've used more. "I'll call and figure out the process."

"Harper, if it's the money—"

"No going there, okay? That's a tired point of conflict." Money was tight now that she had moved off Andrew's couch and into a rented bedroom the next town over from him.

"Fine, but at least let me help you figure out a way to get some cash flow if it comes to that. We have the budget for one more cleaning crew member."

Andrew always offered for her to work at the women's shelter he ran. Being there always brought tough memories to the surface. "I'm fine."

"There is something you can help me out with. Well, my parents more so."

His parents.

A weird, typical jealousy waved through her.

"Sure, anything for them."

"Their friends who own Bella Rosa's Marketplace are stuck in Japan. The man had a heart attack while vacationing. Right at a cousin's wedding while they were cutting the cake."

"That sucks for the heart attack guy."

"Anyway, the couple is stuck in Japan for six weeks until he recovers enough to fly home. My parents are managing the gourmet market for them, and today they're hosting the annual fundraiser for the shelter. Wine tasting, herbal gardeners, painters, authors, and things like that will draw a crowd. It might be nice to have your voice and guitar flirting with the air in the produce aisle. What do you think? It could buy a dog bowl, leash, and a few squeaky toys at the very least."

Harper unlaced her sneakers. "First of all, this dog belongs to someone. Secondly you want me to perform an acoustic gig in the produce aisle of a grocery store?"

"Not just any grocery store," Andrew said. "This is Bella Rosa's. It's the crème de la crème of grocery stores. It's a destination. People get into their cars and drive for miles to experience the gourmet foods, wine tasting, and cheese parties. So what do you say? It pays a hundred and fifty dollars for two hours."

First she'd play the produce aisle, next she'd be back on the corner of Pratt and Light Streets in downtown Baltimore with her guitar case opened for handouts, waiting on the toss of coins from pedestrians wearing their guilt in the deep wrinkles around their compassionate eyes.

Show up and stay in flight, Harper reminded herself.

"I'm curious about the audience. Are the oranges of high-caliber?"

He laughed. "They're the best of the best."

"And the apples?"

"Oh well, don't get me started. You've never seen shinier apples before."

"Sounds like a distinctive audience awaits then."

"Just think, if you get hungry in between sets you're only a grape or cucumber away from satiation."

"Sounds like a dream gig come true."

"Someone important might even discover you. Can you imagine the headline for your future *Rolling Stone Magazine*? Harper Ray, the folk music goddess, played to a crowd of charitable people in the produce aisle of Bella Rosa's Marketplace and now has grown her audience from apples and oranges to millions of human fans worldwide."

Harper cleared her throat.

"Too much?"

"Yeah, yeah. Too much. You had me at a hundred and fifty bucks."

"So yes?"

"I do need the cash, and it has been a while since I've seen you."

"If you need the cash—"

"See you later on."

She hung up before he could break into one of his advice diatribes. Last year, he hired a life coach, a woman named Ivy who ran a wellness center out in Western Maryland, and now he had turned into Mr. Life Coach himself.

"A freaking grocery store." Harper laughed and pet the dog's head. "It's something, right?" She cleared some gunk out of the dog's eye. "Let's get you home."

She called animal control when they opened a little while later, ready to file a report and arrange to have them pick the dog up and find its family.

Harper exchanged all the information possible, including the dog tag number. As she waited for the lady to complete the report and investigate the tag number, the dog stared at himself in a mirror. He tilted his head to the side a few times, barked, and broke into a cute little skipping move.

A moment later the lady came back to the call. "He's a repeat offender. This is the fifth time in two months that he's been brought in by someone."

"So what do I do?"

"I can send an officer to you. We'll bring him back here and fine the owner a hundred dollars. Or you can call the owner and tell her that you found her dog and save her a fine. It's up to you."

At that moment, the dog happily trotted her way and landed in front of her on his funny little skip.

Then the dog snuggled up against her knees, bowing its head and asking for a scratch behind his ears. "Yeah, okay, I guess I can call the owner."

A few minutes later, Harper called.

"Are you missing a dog?"

"A dog? My shih tzu and yorkie mix?"

Harper examined the trembling little dog. "Yeah, I think so."

"You have him?"

"That's why I'm calling."

"How?" She yelled.

Harper pulled the phone away from her ear and glared at it. The woman didn't have all her marbles. "I found him on the street about an hour ago."

"An hour ago? How the fuck did no one know he was missing?" The lady screamed.

"What?"

"I'm so tired of all these people letting the fucking dog out of the fucking house. Can't they see they're driving me crazy here?" Her voice waved on the edge of hysteria.

Harper pulled the phone away from her ears again as the lady continued to curse and scream.

"You can have him. He pisses all over everything anyway."

Harper choked on a sudden rush of panic. "Keep him? I can't keep him."

The lady began to sob. "I can't keep doing this. I can't keep paying fines to get him back. He costs me too much. Please keep him."

"I don't think I—"

"If you don't want him, drop him off at the pound then. Someone else will want him. He's cute, right?"

"You're asking *me* to drop him off at the pound?" Didn't she want one last kiss to his cute nose? Stare into his lovable eyes one last time? Hug him and wish him well?

"Do what you have to do." She hung up.

Harper stared at her phone in horror. Then she glanced down at the little guy. "She didn't even tell me your name." Tears stung the back of Harper's eyes. His little pink tongue stuck out the side of his mouth as he panted. A small little package of cuteness all on his own in the great big world. Unwanted. Unloved. Uncared for by careless humans.

Kind of like how her childhood went.

"I'm so sorry," Harper whispered. "Humans sure can suck. That's why no one can be trusted. They come into your life, promise you beautiful happy endings, and disappoint the crap out of you once they walk out. I'm so sorry you have to depend on humans. I can't imagine a more nightmarish scenario than that."

The dog snuggled up closer to her, laying his head on her leg in a move of complete trust.

Harper's heart swelled and soon emotions flowed.

Fucking humans.

As she sat there and cradled him, her love for him quadrupled. Such an innocent, affectionate being who never asked for his life. He deserved so much more. Harper hugged him tightly.

He soon snored and tucked himself into the crook of her elbow. His little nose and tiny perked ears melted away all the angst and left Harper in a state of complete love. She adored his little grunts and the trust he placed in her so easily.

"You are loved, sweet boy."

Even if only by her.

Harper's tense body relaxed in the wake of his blissful nap.

Soon after, she rose and pulled down one of the ovation guitars from the wall. Then, she lowered herself and began to strum a smooth melody. The dog snuggled up closer to her as the music nestled deeper in her heart. Harper surrendered to the emotions of the melody. Before long, lyrics formed into a song that softened her heart and seemed to soothe the little dog's anxiety. It filled the space with a warm vibe.

Music had always been her go-to as a stress reducer.

She played their new song for an hour, and with each rendition, it grew more soulful. She wanted to remember it for when she and her new little dog needed it most. So she rose quietly and jotted down the lyrics and melody onto a piece of scrap paper from the sales counter.

Once she placed the guitar back into its hanging position, the dog woke and leaped to his feet. His face brightened, and he wagged his tail. He then broke out into a little skip again, kicking his hind legs back like Michael Jackson's signature dance move the moonwalk.

"I'm glad she didn't tell me your name. Because I have the perfect name for you. I'm going to call you Moonwalk."

His eyes sparkled.

"So why five times, Moonwalk? Were you trying to run away?"

He kicked his hind legs back again and barked at her. Then twirled.

"You're silly."

He barked again.

"I'm terrible. I forgot to get you water. You must be thirsty."

Bark.

Harper headed to the breakroom to find a bowl.

She settled on an oversized coffee mug. "You're going to need some supplies, which means I'm going to need some cash."

Moonwalk opened up his eyes wide, waiting on her.

She leaned down and pet the top of his small head. "Thank goodness for the grocery store gig. I'll be able to get you a decent leash, a bed, some kibble, and if we have enough left over, one of those cute doggy outfits."

Moonwalk did his little leap and skip.

"Don't worry, I won't make it a tutu. We'll get you something that shows off your intelligence. A bowtie. Yes! A bowtie."

Harper filled the mug with water and placed it on the ground. Moonwalk lapped it up, spilling droplets all around his little feet. He glanced up at her through his long hair. The little guy would soon need a haircut, too.

"I suppose we should head home. You're going to need to be a good boy while I'm at the gig. My landlord, Shelley, won't be home until later, so we should be good to go. You can have the run of my bedroom. Well, I suppose your bedroom now, too. If we don't get kicked out, that is. Don't worry. We'll figure this out." She repeated that out loud several dozen times, hoping she was right.

4

FLOATING

IVY

Ivy Homestead always considered herself a work-in-progress, but never so much as the day she kicked her best friend, Lila, and Lila's five-year-old son, Tommy, to the curbside. Okay, well, she didn't so much kick them as she did allow them to pass by her in her narrow foyer, clutching suitcases and sad faces, without begging them to stay.

"YOU'VE TURNED ME INTO A BITCH." *Ivy waved her hand madly in front of Lila. "That's not who I am."*

"You've always been a bitch, Ivy. Always thinking you're better than me because you had the better family, grades, college opportunity, an inheritance, a retreat center, a garden oasis, and a flashy life-coaching and video career on YouTube. Just because you open your door to people in need, that doesn't make you a superhero. Stop pretending you're better than the rest of us mere mortals with nothing on our backs but our fucking failures."

Ivy's heart clenched. "That's what you think of me?"

"Screw you and your elitist attitude." Lila's face flashed to an intense shade of tomato red. "I don't need your help anymore. Tommy and I will find a new place to live."

An image of Lila and Tommy trudging along the streets of Hagerstown with their suitcases in hand flashed before her. Then another image appeared where listeners of her Authentic Voice transformational life coaching show dropped their jaws and muttered things like, 'What the fuck? We counted on you having your shit more together than us.'

SOME TRANSFORMATIONAL LIFE coach and green witch she had turned out to be.

She had mangled the beautiful gesture of caring that she had placed before Lila. For someone who had trained her whole life to be a person who helped others in need, she sure had a lot to learn.

Thankfully, Ivy lived and worked in the right place to learn more. Ten years ago, Ivy, her mother, and her late aunt Kathy had inherited her grandfather's estate and transformed it into The Oasis Wellness and Retreat Center. Ivy had access to lush gardens, tranquility ponds, fitness equipment, and guests seeking solace, all things perfect for a green witch whose practice focused on nature.

Almost one year to the day of Ivy and Lila's fight, Ivy still struggled with imposter syndrome. How could she teach others to open their hearts when her last attempt had ended so poorly?

As a result, she had long since stopped recording her popular *Authentic Voice* show and worked behind the scenes at Oasis, cleaning the guest houses and wellness center, creating flower essences, and prepping meals and teas for guests.

Her mother, an energy healer, fought her decision every day, eventually cornering her in the locker room while Ivy scrubbed the tiled floor.

"I bought us a sensory deprivation floating tank." She grabbed Ivy's cleaning towel, twisted it, and tossed it on the counter. "It delivers and gets installed on Tuesday morning. I expect you to float in it on Tuesday afternoon so you can get out of this funk once and for all."

"If your magic touch isn't helping me, how will a floating tank be better?"

"I'm out of answers. Tuesday by two o'clock, you'll be able to float."

Ivy opened her mouth to protest the elaborate purchase, but closed it when she spotted her mother's eyebrow arch way higher than normal. "Fine."

She reached for her towel and lost her balance. She slipped on the wet floor, breaking her fall with her wrist.

Pain blinded her. It sizzled and scorched its way through her wrist until she could no longer feel anything.

The next thing Ivy felt was a cold cloth on her forehead and her mother's healing hands passing warm energy into her sprained wrist.

"Looks like your cleaning days are over for a few weeks," her mother said, kissing her forehead. "That floating tank can't be installed soon enough. The Epsom salt and darkness will heal you faster than you can blink, sweetheart."

TUESDAY AFTERNOON ARRIVED and Ivy entered the floating tank room without argument. She had to admit, she had high hopes after reading about other people's breakthroughs from floating.

She removed her wrist bandage and lay backward in the vat of water, pushing the button to turn off the lights and close the tank's lid. She sealed into the oblong shaped pool of Epsom salt, praying she'd find a way out of her perpetual darkness.

For the next ninety minutes, she floated and waited on some brilliant insight to cure everything. Instead, her nose itched. Then her cheek. Then her forehead. She couldn't itch them because she feared getting salt in her eye. So she simply floated.

With no access to the outside world, Ivy eventually drew her first deep, restorative breath after a year.

Her stress slowly decreased and she fell into the beautiful arms of Zen.

Floating transported Ivy to a strange new plane of reality. She widened her eyes as far as they'd stretch. Blackness covered every nook and cranny. Her breaths and heartbeat filled the space. Nothing else. Not a hum, buzz, ping, bark, cackle, nothing.

Ivy waited on the magic and grew concerned when it didn't appear. What if nothing happened? Would she be doomed to a life of cleaning pools, making beds, and scrubbing toilets for eternity?

She spread her arms and legs and tried to enjoy the warmth of the water.

She liked cleaning, actually. So maybe such a life would be okay.

Did she need more?

Her heart still beat. Her lungs still filled with air. She could still hear birds chirp and people laugh. And when not purposely sealed off into a floating tank, her eyes still revealed the beauty in the Earth's colorful flowers and sunsets.

"Maybe that's my breakthrough," she whispered. "To be grateful for my senses?"

She drew a beautifully enriching long breath, and when she exhaled it, her eyes played a trick on her. There in the center of the blackness appeared a violet pulsating heart. It beat in sync with her heartbeat. After several moments, her imagination grew even more vivid when the heart grew white roots that stretched beyond the bottom of the blackness. A beautiful heart-rooted tree had bloomed in her mind's eye.

As quickly as it appeared, it disappeared.

Then the timer went off and the tank filled with a soft light when its top lifted. Ivy lay still for a moment, grateful for the heart-rooted message. She would keep her mind and heart open to learning what it meant to her life's journey.

SEVERAL DAYS LATER, Ivy stuffed herself into a pair of jeans, promising herself one thing: never again eat junk food. That day, she'd work a table at a local community event at Bella Rosa's Gourmet Market-place, selling her flower essences.

She could barely take a breath once she buttoned the jeans. So, a comfortable sundress it would be instead. She'd be sitting all after-noon, and nothing screamed pain more than tight clothes.

Once Ivy arrived and parked her car outside Bella Rosa's Market-place, she opened up her Facebook app and clicked into her former best friend, Lila's, profile, an activity she did weekly since she kicked them out a year ago.

When Ivy landed on Lila's newsfeed, she spotted a new post of Lila posing in a selfie three days before, her first post in six months.

She and some bald guy cradled a baby in a hospital room. "Our baby girl."

Something popped in Ivy's chest.

She had a baby.

Pop.

Sizzle.

Burn.

Lila hadn't trusted Ivy enough to tell her she was pregnant?

The hurt doubled her over the steering wheel.

Trust was a rare gem that needed constant care. It required atten-tion. It died in the arms of neglect. It was like that new car smell. The second something invaded that space, that scent disappeared forever. One could attempt to recharge it with a fake only to fail. Nothing could replace the authentic pureness of something so delicate.

Lila's skin radiated with a pink glow in her selfie with her new family. Like she carried not a problem in the world. Like never seeing Ivy again would be the best thing for her and her new child.

Ivy stared into her sparkly eyes and a sadness pooled in her.

Lila would always be her sister at heart. Yet she'd never be Lila's again. Tommy probably forgot his Auntie Ivy ever existed, too.

Ivy's anxiety climbed back up her throat from its hiding place where she had put it shortly after her mess up. She squeezed her eyes closed and willed serenity to enter. For the next two hours, she needed energy, good energy, to serve any visitors who might stop by her flower essences table. Her mother should've been the one to work the table that day, but a guest booked a Reiki session. Besides, her former clients, Andrew and Catalina, asked her, not her mother.

They trusted her and the insights she had shared with them last year when they paid her for life advice on how to navigate the guilt of success when others they loved struggled to find their footing.

She squeezed her eyes shut for a last-ditch effort at balancing. Then she opened them, climbed out of her car, and headed toward the entrance of Bella Rosa's.

Fake it, she said to herself as the doors opened to the produce section of the gourmet market.

5

THE GROCERY GIG

HARPER

Barry and Nancy opened their arms wide to Harper, and she fell into their embrace. They smelled of essential oils and aftershave, familiar scents that still brought her comfort. "Thanks again for doing this," Barry whispered. "It's not The Hard Rock Café or Madison Square Garden, but it's full of grateful and generous people who are going to love hearing your music."

"Always my cheerleader."

Nancy cradled her arm. "We'll let you set up. I'll make you a plate of pit beef with all the fixings." She winked, and they drifted into the sea of shoppers there to support a good cause.

The produce aisle of Bella Rosa's Gourmet Marketplace over-flowed with colorful fruits and veggies. When the owners first opened their doors back in the early 1980s, they hadn't skimped on a single detail. They jumped right in when they dreamed up their garden-fresh haven in the tight-knit community of the historic town of Elkridge, about ten miles south of Baltimore City.

Shiny nectarines, plump oranges, and mouth-watering grapes livened the aisle where Harper set herself up to perform. She started with a Natalie Merchant song.

Soon, the crowd that gathered for the annual community festival on that late Saturday afternoon brimmed with happiness as they filled their carts with food for Memorial Day weekend. A woman with snow white colored hair and wrinkled skin waved shoppers over to her and handed them toothpicks with Spanish olives and cheese on them. A middle-aged man wearing a green Bella Rosa apron piled ripened avocados onto each other with astute precision. At one point, he stepped back from his work and eyed it with the pride of a sculptor.

The meat being grilled at the outside patio café by two men wearing crisp white chef's hats teased Harper and caused her stomach to growl. Six more songs before she'd chow on the pit beef and cranberry sauce Nancy had put aside for her. If it weren't for the rain shower, she'd be performing outside amongst the petunias and marigolds instead of inside by the leeks and cilantro bunches.

With her heart wide open thanks to her afternoon with Moonwalk, Harper eased into her set and enjoyed the view.

The gig wouldn't cover her rent that month, but it did provide entertainment value. People-watching had always been one of Harper's greatest pleasures in life, and Bella Rosa's offered her a front-row seat to some comical characters.

A young boy ran past her and over to a shelf stacked with red, white, and blue cupcakes. He sported a contagious joy that lit up his rosy, freckled cheeks. His mother dashed by, chasing him. She stretched her apologetic eyes at Harper. "I need roller skates to keep up with him!"

Harper laughed and continued strumming.

Playing in the produce aisle of a grocery store sat well above entertaining on a street corner on Harper's *will work for food and rent* list. Gigging next to fruits and veggies sure beat the days of playing on the corner of Dorrance and Pine Streets in the heart of Providence when she first ran away with Kate at seventeen years old.

Here, gratitude radiated from the eyes of strangers and, of course, family like Andrew. He stood alongside his wife, Catalina, and his mom and dad.

Some of the shoppers stopped pushing their carts and chatting with their neighbors when she hit a cool note. Their perfect lives coated them in a delicious layer of happiness. Harper enjoyed catching some of that vibe from them. It offered her a momentary break from the stress that waited for her back in her tiny, rented bedroom.

She prayed Moonwalk rested quietly and didn't poke holes in her air mattress with his overgrown nails. She hoped her landlord, Shelley, didn't discover him before she could explain.

She glanced around at the shoppers. They all appeared to have pleasant lives with their fancy apples and stylish yoga outfits. They reminded Harper of her life a little more than two decades before, to a time when a small hole in her jeans or socks resulted in a trip to the mall to replace them. To a time when her parents and sister were sober and happy. To a time when her mom was still alive and cared about things like washing her hair, getting Harper ready for school, and planning Sunday dinners. Back then they'd stroll from their townhome a few streets over and shop at Bella Rosa's for potatoes, carrots, and a fine cut of roast beef, then stop by the snowball stand for their treat on the walk home.

Harper finger-picked "Dust in the Wind" by Kansas, floating on the bittersweet memories. A rush of nostalgia flooded through her as she spotted a large ceramic planter near the lemons. It resembled a similar planter Harper had gifted Andrew and Catalina when they bought their townhome. Its aqua blue and coral colors reminded her of the first of many summers that she and Tess got to hang out with Andrew when Barry and Nancy would invite them to come along on their family adventures. They'd lazily comb the beach sand of Sandy Point State Park in search of treasure. After hours of laughter and hopeful digging for the elusive treasure, they landed happily on beach blankets and sipped lemonade and bit into Hershey bars. Happiness was within reach back then when she and Tess could escape their miserable foster home for a few hours and feel like a part of a real family again. Back then, Harper actually believed that achieving happiness could be as simple as lemonade and Hershey bars on a summer day.

She glanced around the bright and cheery marketplace. An elderly couple giggled as they shook coconuts near their ears. The man turned to face Harper and shook the coconut like a tambourine in perfect beat with the melody. His wife giggled some more and playfully slapped his arm down, offering Harper a happy eye roll.

Bella Rosa's remained a staple in the community. They were the keystone species of Elkridge, summoning the charitable vibes of its neighbors. Ten percent of everything bought that day from the local vendors, the store, and the pit beef barbeque would go to a good cause at the heart of their community, the Life Bridge Community Outreach Center.

Harper, Tess, and Andrew all owed their life to that center. Andrew paid them back by serving on their board. Once Harper got on her feet, she'd begin to donate to them.

One thing at a time. First, she needed to continue to rebuild the trust she'd lost from Tess back when she ran away to Rhode Island and left her alone in that terrible foster home. Sure Kate had pressured her into running away. But at the end of the day, Harper had chosen Kate and Rhode Island over Tess. And for that, Harper would always suffer guilt.

Guilt was her driving force.

Show up. Stay in flight.

The smiley crowd pushing their carts around that day showed up to support the thing that Harper tried to hide about herself: homelessness.

Well, her past self. And if Harper didn't do anything about it, her future self.

As Harper continued to play, she worried about Moonwalk and hoped he wasn't too frightened being by himself. Better than being with that terrible woman who didn't even know he ran away.

She glanced up at the crowd and spotted a woman setting up a vendor table a whole twenty minutes late.

She wore a lacy, bohemian style sundress. Her honey golden brown hair fell past her shoulders in long, thick spirals. She reminded Harper of a prairie girl, one who grew up skipping through a field of wildflowers on a bright, sunny, warm day when the sky radiated deep blue and serenity sprinkled its hope in the air.

The woman offered an elderly lady a strained smile as she bent to secure her box of product under her table. Her knee-length sundress showed off her curvy shape. Her hair curled around her sun-kissed shoulders.

Andrew and Catalina snuck up behind her and surprised her with hugs. They kissed one another's cheeks like friends who hadn't greeted each other in a long span of time.

A few minutes later, someone stopped by her table and talked with her about her little bottles of product. Of what they were, Harper couldn't tell. At one point, the woman waved goodbye to the shopper, and then she turned and glanced at Harper. Her eyes penetrated Harper's and sparked a twitch deep inside.

Despite the delicate upturn of her lips, her eyes were swollen. Her red nose indicated she either had a cold or suffered through a bummer of a day.

Her eyes warmed as Harper's fingers found their way to picking the melody of her and Moonwalk's new song. The song, with its sad and slow minor key, fit the likes of someone suffering from the anxiety of a stuffy nose, whatever its origin.

*T*URN *the light down so I can sleep.*
   Always had a hold on me.
   You gripped too tight and I can't breathe.
   Oh, you live by your name, anxiety.
   Dual feelings that I have.
   I can't find the words to say.
   It courses through my veins.
   Dual words I try to write just to get you out of my mind.
   But you won't leave.
   Anxiety.
   Anxiety.
   Shut the door so I can't go.

I don't need the world to know.
When I'm scared, I tend to flee.
Oh, damned you. Anxiety.
Dual feelings that I have.
I can't find the words to say.
It courses through my veins.
Dual words I try to write just to get you out of my mind.
But you won't leave.
Anxiety.
Anxiety.
Put your hands upon the clock.
Take a breath and try again.
Oh, I've done it all.
It never ends.
Dual feelings that I have.
I can't find the words to say.
It courses through my veins.
Dual words I try to write just to get you out of my mind.
But you won't leave.
Anxiety.
Anxiety.
Breathe.

THE ROOM FELL into silence as the echo of her last strum faded. A few people gripped their cellphones, likely recording her performance.

The beautiful woman with the soft, whispery, kind eyes locked onto her gaze and wiped tears from her cheeks.

Connected to her gratitude, Harper strummed back into the melody and lyrics of a song that obviously touched her.

Ivy

Andrew's sister Harper was beautiful with her dark, shiny hair and light complexion. She was also every bit as talented as Andrew had mentioned back in one of his life coaching sessions. From the emotional intensity of her lyrics, Harper suffered from her own version of a gaping hole. Andrew had briefly mentioned his sister living in Rhode Island with her girlfriend, a woman who didn't appreciate her as much as she deserved. Had her girlfriend broken her heart as Andrew surmised she eventually would?

She commanded that guitar, leading it to magical places. The lyrics had beckoned for the companionship of the worthy acoustic melody she created with her sunburst, shiny guitar. Her words had lodged themselves deep in the pit of Ivy's soul. They transcended the current situation moving her beyond those four walls. Her song brought Ivy to a place of calm surrender where truth bridged the gap between restlessness and wonder.

Ivy's heart fell in sync with the meaningful lyrics. The music that Harper created in that moment resonated with every fiber of her being.

Her soothing voice gripped Ivy and shook her from the shackles of the past year. She put to words everything Ivy couldn't verbalize. The depth of each strum brought to surface hidden emotions that Ivy hadn't even realized she had buried, shining a soft, healing light on them.

Led by something outside her realm of understanding, Ivy glided up to Andrew's sister and hugged her once she stopped strumming. Fresh tears rolled down her cheeks again and onto Harper's tank top.

"I'm so sorry," Ivy pulled away. "I don't know what's come over me. That song. That amazing song stirred me in ways I can't explain."

"Thanks." Harper tucked some loose dark strands behind her ear and tilted her head. "Are you okay?"

Her sincere voice and compassionate eyes brought more tears to the surface. "Yes, just caught off guard a little."

Harper wrapped her hand around Ivy's arm. "I've never had someone cry over one of my songs before."

Ivy instinctively patted Harper's hand on her arm. "It's amazing."

They shared a long gaze, then their hands dropped.

Synchronicity floated in the air. The song. The woman. Andrew's sister. The event. Ivy's intuition sparkled and raised goosebumps across her skin. She knew that something beyond her comprehension was telling her to pay attention to that moment.

The air lightened. The room shone brighter. And despite the stinging of tears in her eyes, a buzz shifted her energy.

"I'm Ivy Homestead. I'm at the table over there with the flower essences." She pointed to her crooked table. "I should straighten that leg out a little."

Harper looped her head through her guitar strap and placed the beautiful instrument on its stand. She extended her hand. "I'm Harper. Harper Ray. I recognize your name. You're the life coach who worked with Andrew and Catalina. I'm his sister."

When Harper's hand landed in hers, a jolt passed through her. She seemed like a kind soul with good energy. "It's a pleasure."

Harper's eyes twinkled as she studied her. "Andrew mentioned you had a way of lifting people. Thanks for the lift."

Her bold intensity spiked another jolt in Ivy. "You're welcome."

To calm her pounding heart, she turned her attention to Andrew speaking with his parents by the door. "With his awesome glasses, he kind of reminds me of Clark Kent."

"He'd be so mad at you for saying that." Harper laughed. "But I have to agree. He does have that nerdy look with those glasses."

Ivy glanced back at Harper. "Well, I should get back to my table and let you play more."

"Any requests?"

"I'm pretty sure whatever you play is going to move everyone in this place. That's a true sign that you love what you do for a living."

Harper folded her hands in her lap. "A living." She laughed. "Not exactly. It's more of a hobby until my lucky break happens."

The woman deserved to make a living with the kind of soulful journey she led people through. As the seconds passed between them, Ivy's heart and mind cranked into action, craving to engage with the synchronistic opportunity before her. "Do you play many private events?"

Harper's eyes grew wide like Ivy asked her if she ever traveled to the moon. "On occasion. Sure. Why do you have one coming up where you need some help?"

Her heart skipped gleefully. She didn't. But that wouldn't stop her.

"I run a retreat center with my mother and occasionally we entertain our guests with a campfire and acoustic music. We're always on the lookout for entertainment opportunities."

"You had me at acoustic music." Harper's upper lip curled, and an adorable blush spread across her cheeks. "When do you need someone?"

Ivy latched onto the woman's sudden rise in energy. "How about your next available weekend?"

"That would be next weekend. Saturday night?"

Ivy curtsied. "It's a date." The words rushed out without proper filtering. Heat blazed across her tingly skin.

Harper pointed to her table. "You've got a visitor."

"Ah, yes." Ivy shook Harper's hand again. "We'll catch up after the event, if that works?"

Harper picked up her guitar. Her arms flexed into a beautiful subtle defined line where her triceps met her shoulder. "I'll be here." She winked.

That wink sent a surprising flutter through Ivy. She stuttered a goodbye before tripping over her foot, turning, and meeting up with her new shopper.

Harper

Once the event wrapped up, Harper fiddled with her equipment. She wiped her guitar and placed it in its case, wrapped up the strap, and secured the capo.

If another gig ever came her way again, she'd be ready for it.

She took her time wrapping up her space because she wanted to stick around for two good reasons. One, Andrew, Catalina, Barry, and Nancy were talking with one of the clerks and she didn't want to interrupt to say goodbye. Two, she wanted to secure the campfire gig. It wouldn't jumpstart the musical career of her dreams, but it sure might pay a few bills and help her stay afloat more than the music store could with its no-show students. It would also be fun to catch more of a buzz from Ivy Homestead. There was something profoundly beautiful about a vulnerable woman who could stir the air with grace and tranquility.

Ivy secured a few bottles of her flower essences into a little baggy for a couple. Her femininity and kindness radiated clear across the room. Harper's head swirled.

Harper's head hadn't buzzed over a woman like that in years. Not since Kate busted through the door of their grungy basement apartment in Providence, showing off her first ever check for an acoustic gig.

Finally, Andrew and Catalina finished talking to the clerk and headed over to her. "Here you go," Andrew handed her two hundred dollars cash. "There's some extra in there from Barry for performing an original piece. Nice job on that song. It was amazing."

"I got misty-eyed," Catalina said. "I've never heard a more raw and telling song."

Harper's face blushed at the compliment. "Thanks."

"So when do we get to meet our new furry nephew?" Andrew asked, swiping his well-manicured hands together.

"I'm free tonight," Harper said.

Andrew and Catalina shared frowns. "We can't tonight," Andrew said. "We already have plans. Tomorrow?"

Harper cocked her head. "Of course." She noticed Ivy heading toward them. "I met your life coach earlier. She's adorable," Harper whispered.

Catalina livened. "Maybe she's still single."

"Last year, she was using a dating app and hated it." Andrew peeked over his shoulder at her, then back at Harper. "Maybe she's into women. You never know."

"Hello," Ivy said in a cheery voice as she approached them. The tear stains from earlier were gone and replaced with a gleam in her eye. "Well, this was a great time. I sold out of my lavender flower essences." She bounced on her heels like an excited kid, causing her long hair to flirt with her bare arms.

"Because they're amazing," Catalina said. "I should've snagged a bottle while you had some."

Ivy's eyes lit up even more. She folded her hands in front of herself and bounced some more. "I'll get one to you." She turned to Harper. "Are you into flower essences?"

Harper would be into most anything Ivy was selling with how she bounced and filled the air with a fun vibe. "I don't have a clue what they are."

"Well, each flower has contained within it a vibrational imprint that is extracted in water. It's a subtle energy that's used in healing work on yourself. They impact the energy fields of the soul to affect well-being."

"Do they really work?" Harper asked.

"If you allow them to." Ivy's eyes twinkled.

Catalina rocked on her feet. "I need some more of the Hibiscus, with the stress I've been under lately."

"Well, I suppose it could help with the stress," Ivy said. "It does increase sexuality and enhance the senses. It's a gatekeeper for romance." She batted her eyelashes at them, and directed her last batting of those long lashes at Harper.

Harper's tummy flipped.

Ivy continued to educate them on the power of flower essences, talking all of them into getting a bottle of their own. Harper didn't believe in such alternative, mystical nonsense, but she did like Ivy. If the woman wanted to sell her ice cubes on a frigid artic day, Harper would've likely filled the back seat of her car with her entire stash to catch more of the buzz.

She needed a good dose of that buzz.

She also needed to learn more about that campfire gig because she needed to figure out a way to feed her new dog and herself. And for that matter, make rent that month.

"I have a question." Andrew cupped his chin and pointed his eyes at Ivy. "Why haven't you released any new videos since last year?"

The glimmer in Ivy's eye dimmed. "I've been on hiatus, trying to reconnect to my roots a little and find a new voice. I'll likely start back up again soon." She raised her wrapped wrist. "This sprained wrist is my motivation now that I can't clean the wellness center for a few weeks. I can't sit around doing nothing. So maybe I'll get back into my work again."

"Perfect. You should do some episodes on the flower essences," Catalina said. "You could do an entire workshop on them. It could turn into a new evolution of your show."

Her eyes twinkled again. Slowly, the prairie girl with the long flowing hair and rosy cheeks reemerged. "That's an intriguing idea."

"I'm craving some of your heart-rooted wisdom," Andrew said.

Ivy perked her head. "What did you say?"

Andrew's cheeks blushed. "I'm craving some of your heart-rooted wisdom?"

Ivy's cheeks now blushed bright crimson. "Wow, that's crazy," Ivy said.

"Crazy?" Andrew asked.

"No, I mean about the heart-rooted wisdom. I had a vision of that the other day."

"Well, then it's settled." Andrew waved his hand in the air. "You need to get back into this. We certainly need you to. We need to uproot some of these bad habits we've planted since your hiatus started. Too much coffee and chocolate."

"Well, I am all about uprooting," Ivy said, bobbing her head up and down as if she had plugged herself back into an energy source and recharged all her batteries. "It could be fun to focus on a new kind of workshop."

"Sign us up," Andrew said.

Ivy's lips curved delightfully. "I'd need a catchy name."

"Maybe something with heart-rooted?" Catalina asked.

Heart-rooted? Blah. Blah. Blah, Harper thought. Talk about a melo-dramatic branding nightmare. That name would cause Harper to bolt with its "heart this" and "heart that" psychobabble probabilities. She had a better idea that stemmed from another word they mentioned. "How about Uprooting?"

"Uprooting," Ivy said on a chime. "It has a ring to it."

Andrew opened up his hands. "Yes! Oh, and you should ask Harper to compose a jingle for it. You know, like a theme song for this workshop."

Gone were Ivy's emotional tears from earlier. Sunshine replaced them when she turned to Harper. "I love it! Would you be willing?"

As Harper's heart flip-flopped around her chest at the potential of such a request, her cell rang.

She glanced down.

Fuck. Her landlord.

Her heart clenched.

"Hey Shelley."

"Why is there a dog barking in your room?"

Harper's heart clenched more. "I can explain."

"Good. Explain."

All eyes trained on her. No one spoke. No one blinked. Except Harper. She blinked like fifty times in a two second span.

Harper struggled to swallow. "Well, I found him on the street today. A car almost hit him," she exaggerated. "He was shaking and scared, so I brought him back home until animal control opened."

"And?"

"And animal control found the owner. She turned out to be a monster."

"I don't want a dog here."

"I'll figure something out by tomorrow." Harper placed her hand over her exploding chest.

"I haven't been able to stop sneezing since I got home."

"I'm sorry about that." Dread pooled. She had moved off Andrew and Catalina's pull out couch two months beforehand. She couldn't impose on them again.

"Not as sorry as you're going to be when you come home to find the dog gone."

"What?"

"If you're not here in thirty minutes to get this dog out, I'll throw him out myself."

"Shelley keep him in my room. I'll be home as soon as I can."

"Half an hour." She hung up.

The three of them looked at her with concerned eyes.

"I have to go."

"Everything okay?" Andrew asked with his panic voice, the one he reserved for those moments like when Harper accidentally set their kitchen on fire or when she tripped while cleaning and spilled bleach on their foster parent's couch.

"My landlord is going to kick my dog out if I don't go get him in thirty minutes."

"What are you going to do?" Even his hair sprang up in stress.

"I'll figure something out." Harper grabbed her guitar and yelled over her shoulder. "Ivy you can get my number from Andrew. I look forward to hearing more about the campfire gig and jingle."

"Sounds great," Ivy said.

"Harper," Andrew called out.

She stopped and waited on him. "What?"

"Go get the dog and come by the house. We'll bring some food home and figure everything out."

"But you have plans."

"You come first." He winked.

Harper swallowed the lump that the brotherly love in that wink created, then darted out the door.

6
___

FAMILY

"Well, here's to moving up in the world." Harper petted Moonwalk's scrawny head, and he flinched. "We scored Cheerios and a walk around Uncle Andrew and Auntie Catalina's pretty neighborhood. Did you enjoy your walk?"

Moonwalk scratched his neck.

"I'll take that as a yes."

She entered their kitchen and peeked down the hall. Tess's door remained closed.

She always worried about her little sister. Would she start drinking again? Doing drugs again?

She opened up a can of organic chicken stew for small to medium-sized dogs, a gift from Andrew and Catalina.

Andrew came into the kitchen.

Moonwalk skipped up to him and his little feet slipped on the porcelain tiles. Andrew bent to pet him, and that's when Harper noticed his bald spot growing larger. Two years ago, they had both landed in the third decade of their lives and that sometimes freaked her out.

She and Kate had always talked about having a family of two kids and two dogs someday. Harper lagged behind that ideal life by a wife, two kids, and one dog. At least she moved one step forward with Moonwalk. Now she needed to find a woman who could tolerate her occasional moodiness and lack of financial stability.

When Andrew stood, he cupped his chin with his hands, something he did right before laying something bad on her. Like the time he told her he'd been kicked out of their foster home because he was bisexual, or when he went off to Florida for four years for college, and then to New York for graduate school. Or when her father got out of prison and showed up at Life Bridge begging for food and a bed.

"What's wrong? Why do you have that look?"

"We need to talk," he said.

"I'm only staying until I can find a place that accepts dogs. I plan to go out hunting today."

"It's not that."

"Then what is it?" She snapped.

Andrew's eyes widened like Harper had slapped him.

"Oh, man. I'm sorry. It's lack of sleep. Even though the couch is amazing. It's more trying to figure out how to get everything cleared out of my rented room this week. It's kind of a mess. I'll toss most of it in the dumpster and start fresh."

Andrew cupped his chin with his strained fingers. "Your father asked us for help."

"Help? You mean like money kind of help?" Harper cringed.

"No, not money. He came into Bella's last night after you left. He'd read in the paper that I'd be there representing Life Bridge."

Had he shown up drunk? Drooling on himself? Smelling like cigarettes? Wearing dirty clothes with grease stains? "Was Ivy still there when he came in?"

He shot Harper a questioning frown.

"I'm just saying. The woman might offer me an opportunity. The last thing I need is my father showing up drunk or high and her finding out he's attached to me biologically."

"Well, she was still there talking with Catalina about some ideas for that workshop. She didn't hear the conversation. And he wasn't out of control. Not by a long shot. Complete opposite, in fact."

"Good for him."

"He's in a challenging place. I was going to talk with you in a few days after everything settled with Moonwalk and the whole getting kicked out of your apartment thing. But timing is at stake. Let me start by saying that he's been sober for a while now. He's not the same man."

Harper wandered into the living room. She sank back against the couch, and Moonwalk jumped up and propped himself in her lap. "I don't care. The damage is done. The blame has been splattered and spilled. I won't forgive him." Harper could no more forgive him than she could herself for causing the car accident that destroyed their family.

"That was the drunk and drug addict talking. He blamed you because addicts need someone else to blame. We've been over this. You weren't to blame for what happened to your mother. You were a kid. You were singing and playing." Andrew squeezed her hand.

"Whatever." Harper continued petting Moonwalk, and he sat like a perfect angel, allowing her the moment.

"There's more I need to tell you than him being sober."

"My stomach revolts against me when we talk about him. We may share a love for Tess, but that's it. The fact that he still comes to you when he's in trouble is so wrong."

"When someone needs my help, I..."

"You offer it." How could Harper argue? Her entire family always relied on his goodwill nature. Not just his, but his parents, too. "I'm so sorry he pulls you in like this. I wish you would turn your back, Andrew. Please do. He's a grown man. He can fend for himself. So can we. And we will. I'll find a place for Tess and myself. Give me a little time."

He steadied his gaze on her and pulled in his lower lip.

"What?"

His shoulders drooped.

"What is it, Andrew? Come out with it already."

He sat taller. "He has cancer."

His words pelted her. They tossed the room off balance.

49

"Are you okay?" He asked.

Harper shook off the shock. "Of course." An image of the man she used to consider her father snapped in her mind. Tubes and wires hung from racks and snaked into his veins.

"It's okay to be upset, Harper."

She bit into her cheek. Then her cell pinged a text alert.

She glanced down at her phone.

Hi Harper, this is Ivy. Andrew gave me your number. I'd like to invite you to come by the retreat center to talk about the potential acoustic gigs and jingle for my workshop. How about today?

Harper leveled a sigh, still mentally tripping over her father's news. The news of cancer clouded what should've been a sunny moment. Would he lose his hair to chemo? Were his eyes hollow? Was he depressed? Was he scared of what death might bring him?

She tossed her phone at Andrew to read.

After he finished reading it, Harper broke the silence. "It bothers me that I care about him."

Andrew placed his hand over her wrist. "You might play the tough woman, but you've got a sentimental vibe in you, too. You have a heart. That's why you care."

"Did he ask you to tell me? He's a coward like that. Just like with Tess's cancer scare. The man has no idea how to take responsibility for something. He always expects everyone else to do his work for him."

"He wants a chance to talk with you. I promised him I'd ask you. That was the help he asked me for."

"Why? To apologize?" Harper stared at Moonwalk. He cleaned his paw like a dog without a care in the world and not one just disowned by his family.

They had so much in common.

"He wants to make amends, I'd imagine. It's a natural desire when facing death." Andrew handed her phone back to her.

Instantly, her breath quickened and she became sweaty and cold. Her peripheral vision faded as a nauseating hum echoed in her head. Harper wanted to bolt. To get far away from the grit of that moment.

So she escaped into the wonderful world that was Ivy Homestead, typing back a response. *Sounds great. What time and where?*

Andrew squeezed her wrist gently. "You've spent a long time building those walls, Sis. I don't want you to worry that I'm going to break them down. I understand why you built them."

Harper swallowed her emotions. In an attempt to stabilize her life by coming back to Maryland eight months earlier, her life fell apart. Once again, she brought Andrew and Catalina into the mess of it all.

She bit her cheek, willing the tears to stop driving up the back of her throat.

The sobs formed, and when Andrew pulled her into his arms and she rested her head against his chest, those sobs turned into a cascade strong enough to hydropower a small city.

"I promise to get my life intact. We'll find a new place to live soon."

He rocked her gently as he used to do so many years ago as a scrawny, pimple-faced teenaged boy. His heart was big enough to fill their pathetic shared foster home with more than enough love to keep them both safe. Harper counted on his big heart more than she should have at that stage in life. "You can stay as long as you need."

He meant it. But, Harper wouldn't take advantage. Who wanted a couple of grown women leeching off them when they should've been planning their future and painting a room with cute bunnies and other baby themes?

They remained in that comfort for a few extended minutes until Harper's cell alerted her to another message. Andrew leaned over to read the message with Harper.

I'll be here any time after 11 a.m. We're located in Sunshine Estates outside of Hagerstown. The street address is 111 Sunshine Way. When you pull in, drive past the main retreat building and the guest cabins. I'll be in the house at the back of the property working on the concept for the workshop. You all inspired me yesterday! I hope it all works out. Knock on the front door when you arrive.

"I like Ivy," Andrew said.

Harper smoothed her fingers over her phone. "Me, too." Then she typed her response back. *I'll be by later on this afternoon.*

Bring your dog, Ivy texted her back.

Harper responded with an animated gif of a cute dog offering an excited hug.

7

SENSUAL JOURNEY

IVY

Harper's animated dog gif reply caused Ivy's belly to tumble.

Harper Ray did something to her. Something that stirred her like no spell in the world ever had.

Ivy lowered herself to her bed and smiled like a giddy girl, thinking back on Harper's wink and how it had turned her inside out with pleasure.

Ivy had never been with a woman, and could only imagine how intoxicating that woman's touch would be. Harper Ray intrigued her. She loved the way she cradled her guitar with her sexy arms. Mmm, and how she nurtured it with a loving stroke, as Ivy imagined she would a woman she admired. How wonderful to be the one on the other end of that attention.

As the minutes passed, desire pooled in Ivy, a desire to be taken on a sensual journey by Harper Ray.

She imagined herself in Harper's strong, capable arms. Closing her eyes, she caved into the intoxicating lure of Harper's lips as they warmed the delicate part of her neck, right below her earlobe. That led to a far more intimate fantasy as Harper's soft lips traveled around Ivy's bare shoulders, collar bone, chest, and then down to her sensitive nipples, engorged with desire and yearning to be nurtured by Harper. Within moments of her imagined touch, Ivy ached for her to take her to a place she'd never been before with a woman.

As the heat passed through her under the alluring plushness of her blankets, Ivy's head buzzed with a delightful lightness that carried her to a blissful place where she floated on an uncharted desire.

Wrapped up in the fantasy of Harper's tempting touch and attention, Ivy's pulse spiked to brand new heights, causing her breaths to quicken and her body to quiver in ecstasy. She steadied in on the sweet spot that she imagined Harper would continue to nurture with passionate sweeps of her hot tongue over her sensitive, tingling erogenous zones.

The heat intensified. One spark created another, and another, until she went into full sensory overload, panting, writhing, and moaning for more. She could no longer sustain the buildup. Wrapped up in pure pleasure, Harper Ray unknowingly delivered Ivy one of the greatest, most intense orgasms of her life.

Ivy clung to the gift of that orgasm, not wanting it to wane, banking on it to stay ablaze.

When it eventually subsided, she lay breathless, completely taken in by the catalyst of that orgasm: a woman. A woman who had moved her to tears the day before.

She closed her eyes and attempted to settle her beating heart through long, deep breaths.

Eventually, Ivy landed back on Earth, taking in her room, the sunrays sprinkling through the curtains, her reality.

Ivy rose and went to the bathroom. She splashed water on her face and stared deeply into the eyes of someone new, a far more interesting version of her former self from a few minutes before.

"What have you done to me, Harper Ray?"

She exhaled a long breath.

She felt alive and refreshed, like she'd emerged from deep in the ground and inhaled fresh air for the first time in months.

After showering, she headed back out to her bedroom and

grabbed her late aunt Kathy's journal, rubbing her hand over its paper cover. *Twenty Rules for Life* by Kathy Walsh. *Life insights as taught to me by my father.*

Ivy opened the book, and in it rediscovered the essays that first brought her "Authentic Voice" show to life. *How to find your purpose, how to be a better friend, how to forgive, and how to live your best life.*

Her aunt's life lesson journals became the foundation for her life coaching principles and self-love rituals that she shared in her videos over the years. Her aunt's spirit had helped her transform others' lives into ones full of passion and teachable moments.

Ivy now felt ready to get back to her passion.

She had Harper Ray to thank for the prod. Her song. Her soul. Her allure. They impacted her and jolted her back to life.

Yes, it still hurt that Lila had moved on without her.

She moved on.

That's what Ivy had to do, too.

She glanced at the clock. She had some time to create something new. She couldn't spend the rest of her life wallowing over the loss of something she had no power to regain.

Or could she regain a part of it?

Besides sending Lila a few text messages begging her to come back, what had she done to prove she wasn't a selfish monster? Part of Ivy didn't want to reopen that can of potential disaster. But to be worthy of living her path as a life coach, educator, and healer, she needed to take the higher road.

She was a fixer, after all, even though that quality often got her into trouble. That quality had also landed her on the couch of one of Maryland's greatest therapists at one point. That therapist helped her navigate the complex world of givers and takers and how that unbalanced combination often resulted in her codependency issues. That was a fancy way to say she cared far too much about keeping checks and balances and grew frustrated when reciprocity died.

Hence her flip out with Lila.

She couldn't ignore the strong pull to get back to what her heart desired.

She grabbed a notepad and cozied up on her fluffy rug in her meditation room. After some deep breathing, Ivy jotted some notes.

She wrote about Lila. Not directly, but symbolically through what she loved most, nature.

Everyone has a stake in being part of the healing. Let's take nature as an example. It hurts to see the destruction of our planet. We go for walks and find trash sprinkled in the brush, invading our waterways. We witness trucks roll down the street spewing toxic, black smoke into the air we breathe, the same air that birds and squirrels and other creatures also depend on. They are innocent to the failures of humans. It's when you become aware of the issues humanity has brought onto itself that you can make changes to help heal the anxiety.

Listen to the world. What is it saying? How's it asking you to show up?

Ivy wrote for the next fifteen minutes, then she reread her words. Could it be her "Uprooting" introduction script? In her past coaching and video workshops, Ivy focused on her aunt Kathy's life lessons. Now she had one of her own to share.

She'd always navigated to her aunt's wisdom, not trusting her own. She needed to brave up and share her vulnerabilities, fears, and failures with listeners. *Learn it. Share it,* as her aunt often said.

She placed her hand on her heart and pictured the heart-rooted pulse. To live in peace, she needed to be true and humble, and most importantly loving.

She stared up at her ceiling.

"Uprooting" was a great name. It lent itself to some pretty cool concepts, one of which pulsed wildly in her mind where her ego always overpowered.

Her ego had blocked her for long enough. It led her down a lonely, fruitless path. She journeyed without purpose. Well, no more. Everything in her begged her to stop, turn around, and start over.

A fresh slate.

A reinvention.

A new chance to earn back trust in herself so she could help others start their new journeys, too. She couldn't do that as long as her ego led the charge.

She sat tall.

Lila wouldn't open the door on her own.

Ivy had to open it.

Lila banked on that.

"Yet I failed to do so," Ivy said to herself as she stood. "Of course she never told me about the baby. She assumes I don't care."

Ivy paced the floor, enjoying the tickle of the carpet under her bare feet.

Thirteen months had carved out plenty of healing space. All the rotten things they tossed at each other that day had time to turn from boulders to dust. Time to sweep away the mess and get busy doing something meaningful – helping people live better lives.

They both deserved a second chance. After all, second chances granted people an opportunity to straighten things. Without that opportunity, things might stay cemented in darkness.

She could redeem herself with a simple, long-overdue action.

She picked up her phone and began a text message. *Hey you!*

Way too casual to be the ambassador of friendship sailing in to shrink the large gap of those thirteen months. She needed to call. To let Lila hear her voice. To inflect on the right words so Lila would hear love.

She called and got her voicemail. "Hi Lila. It's me, Ivy. I hope you're well. Tommy, too. I saw your picture yesterday. You had a baby," Ivy whispered on a cry. "I'm happy for you." She paused. "I miss you and love you. Take care."

She hung up and bent over at her knees, releasing a gush of pent up anxiety before she rose again.

"Now, I'm ready to rock and roll."

She picked up her notepad and chewed on the end of her pen as she considered the end of her script.

If you'd like to learn how to live a more balanced, authentic life and navigate stress, come join me online for a brand new self-love workshop called "Uprooting."

She hoped Harper would take her workshop.

Harper.

There went her skipping heart again.

She turned to the dry-erase board for focus.

Pulling off the cap to a marker with her teeth, she zoned in on the blank white board. "What will it be today?" She placed the tip of the marker to the board. "Where do you want this day to take you?"

I deserve happiness, she wrote in cursive letters.

She stepped back and enjoyed a grateful sip of her water, savoring the momentary lightness the lemon stirred in her.

"I deserve happiness," she said aloud, testing its virility on her ears. She did. She took the high road and opened the doorway.

Ivy stepped up to the board again and wrote another affirmation. *I'm at peace.*

The magic in writing and proclaiming aloud such powerful statements grounded her instead of causing her to scratch at things she couldn't itch.

"I'm on a roll."

She wrote yet another bold proclamation. *I celebrate myself.*

She placed the marker down on her glass-etched desk. Time to open up her chakras. For that, she stepped outdoors.

She crossed the length of the front yard with its lush pollinator-friendly grass, heading to the other side of the sprawling rancher home. As she rounded the side of the house, she headed through a side gate that led to her backyard garden, filled with greens and fresh-scented plants. She stepped through the gate and glanced at the gazebo with its pretty red and pink flowers. She headed toward the trail that led to a forest of trees at the outer edge of the paradise.

The tranquil yard, accessible to retreat guests through the side gate, coated her in whimsy. Ivy sealed her eyes closed for a moment. A light breeze blew across her cheeks and teased her senses. She glanced at the patio. It sat simple and elegant with white wooden lawn chairs circled around a fire pit. A small hibachi grill sat by the corner of the stone area.

She smelled the fragrant flowers as she visualized activating her root chakra, the chakra of stability, security, and basic needs for things like food, water, shelter, and sexuality. She lingered on that chakra for a few extra moments before working her way up her entire system.

Ivy touched a nearby leaf. She admired how the sun sprinkled its golden rays on it. The smell of honeysuckle danced in the air, filling Ivy with a sense of peace.

She wandered farther into the garden.

Recently, she had spent a lot of time pondering her purpose in the aisles of her late grandfather's garden. Even after ten years since moving in after his death, Ivy still couldn't bring herself to call the green haven *her* garden. It would always be his. It's where he lived his life before he grew sick. He thrived in that oasis and taught Aunt Kathy and her mother everything to be successful green witches.

Ivy always wanted to be a witch, too. Her aunt helped her gain comfort in the name witch, referring to it as an enchanting way to describe the work they did. They reveled in the natural cycles of mother earth and appreciated the power and energy shared with all seen and unseen.

"Humans can only see one percent of the visible light spectrum. Can you imagine what else we're missing in the other ninety-nine percent?" Her aunt would ask, always bringing Ivy comfort by reciting random facts like that.

Ivy glanced at the sky. "Today this green witch will do for others before herself."

The potential wafted in the air.

Yesterday, that same affirmation worked. She stood in the same exact spot and stated the same exact phrase. And within a few hours, she had met Harper Ray, a woman who sang from her soul with "Anxiety." She had to be a woman who was torn herself to have written such a moving tribute to an emotion that ransacked the heart.

She had no place to live with her dog, according to Andrew.

Ivy wanted to help if she could.

She continued her stroll, admiring the fragrant scents of lilacs, hydrangeas, and wild lilies. She scanned the garden and attempted to push flashes of concern away over whether Lila would return her call.

What if she didn't? Had her words and actions created so much pain that Lila would never be able to stop hating her?

So easily her emotions took a nosedive.

She still had a long ways to go before getting back to balance.

Ivy kneeled before a patch of weeds and took her worry out on them with her one good hand. She yanked them bunch by bunch. The power in cleansing the dirt around the precious flowers usually offered her temporary relief from the anxiety lurking around the dark recesses in her.

She folded in her bottom lip to stop the tears. *Why did I ever say such terrible things that day? How can all of those years mean nothing now? We swore on the blood of our fingertips that we'd forever be sisters. We promised. Do promises no longer matter? Is that what happens in adulthood? We become rigid and unable to get past hurt? Hell, we survived falling off the wall by the river with lollipops in our mouths. How can we not get past this?*

She dug her hand into the composted soil, squeezing it hard between her fingers and enjoying the coolness when her mother snuck up behind her and kneeled by her side.

"You're mad. Why?"

Ivy sniffled and wiped her runny nose with her wrapped wrist. "Just thinking about things I regret and wishing I could do something more to set things straight."

"Ah, Lila regret." Her mother yanked with equal fortitude. "Sometimes people are in our lives for only as long as we need them to be. Then they move on. That's okay. It's no reflection of you as a person. It's simply life."

"I know," Ivy whispered.

"Then prove it by being a little gentler with the dirt." Her mother poked Ivy's side.

Ivy laughed. "I met a woman yesterday at the event who planted an idea." Ivy sat back on her heels and flung the dirt from her hands.

"The last time a woman planted an idea in you, we ended up opening up a wellness retreat center in the middle of the woods. Granted, that woman was me, but still, I don't want any competition." She squeezed Ivy's cheek, lovingly. "So what was this woman's idea?"

"Well, I've been in a rut with my life coaching since Lila and all."

Her mother puckered her lips. "Is that what we're calling it these days? A rut?"

"Yes. Anyway, one thing led to another and I got to talking about flower essences to her, Catalina, and Andrew, Barry and Nancy's son from Life Bridge."

"Ah, yes. It's been a while since I've been out there to volunteer."

"They said hello. Anyway, the woman is Andrew's former foster sister from before Barry and Nancy. One thing led to another and we all started tossing ideas out to each other about the flower essences and crafting a workshop around them. Then that led to Andrew's sister, Harper, suggesting the name 'Uprooting' for it. It kind of felt like a moment."

"You got an intuitive hit?"

"I did."

Her mother sat back on her heels, too. "Yet you're still harboring anger toward Lila. The two can't exist on the same frequency."

Ivy yanked up another bunch and placed them on her lap. She pet them like she would Lil Boy, her aunt's dog who still lived with them and now served as the center's mascot. "I left Lila a voice message congratulating her on her new baby."

"Baby?"

"She had a baby a few days ago. I saw it on Facebook."

Her mother swiped her forehead with the back of her hand. "Hence the angry weeding."

"Hence." Ivy tossed the bunch of weeds to the ground. "I'm glad I left her a message."

"She may not call you back. Are you okay with that?"

"That's a silly question."

"And the reason you called her?"

"To squash guilt and take the high road."

Her mother patted Ivy's knee. "You know what I'm going to say to that, right?"

"Not to be disappointed."

She rose to her feet, groaning. "A workshop is a great idea. That Harper woman is a smart, creative cookie. 'Uprooting' is brilliant."

"She is brilliant. I asked her to perform acoustic guitar and vocals for our guests around the campfire."

"Fancy."

Ivy shifted her weight onto the ground and stretched her legs out in front of her. "I sensed something special flow between us at the event. Like she and I were meant to share the same space and have our conversation. She sang a song that touched me deeply, and I felt instantly connected."

Her mother remained still, lending a listening heart.

"There's something about her that I need to pay attention to. I don't know what it is yet. There's something though. It's like the universe opened up and shined a light down on her head and whispered to me to take notice."

Her mother didn't blink for a good long twenty seconds at least. "You said the same thing about Lila."

"That was different."

"Now you're trying to right that wrong with this other woman."

"I'm so not doing that," Ivy said.

"Yeah, and I'm a super model."

Ivy tossed a clump of dirt at her.

Her mother bent over, hands on knees, and studied Ivy. "I'm just giving you a hard time out of fun."

Ivy rose to meet her bent over stance. "After all these years working together, I've figured that out by now."

Her mother headed away from Ivy, back toward the retreat center. "Come on, we've got some tea to brew for some thirsty guests. After that, the tank rooms need to be mopped. You can hang out with me while I work."

"What happened to the new cleaning person?" Ivy asked, trotting a step behind.

"She quit. She fears dogs."

"She fears Lil Boy?" Lil Boy was as goofy and mild-mannered as any big, slobbery dog could be.

"We'll hire a cleaning company. Eventually, your wrist will heal. So you can reclaim your cleaning spot if you'd like."

"If I do get back into life coaching and the workshops, we should consider hiring someone else. Like a live-in someone else. This time someone who might lift a finger and do something. Lila didn't work out in that capacity, but we'll find someone else."

Her mother opened the door to the kitchen area of the retreat center. "You've got dirt all over your face. Go shower. Get ready for your new pet project."

Ivy chuckled and followed her through the door. "Wait until you hear her play."

"Does she want a cleaning job?"

"Catalina and I were chatting at the event and she mentioned that Harper was looking for work. But Harper's too talented for that."

"Says the talented green witch and life coach turned house cleaner."

Maybe like her, Harper also suffered from imposter syndrome. Why else would she be playing grocery stores and agreeing to play around a campfire at a retreat center?

HALF AN HOUR LATER, freshly showered again and now more balanced, Ivy readied to record her script from that morning.

She sat on a stool before her video camera and spoke instead through a stream of consciousness about serendipity, synchronicity, and intuitive hits. In that time, she had recorded a brand new video episode. She couldn't wait to edit and share it with her social media followers.

More ideas bounced around her head as she slid into a different outfit: a pretty skirt and tank-style shirt. She'd record those ideas later on after meeting with Harper.

As she smoothed her hair into place, the sound of a car door being slammed shut came from the driveway. Not once. Not twice.

Three times. Each time the slam grew more intense. Midway through pulling her undies up under her skirt, she ran over to the window to see the fuss.

Harper Ray, wearing a tight pair of blue jeans and a T-shirt, bent down beside her driver's side car door and lifted it, body slamming against it. She stepped back and waited, her hands splayed out in front of her as if ready to catch the door, should it have fallen off its hinges. The car, a faded blue sedan with white spots on its bumpers and sides, resembled something that had been driven over landmines in a warzone. A crack stretched across her windshield above the driver's viewpoint.

Harper cupped her hand over her eyes and glanced at the house. Ivy jumped backward behind her curtain. A moment later, she peeked out again. Harper's thick, dark ponytail hung at her shoulders. Harper was beautiful with her ivory-colored skin and toned physique.

She shifted on her tattered sneakers as if deciding if she should get back in her car and speed away or take a chance on the weird flowery woman she met in a grocery store the day before.

Eventually, Ivy headed toward the front door and waited.

When would she knock?

"Knock on the darn door," Ivy whispered.

When she did, Ivy beamed to life.

She opened the door and a set of dark eyes met hers. Harper Ray with her little nose and messy ponytail was adorable. So adorable. She wore a T-shirt from Bella Rosa's. Ivy had one just like it.

Wisps of Harper's hair sprang from her loose ponytail as if trying to run away from her stress. Dark smudges smeared on her jawline, likely from the car door grease.

Harper glanced around the front yard, pointing her eyes down at the pruned bushes that covered Ivy's front bay window. When she swept her eyes up to Ivy, everything from her roots to the dark circles under her eyes screamed *help me*.

Hot damn, if those two words didn't get Ivy's heart beating, nothing did.

8

HOPE IN THE AIR

HARPER

H arper closed her eyes, banking on the fluidity in that moment as she prepped to knock on Ivy's front door.

Show up and stay in flight.

She swallowed hard considering the potential. If she did get the job, she'd have to find an affordable place to live nearby. The nearly seventy mile drive from the Baltimore area to western Maryland would kill her and what was left of her car.

She steadied her fist for the knocking, drawing in a ridiculously large breath to sustain whatever she might experience on the other side of that door.

When the door opened, Harper didn't expect a half-naked Ivy.

"Your skirt is kind of um..." Harper glanced at Ivy's lace panties. They were sexy as hell, hugging her thighs. She couldn't *not* look at them.

"Oh my gosh." Ivy pulled her skirt out of her panties and chuckled nervously. "I must have... er... Oh who knows what I must have done. As you can see, I need help with more than a jingle for my workshop. I can't even dress myself properly."

Ivy's flowing hair hung around her shoulders like wild vines in the forest. She stood an inch or so taller than Harper. She scanned the length of Ivy. A pendant flirted dangerously close to her voluptuous cleavage. Her wide hips accentuated her leaner torso. A black and white "thank you" tattoo adorned her wrist. Red polish coated her toenails.

She smelled fucking amazing, like a garden full of gardenias.

When Harper craned upward, she noticed Ivy's curious eyes full of laughter. Freckles dotted her plump cheeks, and a tiny mole, the size of a pinhead, sat right above the upturned corner of her full rosy lips.

Harper attempted to look away from her undies debacle, but couldn't help staring as Ivy continued to fret with her skirt.

"You look a little shocked," Ivy said. "Never seen a woman wearing her skirt in her undies before?" Laughter curled up around her words, spreading a blush across her face, down her neck, and possibly everywhere the sun didn't shine.

"Oh, I don't shock easily."

Ivy extended her hand. "Let's start over. Hi, I'm Ivy Homestead. I'm a vlogger, life coach, and lover of plants and flower essences, and soon to be host of a new workshop called, 'Uprooting,' named by a talented musician named Harper. Oh, and occasionally, I'm clumsy and forget to check my wardrobe before opening the door to a potential new partner."

"Bold, too." Harper shook her hand firmly.

Ivy released her firm grip. "Partner, as in campfire entertainer." Ivy corrected herself on a deeper blush.

Ivy's blush tickled Harper. "And jingle partner too, right?"

"Jingle partner. Entertaining partner. Sure, you name it, Partner."

There went her blush deepening even more. Damn it. Ivy needed to stop doing that or else Harper might do something foolish, like flirt with her.

Never mix business with pleasure, she recalled her father whispering in her ear once when she asked to run a lemonade stand with Andrew. He was wrong about so many aspects of life, but Harper had to agree with that one. Mixing business with pleasure could be hazardous.

She needed work, and she couldn't risk offering the woman a sudden longing gaze and wind up without an opportunity to help lift her to higher ground.

She sank financially, and fast. She thought of heading back to Rhode Island to recoup some of her odd jobs, but couldn't now. With Tess's depression, her father's cancer and how that might affect Tess, and her new responsibility with Moonwalk, she needed stability, something to keep her afloat until she could regain her footing and go after her dream again. None of her demo tapes produced any quality gigs. So campfire songs she'd sing, if Ivy offered up the chance. Harper didn't want to ruin that. Though, Ivy's twinkling eyes hinted to Harper that she might not mind catching a flirt or two from her.

They stood smiling at each other like women on the verge of something more daring than wearing their skirt in their undies.

Harper turned over her shoulder and scanned the wild fields and dense trees that surrounded the grassy yard. The scent of honeysuckle swirled around her. The cicadas sang in waves. The sun's rays sparkled against the leaves. Harper's heart pounded in her chest at the opportunity that could lie before her.

"So where's your dog?" Ivy asked.

Harper turned back to Ivy. "His Uncle Andrew is watching him."

"Shame. I would've loved meeting him." Ivy's striking blue eyes played a tune on her heart. "My dog, Lil Boy, would've, too." She ushered Harper into her home and glanced around. "I guess he's with my mother. He wandered in here a few minutes ago. He likes to saunter around and greet guests. He's like a mayor around here, expecting everyone to stop and say hello."

Harper had no clue how Moonwalk would be with other dogs.

"This is quite a place you have here." Harper peered out the large window. Everything was so green. So alive.

"It's a lot to handle. My mother, aunt, and I opened up the retreat center about ten years ago, and life hasn't slowed down since. I'm not complaining though. Maintaining and cleaning the place has been my self-therapy over the past year. A little misunderstanding with a friend of mine. That's all behind me now." She lifted her wrapped wrist.

"The cleaning or the friend?"

"Hopefully just the cleaning. Time will tell with my friend."

Harper glanced around the room. Dust bunnies floated around the baseboards and the streaks in the windows could've used a good hosing. "Who's doing your cleaning work now?"

"Why? Do you clean houses?"

"I cleaned hotels when I lived in Rhode Island." Harper learned to say that with confidence ever since Andrew reminded her that she was an entrepreneur at heart. She chose to mop floors and clean toilets. She could just as easily have studied for her GED, gone to college, and gotten a job sitting at a desk all day like the average miserable person did. She chose a life of freedom instead. How else would she be ready for her dream to launch if she got stuck working on spreadsheets all day long?

"Want a maintenance job?" Ivy asked on a chuckle, walking them farther into the living space.

She'd take any kind of job from Ivy right about then. Her muffler dangled on the drive there. Her jeans were getting a new hole in the crotch that she'd have to patch. Moonwalk needed to visit a vet for a checkup. She needed to find a new place to live.

Harper was resourceful. Another good trait she picked up from her father, the bastard. "Tell me more about it. What kind of maintenance do you need?"

Ivy turned around. "I was joking." She searched her face. "Were you?"

Harper would shovel shit out of a horse barn at that point. She had like five dimes to her name. That little dog had an appetite the likes of a stallion back from a month-long trek across the plains. "I can juggle multiple things."

"Like your car door and guitar case?" Ivy glanced at Harper's case.

Harper lifted it slightly. "What can I say? I'm a woman of all trades."

"That comes in handy, especially when a landlord kicks you out."

Harper gripped the guitar case handle tighter. "That she did."

"I was confused and concerned when you bolted, so Andrew filled me in."

Harper switched her weight back and forth.

Ivy eyed her with mischief, as if excited to see a new topic for her revitalized self-love business come to life. She turned on her heel. "Come on let me show you around." She spread her arms wide. "This is my go-to room for chilling out with a good book. Do you read?"

Harper would say she ran marathons and jumped out of airplanes if it helped her stay the course that lay before her. A music and cleaning gig all in one? That spelled stability in Harper's book. "Here and there."

Ivy motioned to her massive bookcase lining the long end of the room. A fireplace with a used log reduced to a weakened pile of ash balanced the wall of books in its center. "I sometimes used to record my videos in front of this wall. I reference a lot of the books when talking about certain topics. My aunt introduced me to many of these books when she was alive. These are her collection. Are you into self-help type things?"

If pretending to enjoy long diatribes about self-help would be her ticket to a better financial foundation and get her back on track, then she'd better not answer truthfully. "Sure, I suppose."

A smirk rested in the tiny lines around her lips. "You strike me as a nice person, and I've heard enough of your music. You'd do a fine job as the Oasis entertainer. If cleaning is your thing, we sure could use the help with that, too. It's a big place and my mother has a bum hip flexor."

Was it her long hair or curvy hips that made everything seem so sunny and fresh? She could've demanded she scrub every nook and cranny with a toothbrush and Harper wouldn't have been able to resist. "How soon would you need me?"

"Today, next week, a month from now? Whenever."

A month. A lot could happen in a month's time. She could end up sleeping under a big tree in the park again, wrapping Moonwalk up into her jacket to keep him safe and warm.

Students dwindled at the music school, so that wreaked havoc on any stability. Sunny's diner didn't work out because she sucked at waiting tables with a smile when people were rude and left her a dime for her hard work. None of her demo tapes produced a profitable gig. Of course, Andrew and Catalina would never allow her to sleep in the streets, but she wouldn't tell them if it came to that again. They had their life nicely arranged, and were planning to foster a few kids once Tess eventually moved out and they fixed up the extra bedroom in their home. Harper wouldn't delay all that by overstaying her welcome. "The sooner the better."

"I sensed that from your car."

How did she end up being thirty-two years old and still desperate? "That's a temporary car until I get more settled. I recently moved back from Rhode Island."

"What brought you back to Maryland?"

"My family."

Ivy moved in slightly closer, and her subtle flowery scent swirled in Harper's head. "Family is everything. I did the same thing ten years ago when we inherited this place from my grandfather. I was working as an office assistant in a high-rise building in downtown Pittsburgh. I hate cities. I hate crowds. So when word came that I could build a life back here in Maryland, I jumped on the next flight home."

"Why would you live there if you hated cities?"

"My ex-boyfriend." She bit her lip. "That'll be the last time I ever uproot for anyone. This is home now. This is where my soul comes alive." She surveyed the beautiful space. "Do you like how I tossed in the word uproot?"

She tilted her head and glanced at Harper suggestively.

Harper traveled her gaze around her sunshiny face. "Nice one."

"So were you serious about the cleaning gig?"

"Yes." Harper dotted her word with great care to accentuate just how serious.

"We have ten guest houses to keep clean, plus the wellness center and gardens. It's a full-time job. We were set to hire a cleaning company until we could find someone to hire directly. We prefer to have one dedicated person on hand."

The survivor in Harper went into overdrive, stepping up and claiming the golden ticket. "I'm your girl."

"You're a musician. Do you want to be swapping water around the floor with a mop?"

"I do my best lyrical brainstorming when I'm cleaning."

Ivy considered her for an extended moment with a deep squint. "Okay then, let me get my mother so she can meet you. She does all the official hiring." Ivy air-quoted. "I'm pretty sure she'd be impressed with the way you take care of your car, so—"

"My car got me here, over sixty-eight miles of interstate, so—"

Ivy giggled again. "So yes? You're serious?"

Harper attempted to stay grounded with a lackadaisical stance. "As serious as they come."

Ivy trekked across the living room space toward a small white table where her cell sat. A bright glow filled the room. Plants of all sizes and shapes covered most of the wall-length windows and sat on top of the various tables strewn about.

"Can you come to the main house, please," she said into her cell. A moment later, she turned to Harper. "Want some tea?"

She nodded.

She followed Ivy through a set of French doors into a vibrant kitchen. Everything was so white—the cabinets, counters, appliances, ceiling fan, and floors created a sharp contrast for the red curtains, tablemats and chairs along the island.

Harper eyed a layer of dust along the edges of the ceramic tile. If her father entered the house wearing his white glove back in the days before he discovered drugs, Harper would've been scrubbing the floor on her hands and knees.

A woman wearing a flowery over-sized shirt and white cargo shorts sailed through the back door, waving her well-worked arms in front of her cropped brown waves. Either she was flinging a cobweb off her face or she was performing tai chi. Before closing the glass door with her plump hip, a big adorable squishy dog with pristine white fur, a gigantic head, and a burly chest barged in between her legs and hobbled over to Harper. His whole body wagged along with his stubby tail. His tongue hung out the side of his mouth and his jowls blubbered.

He pushed against Harper's knees, demanding attention.

"Harper, meet Lil Boy," Ivy said.

"Good gracious," Harper said, grabbing his pudgy neck and massaging it. Her fingers got lost in his squishy folds. "Where did they come up with the bright idea to call you Lil Boy?"

The dog responded with an eager pass of his wet tongue on her nose. Harper bowed to meet his cuddle.

"He'll lick you to death if you stay down there too long," the woman said.

"Death by licks it is." Harper stretched her face.

Once the greeting ended, Harper rose and extended her hand to Ivy's mother. "I'm Harper. It's nice to meet you."

"Annie." She accepted the handshake, squinting at her as if uncovering one of Harper's many dark secrets.

Deliberately moving on from the awkward stare, Harper said, "Nice place you have here."

"It's a monster of a place to maintain." Annie wiped her hands together as if the words themselves left a smudge of grease on them.

"Harper has experience with cleaning houses. Don't you, Harper?"

Harper raised her chin. "I do. And I'm available."

Annie cupped her chin. "Is that your clunker parked out front?"

"It is. She's a bit rough around the edges, but she's like that family member you can't kick out."

Annie put her hands on her hips. "I like that. Loyalty." She lifted her chin. "You're a musician, right?"

Harper touched the side of her guitar case with her sneaker. "I'm that, too."

"She's a woman of all trades," Ivy chimed in.

"So technically you can maintain and entertain?"

She'd maintain, entertain, and run around the yard in circles if they needed. "I'm going to level with you. I need a job. I moved back to Maryland a few months ago to take care of some family stuff. Finding gigs isn't easy. I like cleaning. I like gardening. I can fix things. And yeah, I can entertain guests around the campfire while I'm at it, too."

"The guests do love their campfires," Ivy said.

"Then it's perfect. Win-win." Harper rolled her shoulders back, staving off the pathetically desperate ring to her plea. Her inner sales-person sprang into action. "The guests love music. Your floors need mopping. Your plants need pruning. You get it all with me."

Ivy swiped her hands together as if sealing the deal. Annie remained calm, the obvious analyzer of the two, testing and retesting. Ivy, on the other hand, seemed to jump in without asking how deep.

"I'm also a good organizer. I clean bathrooms like a champ. You'll never find a dust bunny in the corner. I can have those rotting branches under the bushes in the front yard cleaned up before you even ask."

"How much do you want?" Annie asked.

"As much as you can give me."

Annie smirked. "Another one who sells herself too short, just like my Ivy. I'm going to ask you what I always ask her, what kind of answer is that?"

Harper's skin burned. She searched for a reasonable figure without tossing herself out of the race. Hagerstown was over an hour's car ride each way. Of course, she'd rent an apartment closer, so that wouldn't be an issue in the long term. She technically would be working two jobs for them with the campfire music. So there was that.

Harper opened her mouth to steady for the launch of a good answer as she calculated her expenses. "Um. Well, um." Rent, car, gas, food, Moonwalk's vet and food. "Two thousand a month would work," she said confidently.

Annie pursed her lips and darted her eyes at Lil Boy. He sat like a statue staring out the glass door at the green world.

The pelting of uncertainty hammered against Harper's temples.

"What if we toss our in-residence apartment into the compensation mix? Would you be willing to take three thousand a month?"

Was the Earth round? Did clouds float? Did trees grow leaves? "Did you just offer me a thousand dollars more plus an apartment?"

She expelled a winded breath and stared at her for a longer than comfortable moment. "For the cleaning gig, the two grand and apartment would be suitable. But you need compensation for the musical entertainment portion, too. We don't expect you to do that for free. No wonder you're an out of work musician. You have no idea how to sell yourself. We're going to fix that. Now, are you interested in my offer?"

Harper swallowed hard. "I am," she said like a serious professional who considered amazing job offers all the time. While on a roll, she may as well have kept up the momentum. "There's one small thing."

Annie's eyes widened. "What would that be?"

"I promised my sister that we'd get an apartment together. She's just like me. Calm. Quiet. Respectful. Helpful, too. And she loves gardens. Of course I'm not asking for a job for her. We'd pitch in whatever money to make up for her living with me. Whatever that is."

"It's a two bedroom apartment. As long as she doesn't smoke, drink obsessively, or bother the guests and us, then she's welcome. Any bologna with either one of you and you're out. Simple as that." She swiped her hands together again. "Got it?"

Harper's heart twirled. "Absolutely."

"Just so we're clear, this isn't a handout. You're going to work your ass off. Got it?"

"Got it. I'm going to earn my keep. I expect you to put me to work."

"Fine." Annie reached into the space between the fridge and the counter and pulled out a broom. She handed it to her. "Make sure you get under the stove. God only knows what's under there."

"Mom?" Ivy asked in disbelief.

"What? The woman wants to work and I can't say I disagree."

Harper bent down and shoved the broom under the fridge. "Thank you, Annie," she said. "I appreciate the opportunity."

Harper continued to sweep under the fridge until Lil Boy's paws shuffled away as he followed Annie back out to the green paradise.

Ivy tapped her shoulder. "Get up off the floor. She's messing with you."

Harper climbed to her feet and placed the broom against the counter. "She's tough."

"She's not really. She volunteers her energy healing at Life Bridge, and so she knows Barry and Nancy. After I told her about you, she called them to confirm that you weren't some ax-wielding psychopath. She mentally hired you as a guitarist before you even arrived. The cleaning gig is a bonus for us. Barry told her you prefer to keep things real. So she broke into her bad acting and attempted to keep things real."

"So that was all just a song and dance a moment ago?"

"We may not know our way around a guitar, but we know how to have some fun." She wrinkled her nose.

"What else did Barry say?"

"That you don't like handouts, for starters."

"For starters?"

She laughed and stood taller. "That you and your sister, Tess, are good people and could use a lucky break."

Harper didn't like Barry and Nancy airing her troubles to strangers. They could've given her a heads up that Annie called them.

Harper picked up the broom again and headed toward the dust along the baseboards.

"Do you at least want to see your new digs before you officially say yes?"

Her new digs. Gosh, that had a nice ring to it. Sure, she'd never written cleaning lady on her list of dream careers, but it sure beat the hell out of sleeping on a street in the middle of Federal Hill in Baltimore with her new dog. "Lead the way."

As they proceeded down a hallway toward the back of the house, Harper mentally noted the décor. Earthy. Plants dotted every nook and cranny. They even hung on the walls as sconces. She kept her eyes on one as they rounded the bend in the hallway, descended a short flight of steps, and came upon a locked door near the garage. A philodendron vine snaked along the border of the wall.

"Here we are."

Ivy unlocked the door and they entered a small living space equipped with an oyster colored two seater couch with plush cushions and royal blue and magenta pillows. Harper would be able to sprawl out on it and spend lazy weekends snuggling, reading, and playing guitar without infringing on anyone anymore.

A large flat-screen television hung on the wall and a few floor plants in various heights outlined the country décor.

Harper's hope rose even more when they entered the kitchen nook. The efficient space spoke to that part of her heart that her music also did. It beckoned her to slide her finger along the smooth, shiny, ivory granite countertop and imagine what it might be like to cook bacon and eggs on a Sunday morning while coffee brewed in the fancy coffee maker. A blender and food processor sat on the counter, along with a two-slot toaster oven and a steel jar with every kind of food prep utensil a fancy chef from one of those five-star restaurants in Newport might use.

"Over here are the bathroom and the two bedrooms." Ivy led her farther into the cozy space. "The bedrooms are small and simple. And pretty easy to manage. We'll get to those in a minute."

They entered the large bathroom. A huge Jacuzzi tub sat in front of a window overlooking paradise. The shower was a stand-up stall with shampoo, conditioner, and bath soap dispensers. "My grandfather loved practicality."

"So he lived here?"

"Yep."

"Did he run the wellness center?"

"Nah. It didn't exist. He ran a wilderness camp on the property instead. The property was a mess. We tore down a dilapidated barn that he used to use for restoring old cars and replaced the old, redwood clapboard on the house to get the property in better shape. The yard was a sprawling, overgrown mass of grass that needed a machete, as well. Eventually, we built the wellness center and restored the tiny guest houses with the savings he left to us. It was a ton of work, but we didn't complain. This place was a gift to us all."

Ah inheritance. Some people had easy lives, Harper thought as she marveled at the pretty towel set hanging from a pewter-colored rack. "Sorry to hear that he died."

Died.

Dead.

What her father would be soon.

Her heart pinched, despite the distaste that still circled around her mouth from his years of drunken stupidity.

"He's in a good place now. We keep his memory alive with his beloved gardens and guest houses. Which is where you'll now come in. Not with my home. The retreat center and guest homes, of course."

Harper reserved her desire to run circles in the bathroom. "I appreciate your generosity, and rest assured that I'll take good care of it all."

"There's one thing I need to let you know." Ivy exited the bathroom and opened a door at the end of the small hall. The sun filled the cheerful, rosy space. "We get a couple of houseguests who like to pop in once in a while uninvited."

As long as they didn't try and climb into her bed and fuck with her sleep. A tourist bus full of guests wouldn't keep her from jumping at the opportunity to not have to impose on Andrew and Catalina anymore or sleep on the ground. Hell, she'd spent enough nights in the communal bedroom of the Life Bridge shelter. She could navigate houseguests blindfolded. "That's fine."

"These aren't your typical houseguests."

"Are they ever?"

"They're field mice."

The hair on the back of her neck rose. "Mice?"

"Our former live-in maintenance person had a cat who took care of them. You're welcome to bring a cat along. Unless Moonwalk likes to deal with mice?"

Harper glanced around the room, at the acorn colored headboard and light pink eyelet bedspread. "Time will tell, I suppose."

"I don't tell you that to chase you away. I wanted to be honest. They're harmless. Once in a while they get into the pantry, but nothing too crazy."

Ivy spoke as if telling Harper about a frisky cat knocking over her water or stomping on her alarm clock. Like having mice crawling around the house was normal. Like everyone had to deal with them, one of life's annoying little inevitable things. "Are there any in here now?" Even uttering the words, as whispery as she did, caused a rapid pulsing of shocks to flood her as she scanned the corners of the room.

Ivy tilted her head toward the floor. "No. Not now. I did a cleansing before you came in. That keeps them away for a while."

"A cleansing?"

"Sage works best on them. It settles them down. Either that or they can't stand the scent of it. Anyway, eventually they come back." Ivy spoke about them as if they were real guests.

"Have you tried mousetraps?"

Her hand flew up to her chest. "I could never." She shook her head. "No way. I prefer the natural, circle of life methods a cat offers over manmade torture devices."

Harper wouldn't let a few mice get in the way of her opportunity. So if she had to share her space with one and toss out a cereal box here and there, then bring it on. Mice would be easier to deal with than real guests anyway. People always wanted to dig, analyze, and judge. Maybe the mice would turn out to be great companions. They'd do their mice thingy. Harper would do her people thingy.

Harper could make it work.

Mice or not, the place had a home vibe that caused her heart to skip. She was seven again, riding her pink bike with silver tassels alongside her beautiful sober mother who hadn't yet broken her spine in a car accident that Harper caused. Back then, freedom and hope swirled together. Everything was so pink and shiny.

She considered the plush rose carpeting, the tasteful pictures of nature, and the rich green of the plants. She'd put up with anything to stay in that zone of freedom, hope, and all things pink and shiny. If she focused deeply enough, her imaginary butterfly wings lifted her, fluttering with the delicate breeze.

Then the familiar trickle of doubt entered.

Lucky breaks like that didn't happen in the real world without a price attached to it. Harper learned to never let her hopes float too high. Better to settle those feelings before they sent her too far over the edge of sensibility. "What's the catch to all of this?"

"The catch?"

"There's always a catch. This is too good to be true."

"There's no catch. The compensation is equal to that of the average hard-working person here in Maryland. This is seriously not a handout."

Harper had never earned an average paycheck. She always landed just above the poverty line.

Ivy's eyes warmed. "You've been through some rough times, huh?"

She didn't want Ivy viewing her as anything short of industrious and strong. "No different than anyone else."

Ivy clutched her shoulder, squeezing it gently. "Well, you're in the right place, if you ever want to unload sometime. I'm a good listener." Ivy lowered her hand.

The woman had appeal and knew how to soothe an anxious heart. Her smile settled Harper. It warmed her like a cozy blanket on a cold winter's night, wrapping itself around her and keeping the cool draft away. It could be quite distracting if Harper didn't keep up her guard a little. "Thanks. I'll keep that in mind."

Ivy backed out of the room and headed to the second bedroom. She opened the door and revealed a smaller room with oak furniture and cream-colored walls.

Harper glanced around. "It's beautiful."

They shared a grin before Ivy led them out of the apartment and toward the short steps up to the main house. A door to the outside sat at the top of the steps. Harper peeked out at the greenest yard she'd ever seen.

"There's seriously no catch." Ivy glanced over her shoulder at Harper. "Truly."

Harper followed closely behind her, and finally they landed back in her kitchen.

"My mother and I are busy with running the center, tending to the guests, and well now, for me, running a new workshop. That's it." She widened her eyes. "Will you be happy with the work?"

Was Harper dreaming? Harper would've accepted the job for the free rent alone. The opportunity to prove herself as someone creative and valuable was icing on the cake. Where could it lead? It was the first promising thing to land in her lap since she moved back to Maryland. "It's everything I want right now."

"I'm glad. You know, you can move in today if you want and start work tomorrow."

"Sounds like a great plan. If you want to draft a list, I'll get right to it. I'm your girl." The silly remark rolled out between them. "Meaning I won't let you down."

Ivy's smile turned mischievous. "I knew exactly what you meant."

Harper backed away. "Right then. So I guess I'll go to Andrew's, pick up my dog and some belongings and come back in a few hours."

"Will your sister be coming back with you today, too?"

She'd have to talk with Tess about living an hour away from their father and Andrew. "Possibly."

"Well, I'll have some fresh lemonade and home-baked cookies on your kitchen counter waiting for you, and treats for your dog."

Harper wanted to jump up for joy and fist pump the air. She wouldn't have to overstay her welcome at Andrew and Catalina's another second. She'd have a warm, beautiful bed to sleep in that night. She'd get to save that charming dog and be there for Tess. She'd get to do some physical work and play some guitar without the annoying distraction of worry pressing on her chest like a set of heavy dumbbells.

A butterfly would've fluttered and twirled in the face of such joy.

Harper wanted to as well, but didn't want to celebrate prematurely. So she settled on, "Fantastic. I'll be sure to stop and get some milk on my way back."

Finally, she had the financial aspect of her troubles covered. She could afford milk again!

When she climbed into the driver's seat of her beat-up car, she prayed it would get her back and forth without issue. She glanced at her cell and noticed a text from Andrew.

"Don't come home yet. I'll explain more when I see you. Wait until five. By then everything should be clear. Moonwalk is doing great. He's a cutie."

Was Tess drunk or high again? Had she relapsed? Why else couldn't she go home?

She went to call him, but flung her phone to the passenger seat. Better to surprise them both.

So she drove down the driveway that led back to civilization, back to where the chaos of her life typically spun like an angry tornado on those *not* lucky enough to inherit paradise.

9

SURVIVORS

Harper wished for a day when she could leave the past in the past. As life would have it, somebody always came along and fucked that up. Harper never liked dredging things or people up who served as nothing more than bad news. Nothing ever good resulted from sticking a shovel in the ground and yanking up things that were meant to stay out of the light.

Harper wished she would've taken Andrew's caution to heart and not shown up to his house until five o'clock.

There in Andrew's living room, Harper stood before Harold Ray, the man who knocked her mother up some thirty plus years before. The man who blamed his child instead of himself for fucking up a family's life.

"Tess invited him," Catalina whispered as she handed an excited Moonwalk to her. "The cancer and all."

Andrew steered Harold away from her.

Harold, with his grizzly, pathetic, scruffy gray hair, and eyes that drooped like a sad, creepy clown, fought Andrew's efforts.

Harper's feet decided to form a mutiny against her orders to turn and bolt in the opposite direction of him, back out the door and to her new home in paradise.

Moonwalk wriggled in her arms, so she let him down. He skittered away toward Harold of all people. He sniffed his sneakers and did his little Moonwalk skip.

Moonwalk was a poor judge of character.

The room and everyone in it disappeared from around her. They stared blankly at each other, waiting on the other to make a move.

Harold swallowed, cleared his throat, and stepped forward. Harper, in turn, stepped back. He put up his hands in surrender. "I'm not here to make trouble, Harper." His voice sounded old and tainted with the foulness of the bleak prison walls and gray skies from which he emerged. "Andrew said you wouldn't be back until later. I was going to leave before you got here, but Tess invited me to sit and talk."

Harper stopped herself from telling him to fuck off.

"I'd like to make peace with you." He bit his cracked lips.

God, he could use a bath. Had he spent the early afternoon rolling around in the street dumpsters fishing for scraps from other people's trash? Her father, a dirty bum with scraggly hair had gray teeth that likely hadn't seen a dentist since the days when her mom would serve them big bowls of buttery salted popcorn and cocoa by the fireplace in their home. The home she, at one time, loved. The place where some strangers came in with their large black plastic bags, latex gloves, and face masks to trash all of her toys, blankets, and Polaroid pictures. The same man who never failed to blame his little girl for what would become their worst nightmare ever.

In that moment, he stuck that shovel in the ground, piercing her skin and reopening all the wounds she'd worked so hard to heal over the past two decades.

Her eyes traveled over to Tess who wrapped her hair in a ponytail and pretended not to notice the awkwardness.

Harold shifted his weight, stuffing his worn hands into his front jean pockets. "I heard you played at Bella's. You were always so talented with the guitar."

A flashback of them sitting around a campfire playing guitar and singing invaded her better senses. "I'm not doing this." She stepped back another foot.

"I understand," he said.

Harper glanced around the cozy and welcoming space and paused at Tess who pretended not to notice that Harper stood four feet in front of the man who ruined their lives.

She glanced back at her father. "You should leave."

A disappointment he hadn't earned the right to smeared across his face. "One cup of coffee. That's all I'm asking."

"Harper," Andrew whispered, coming up to her side. "One cup."

Her father reminded Harper of her own ugly side, the one she'd shoved into the ground and covered up with the firm side of a shovel too heavy for her own good. Sorrow and lost hope seeped into the creases alongside his tired and desperate eyes.

"He's dying, Harper," Tess said. "The least we can do is offer him a cup of coffee."

She glared at her sister, the same scared little sister who would bury herself under Harper's covers during a thunderstorm. The same set of desperate eyes that pleaded with her not to leave her behind and trek to Rhode Island.

"I need time to think." Harper raised her stance to protect against the power of everyone's regretful gaze.

She inspected Harold. A brightness shone in his dark eyes, one that spoke of promise and a chance at redemption. She didn't want him carrying that away with him, as much as she didn't want him carrying the torture that trailed him for the past decades.

How could she hate and love him at the same time?

"I'm getting a piece of my liver removed tomorrow," he said. "My cancer spread there, too. I'll be at Mercy Hospital for a day or so if all goes well. Tess is bringing my guitar. You're always welcomed to play it."

She offered him one single drop to quench his thirst by way of a nod. He accepted that nod as if she'd placed a hefty load of gold in his arms.

"I'll leave now."

He walked out, leaving Harper stupefied with misty eyes.

Fucking Tess.

She glared at her, then sat on the couch. Moonwalk jumped on her lap and circled until he found his sweet spot.

Harper restrained herself from lashing out. If Andrew hadn't been eyeing her from the other end of the couch, she might've unleashed all the anger she'd spent the last two decades swallowing.

Tess was like an eggshell. Bump into her the wrong way and she'd crack. Say something in the wrong tone, and she'd turn into a five-year-old, tossing herself to the ground in a tantrum, kicking her feet, and pounding the floor with her fists.

So everyone treated her delicately. They avoided truths that should've been stated and tough love that should've been doled out, all for the sake of keeping the peace.

She had no right inviting him to the house.

Trying to keep peace was tricky. Life tossed curves. If people spent a lifetime avoiding all the curves, they'd have no clue how to work with them. Instead, when finally faced with one, they'd fall off the edge of it into a deep abyss where all the arm flails and screams they'd grown accustomed to in life would fail them.

That's why Harper loved butterflies so much. Strong and resilient, they never faltered out of avoidance. They flapped their wings and faced nature with a will to thrive in the midst of winds, gusts, and whatever else Mother Nature decided to toss at them.

Tess never learned to flap her wings.

Harper reminded herself of that as they gripped their pride in their rightful positions. She wanted to help, not worsen things. To encourage, not break down. To be the wind for a set of wings Tess might one day discover.

She had a part in Tess's struggles. She left her alone at a critical time under selfish conditions when she ran away with Kate to Rhode Island all those years ago. To worsen the matter, those selfish considerations never did materialize past heartbreak.

"Are you mad at me?" Tess asked.

Her hair was matted at the ends, creating a dusty halo as depressing as death. Her eyes lost their shimmer. If Harper told her the truth, would she end up swallowing too many pills and killing herself as well?

So Harper lied. "Of course not."

Tess smiled weakly. "Thank you."

She'd become an expert liar over the years. She learned that gift from her dear old father. If ever there was a master, it was he. So she pretty much learned from the best. She used to be able to score free meals, spare change, and rides around town by telling small fibs. He admired her for it, and that rare accolade motored Harper to stand on the side of the street, lifting her thumb. Each time someone would pull over and invite them to hop in for a ride to the store, they'd dump a handful of change into Harper's palm to buy treats.

Harper gained one valuable thing from that man. She ended up a survivor.

Tess was a survivor, too.

Under the wise and strong gaze of Andrew, Harper swallowed her pride. "Are you okay?"

A watery glaze shone in her eyes.

It gripped Harper, wrestling her into discomfort.

"As long as we're okay, I'm okay." She picked up her water glass and sipped. "Would you like for me to brew some tea?"

Just like that, they swept any trace of a would-be fight under the floor mat and went about pretending their world had balanced itself out and that a big looming concern didn't cloud the days ahead. "Sure."

Tess headed into the kitchen.

Andrew joined Harper at her end of the couch. He tapped her wrist.

"You're a great sister."

"I'm angry right now."

"Well, you do a great job covering it up."

"I always do."

That three word statement covered Harper in a layer of unease. Tess annoyed her and amused her equally. The two emotions battled one another as she chewed her gum and settled into comfortable silence with her brother.

"It's nice to have you here," he said.

"Yeah, well about that. I did come across some good news to help salvage this day."

"Oh?" Catalina plopped down on the couch next to Harper.

"I'm moving out today and inviting Tess to come with me."

Andrew stretched his eyes. "Moving out? Today?"

"I got a job at Ivy's wellness center. Barry and Nancy had put in a good word for me. It's a live-in position where I'll be maintaining the property and entertaining the guests by campfire at night. The apartment has two bedrooms, and they're fine with Moonwalk and Tess coming along."

Andrew scratched his head and averted her eyes.

"This is good news, Andrew." Harper said. "It means you have your place back and you can start working on the remodel for your future family."

Tess cleared her throat from the kitchen opening. She gripped a sugar bowl between her hands. "Thanks, Harper, but I'm not going to move in there with you."

Harper stood. "Why not? It's paradise. You'll have your own room. There's a garden and tall green grass with lots of pretty dandelions. They have an adorable dog named Lil Boy, who isn't so little. You'll love it, and they've already confirmed that all three of us can move in today. We can grab our bags and head there now. I start work first thing in the morning. I'm pretty sure that once I get to know them, and they get to know us, that we'll find some odd jobs for you, too. They have guests, which means they'll need extra hands. It's perfect. Grab your bags."

Tess squeezed her hands against the delicate bowl. "I'm moving in with Dad. He has a double-wide trailer, so there's plenty of room."

Alarm bells rang in her head. "Why would you do that?"

Tess lowered the bowl to the coffee table and pointed her eyes at Harper. "Because he needs help. He's dying and can't manage on his own. One of us has to swallow our pride and pitch in. It may as well be me because you're incapable of being within a foot of the man."

"Can you blame me?"

Tess winced. "He's changed, Harper. He needs me. And right now, I need to be needed."

Harper swallowed the strange emotions swirling in the back of her throat, a mix between hurt and frustration. "I think it's a mistake."

"If it is, then it's a mistake I'm willing to make. I don't want any regrets."

They squared off at each other.

Tess stood tall with a confidence Harper hadn't seen before.

Harper backed up a step and nodded. "Very well." She continued to hold her gaze. "The invite is always there for you."

Tess eased into a long exhale. "I'll keep that in mind."

Harper glanced at the clock. "I suppose I should get my stuff together and get back on the road."

"I know you're upset with me."

Harper turned back toward Tess. "Not with you. With your decision. It's only because I care about you."

"Will you still visit with me and Andrew?" Her voice cradled the same plea as when Harper had left her for Rhode Island many years before.

"Of course I will. I'm not *that* upset."

"But it's so far away."

"I'm only an hour's drive. That's a typical work commute for most Marylanders."

Tess curled her lip upward. "Yeah, but with your car."

Harper laughed. "Yeah, well, that's all going to change soon hopefully."

"Yeah, hopefully."

It would. It had to. Life had dumped enough heaviness on them for ten lifetimes. They deserved a break from it for a change.

10

SEXY GREEN WITCH

Living in survival mode for most of her life, Harper tended to question a lot of things. Like Ivy's podcast playing through her car speakers on the drive back to Oasis.

She listened in to get a better read on her personality for when she composed the jingle for her workshop.

Well, that exercise proved futile. Ivy shoveled a bunch of nonsense on forgiveness, and from what Harper could surmise from her sunshiny spirit, Ivy had no business rattling off her positive words on the subject. Someone that happy would never understand how bitterness leaves its mark.

When we forgive someone, we free ourselves. The weight of the world falls off our shoulders.

To forgive someone is hard. It requires an enormous amount of strength to let that hurt go and observe it with a neutral eye. Many might argue that to keep that hurt alive would require even more strength over time.

Essentially, we forgive to free ourselves.

Forgiving someone for their horrible actions doesn't mean we're accepting those actions as being okay. Absolutely not! They hurt us. In no universe is this acceptable. We're not justifying the wrong they've caused. That being said, we can forgive people without condoning the act.

"Sorry, Ms. Flower Essence, but I do not agree with you," she muttered, tapping her steering wheel repeatedly.

A defensive argument brewed in her overanxious mind. Life wasn't a fucking bowl of lemons turned into delicious lemonade that one sipped on a sunny summer day on a big, sprawling porch.

Harper turned her focus to Moonwalk who snuggled up against a stuffed teddy Tess had given him. "You probably like what she's saying. In fact, you seem to like everyone and everything. You'd probably crawl right back onto that mean lady's lap who let you run away."

Moonwalk didn't pay her any attention.

"You and Ivy have bigger hearts than I do, that's for sure." Harper bit the inside of her cheek. "Here's what we're going to do. We're going to work hard. Pay off all debt. Then in a few months, you and I are going to get out of Maryland and try something new. We'll bury all these stupid memories and start fresh. If Tess wants to stick around and pretend that man is a saint because he's dying, well, so be it. It's her wasted time, not mine. We'll get right back out there peddling my demo tapes. With you as my sidekick, someone will take a gamble on us. After all, we're both survivors."

She twisted her mouth. "Speaking of surviving, Lil Boy isn't so little. I don't want his size to freak you out." She pet Moonwalk's head, and he closed his eyes blissfully. "You like that, huh?"

He snorted like a guinea pig.

"Like I said. We'll figure this out together."

WHEN HARPER ARRIVED BACK in the driveway in front of the sprawling rancher with the bright white wrap-around porch, she settled her anger back down to its hiding place. She couldn't afford to screw anything up by stoking her bitterness over the sore topic of forgiveness. So she swallowed it and rested on the beautiful opportunity that sat in front of her.

She climbed out of the car and placed Moonwalk down on the

bricked surface. Then she opened her back door and proceeded to gather some of her items.

She pulled out her guitar case first. Then Ivy opened the front door and walked toward them. She greeted them with her shiny smile and opened her arms for Moonwalk. He ran toward her, wiggling his butt.

"Oh, your little nosy poo." She rubbed her petite nose against his and he snorted again. "Oh, Lil Boy is going to love you."

On command, Lil Boy ran clumsily out of the extra-large doggy door at the far end of the porch and straight over to Harper. His big paws and little, floppy ears stole Harper's heart again.

Her arguments over Ivy's podcast quickly faded as Ivy lowered herself with Moonwalk and Lil Boy licked his nose.

"I can't take the cuteness." Ivy pet Lil Boy as she hugged Moonwalk. She danced that line between sexy and nurturing, and Harper's resolve to be a lone survivor with a stoic heart blew away and left her gooey and warm inside.

Harper bent to get in on the petting action, and Lil Boy kissed her face.

Between the affectionate kisses from Lil Boy and Ivy's sparkly eyes and plump cheeks, Harper was swaddled in sweet goodness. With the power of cute doggy noses and floppy ears, she was free of the stress that she'd left behind in the front seat of her beat-up, rusted car.

Lil Boy kept passing his big tongue over Harper's face. "Moonwalk isn't going to be happy if you keep this up."

Ivy giggled. "Moonwalk doesn't care. He's got his own little kissing going on over here."

Lil Boy tapped Harper's chest with his big paw and knocked her back on her butt. She landed against her guitar case.

"I clearly haven't taught him manners yet. We're still working on the sit command. So expect big, wet, messy tongue licks for a while. It's been seven years since I started his training and I don't see him learning to sit on command any time soon."

Lil Boy straddled Harper, and she giggled like a fool. "I'll take it. I haven't had someone get this excited to see me since, well, ever." Harper pushed up and sat back on her heels.

Ivy stood and cocked her head, lingering on a seductive smile.

"Well, now that we've gotten that out of the way." Harper stood tall to brace against another Lil Boy explosion of emotions. "I've got all my belongings in my car and am ready whenever you want to put me to work."

"Wow. A no-nonsense woman." Ivy placed her hands on her hips. "So, I take it your sister will be up later in the week?"

"No, actually. She's got other living arrangements."

"Is she worried that she's not welcomed?"

"No, that's not it at all. She was humbled that you were willing to let her stay with me."

"Then why isn't she?"

Harper leveled a gaze. Maybe the light playing with the delicate blue spokes of her eyes or the love in Moonwalk's expression eased Harper's resolve to stay guarded. She blurted out the truth. "Our father has cancer and she's staying with him for a while."

"Oh, gosh. That's terrible." Ivy placed her warm hand on Harper's arm. "Is there anything we can do? I can teach him some relaxation techniques. My mother can do an energy healing on him."

"Oh, I don't think so." Her father didn't deserve that kind of grace.

Hurt fell upon her gentle face.

"He doesn't believe in energy healing. He's a typical westerner who believes in pills and doctor visits. That's all."

"Well please keep that offer in mind. My mother works wonders on relieving patients with pain."

"Will do."

"Well," she said spinning in a small circle. "How about if we start with a tour of the facility itself?"

Harper swiped her hands together. "Sure."

Ivy dropped her eyes to Harper's guitar case. "Is your guitar heavy?"

"Nah."

"Good. Take it along. You never know when inspiration for the jingle might strike."

Harper laughed and grabbed it.

A few minutes later, they arrived at the main retreat center. "We're standing in the lobby. This is where guests arrive and check in." She extended her arm to lead Harper's eyes around the large receptionist area where a few friendly-looking staff members talked with guests. "We can start in the wellness center and then head into the meditation garden."

Lil Boy and Moonwalk fell into pace beside her, and Harper quickly followed. They hurried past a big room that had a tripod and camera. Harper recognized the ugly black backdrop from the video podcast she'd listened to on her drive over. She stopped and peeked inside, spotting her camera. "A Nikon lover, I see."

Ivy's skirt swooshed as she turned toward Harper. Her bare arms curved delicately; a lone aquamarine bead hung like a teardrop at her chest. She was fresh and free, her lips full and naturally rose-petal pink, her hair untamed and shiny with a hint of honey-colored streaks drizzled throughout.

She could easily step into a trendy clothing store's commercial, running through a field of wildflowers while showcasing their latest fashion.

"I don't know about lover. But opportunist." Laughter colored her voice.

Was she referring to herself in the context of the camera or life? Harper was terrible at concealing her facial emotions, and Ivy appeared to pick up on her confusion.

"My grandfather used to love filming the butterflies in the garden. He was the Nikon lover. I'm the opportunistic inheritor of said piece of equipment."

Butterflies.

Show up. Stay in flight.

"Are you a lover of Nikons?" Ivy asked.

"My ex, Kate, filmed with a mirrorless Nikon camera when not performing."

"Is Kate any good?" Her eyes sparkled playfully.

That sparkle caused something in Harper's heart to twitch. "She's better at performing."

She cocked her head. "And what about you?"

Her inner thighs twitched now, too. *Focus, Harper. Job. Money. New boss.* "Why? Do you need to hire a video person, too?"

Ivy laughed. "I couldn't work under that kind of pressure."

"Pressure?"

"You're a musician. You're used to people watching you perform. I suffer enough from imposter syndrome on its own accord, never mind someone watching me do my fifty retakes."

"Imposter syndrome?"

"We can talk about that in the salt room one day." She picked up her pace, leading Harper through a beautiful maze of greenery. "Let me show you where all the magic happens."

Harper repositioned her guitar over her shoulder and followed.

Ivy took Harper on a tour of the paradise she and her mother created after they inherited the estate. They first stopped in the meditation room. A large wall of windows bathed the space in natural light. Several colorful meditation pillows in shades of orange, yellow, and peach dotted the planked wooden floor. Calming brushstroke paintings decorated the walls. The soothing sound of water drops and wind brought the room into balance.

Ivy plopped down on a pillow and motioned for Harper to do the same. "This is my favorite space in the center. It was my aunt Kathy's, too. She taught me how to meditate in here, and now I love to lead guests on meditative journeys. Do you meditate?"

"Music is more my chill-out method."

She folded one of her long, curvy legs up to her chest and rested her chin on her knee. In the soothing light, her eyes shimmered. "Can you play something?"

"Now?"

"Yeah. Some light strumming. I love the way you play."

Harper lowered her guitar case. "Any requests?"

"Surprise me." She ran a hand through her long hair.

A moment later, guitar in hand, Harper strummed a few chords lightly. "So your aunt Kathy passed away?"

Ivy rocked herself, chin still propped on her knee. "Yes. She took an extended research trip to the jungles of Colombia and got sick. She didn't want the vaccines. She was all natural. And it got her in the end. Aunt Kathy wouldn't have wanted us to sit around and mourn her too long. She was something else." Nostalgia glazed across her face. "The nicest, most forgiving person I ever met."

Harper wondered if her aunt Kathy would've been able to forgive someone like Harold for his fuck-ups.

As Harper strummed, a soothing melody formed. Ivy lowered her knee and stretched her legs forward.

"I love the sound of that. It has a forest ambiance to it. I can picture myself strolling barefoot across crisp, fallen leaves, mourning doves calling out in the distance, and the sun sprinkling its rays on the trunks of massive trees older than any generation alive today."

Her words resonated with Harper, causing her fingers to intensify the acoustic range. "I can see the scene opening now. You, wearing that flowy skirt with a willowy top that blows in the breeze. Your hair pulled up at the sides and pinned in the back center. You're tiptoeing through the woods, stopping to delicately touch each leaf as you pass it by. Peace settles into your laugh lines as you glance into the camera lens."

Ivy's lips parted and her eyes eased from their brightness into a more romantic gaze. "With that exact song playing in the background."

Harper's fingers traveled across the fretboard, creating a sound that fed her soul what it needed to be focused, clear, and creative.

Ivy grabbed her cell. "Keep playing. I'm recording. We need to remember this melody."

They spent the next several minutes enjoying the venture into the musical sphere of that jingle. When Harper was satisfied with a suitable closing, she lowered her head and allowed the comfort of the silence to resume and compose her.

"Is that an original?"

"Sure is."

"Was that your first time playing that song?"

"Sure was."

"You're amazing." Ivy stood and offered Harper a hand off the pillow. "I've always been fascinated with the guitar."

"Do you play?"

"No, but I'd love to learn."

"I'll teach you one of these days."

She lolled her head to the side, stealing the breath from Harper's lungs with her piercing eyes. "I would love that." She fluttered her lashes, and the color rose on her cheeks. "Come on, let's continue our tour."

They left the meditation room and came up to another space nestled behind a grove of beautiful tall floor plants with giant leaves. Ivy opened the door to the Pilates room with her hip. She eased Harper into the quiet, walnut-colored room with its fancy Pilates equipment. Each of the five machines was elevated about a foot off the floor with a silver steel frame and was accented with oak wood trim. The room itself was decorated straight from a Pinterest board with warm, distressed barn doors with various-sized window panes and large mirrors that created an enlarging effect.

Ivy's eyes strolled down the length of Harper. "Ever do Pilates?"

"Never Pilates."

"We'll have to treat you to a session sometime." She pulled Harper backward by the arm. "Come. Let me show you the pool."

As they traversed the length of the open retreat center, Harper's eyes journeyed around the pristine décor with its large windows overlooking an expansive canvas of greens and colorful flowers. The floor, set in geometric angles, turned what could've been a boring open space into an interesting delicacy for the curious eye. It provided a comforting and relaxing environment for mind, body, and spirit. A luscious interior garden divided the spaces, creating an intimate ambiance. The air flowed with the use of gradients of natural and pathway lighting.

Surrounding the central areas were smaller relaxation rooms that provided detoxification experiences like infrared saunas and even a sensory deprivation floating tank. "These peaceful rooms are meant to allow guests the opportunity to disconnect from everyday stress and distractions," Ivy explained in a silvery tone as they passed them. "This is the time of day a lot of our guests will come back from hiking and want to relax before early evening tea in the garden. Our staff members cater to their every whim, providing them with warm towels and fluffy bathrobes."

The center used warm tones and cool textures to further support a sense of relaxation and comfort.

"As you can see, it's a large space that accommodates not only our retreat guests, but also our monthly membership guests."

Moonwalk sniffed everything in his path, and thankfully restrained from lifting his leg to mark his territory. Maybe he understood that he'd won the dog lottery and needed to behave himself.

Ivy placed her nurturing hand around Harper's wrist. "Be sure to book a treatment session. Especially one in the floating tank. Have you ever been in one?"

Harper hated being boxed into an elevator, let alone a tank of water. "Can't say it's on my bucket list."

Ivy paused on the end of a breath like a thought had trickled into her mind and she volleyed it back and forth. "What do you say we brew tea for the guests?"

"Whatever you need."

Harper followed her through the angled maze of lush greens, back out to the reception area, and off to a beautiful teak kitchen area. She helped her make tea by putting on a large kettle of water to boil. Ivy squeezed lemons into a large teapot with painted pink roses on it. She also squeezed some lemon into a glass and poured filtered water into it. She handed it to Harper. "In case you're thirsty."

"Thanks." Harper sipped, and Ivy's eyes trailed her. A thrilling shiver traveled down her spine. She tried not to do something stupid like spill water out of the side of her mouth.

"So now that we have a jingle, are you going to join my 'Uprooting' workshop with Andrew and Catalina?"

If it means more face time with you, sign me up. "If you'll have me?"

Ivy swallowed the beginnings of a thought, and brushed some wispy pieces of her honey-streaked hair behind her ear. A tease filled her pretty blue eyes. "I will gladly have you." She bit her lower lip and stole a quick peek at Harper, then darted her eyes around the space. "It's been a while for me, I have to warn you."

Hot, delicious flashes flicked at her from all different directions. "Really?"

Ivy's eyes opened-wide as if Harper had caught her naked. "I mean with the life advice stuff."

"Of course. What else would've you meant?"

"Exactly."

"Yes, exactly."

A palpable pulse zapped between them. Harper sipped her lemon water, trying hard to ignore the desire to brush more wisps behind Ivy's delicate, diamond-studded ears. "Tell me about your ideas for the workshop."

Ivy eased back into her comfort zone. "I'm hoping to teach people how to take control of their lives by digging up the old stuff they planted and replanting something new. People who have had tough times need to know they have someone on their side. I want to be that someone for more people. You know?" A wishful glow spread across Ivy's face.

"Yeah. I bet a lot of people would like something like that."

Harper could tell she liked to fix people up, swipe her hands, and lay her head down at the end of the day content that she helped another person to live a better life.

"Would you like something like that?"

Someone as innocent and peaceful as Ivy likely never had her heart ripped out of her chest or lived through the kinds of horrors that kept Harper awake at night. She'd tread carefully with her, divulging only the parts that normal people experienced. Things like losing a pet fish or not getting the job of her dreams.

"Sure. I love to dig. Especially in dirt. Which sort of reminds me that I've got work to do for you. I'm looking forward to getting my hands dirty in the garden and in the cleaning. And of course, I'm totally excited about chilling out by the fire with my guitar and polishing up your jingle."

"I can't wait to sit and let your music wash over me like it did just a few minutes ago and, of course, yesterday." A calmness settled around Ivy. "I guess we're both in the right place at the right time."

Harper ran her finger over her wet glass and raised it. "Here's to being in the right place at the right time."

They clanked glasses, and Ivy sipped. She peered over the edge of her glass into Harper's eyes. "If you ever want me to perform a good energy spell, let me know. It helps with stress and balance."

"Good energy spell?"

"It's when I create a field of energy around you. This field of energy will help to protect you against anything negative."

Harper widened her eyes.

"Don't worry. I'd only cast a spell if you asked."

"Maybe a spell cast on a few others who've pissed me off in life, sure." Harper chuckled. "But I'm all right."

Ivy gripped her water glass and pointed her eyes at Harper. "I sensed anger and anxiety from you when you arrived. Maybe it was the traffic?"

"Yeah, the traffic."

"A lot of times we carry anger around with us, and that anger can cause stress. It comes at us from all different directions, can wreak havoc on our immune systems, and keep us from living happily and in balance. If you ever feel that way, ask me to do a good energy spell for you. Okay?"

Ivy was a nice person with a good heart. "I bet you don't have too many enemies in this world, huh?"

"Oh, I do." Her eyes took on a sadness.

"But you're so easy to forgive people. How do you have an enemy?"

Her lip twitched. "How would you know that?"

"I listened to one of your podcasts about forgiveness on the drive over. To get an understanding of your work so I can compose a proper jingle, of course."

"My what?" Ivy stepped up to her side with the eagerness of a puppy steadying for play time.

"Your podcast on forgiveness," Harper said focusing on the sizzling tea kettle on the burner. "The one about why we should forgive people who have wronged us."

Ivy cocked her head. "You listened?" Her voice rang with a charming excitement.

"How do you still have an enemy in the world if you forgive everyone?"

"Because my best friend still hasn't forgiven me."

"What could someone as sweet as you have done that could be unforgivable?"

Ivy's forehead creased.

Harper tripped over how to proceed. "I've done things that aren't forgivable, too, and others have done things to me that are unforgivable. That's why I don't believe that we can simply reduce the pain of something hurtful and life-altering with a simple *I forgive you*. It's more complicated than that. Even you've suffered that dilemma."

Ivy narrowed in on the lemon peels, searching for the right words. "Hmm."

"Please defend yourself and prove me wrong," Harper whispered.

"Here's where that imposter syndrome comes in." She swallowed hard.

"Do you not practice what you preach?"

"I don't preach. I share." She pulled in her lips tightly and settled her eyes back on Harper. "I fucked up big time with my friend."

Her use of the f-bomb settled Harper down in a comforting way. The ever-peaceful and rooted Ivy was perfectly relatable on top of being beautiful. "Big time?"

She glanced around the space like she didn't trust herself. "Yes. I've spent the better part of a year reconsidering everything I said to her." She stepped closer again, placing a hand on the counter. "Part of the problem with having an ego, and we all do, is we're too busy defending and justifying ourselves. As a result, we fail to get to the root cause of the tipping point. We were both wrong and right. It took me a whole year to wrap my stubborn mind around that. I recorded that episode before that incident happened. I haven't listened back to it since then. I'm sure I've got some things to update with it."

"Do you deserve to be forgiven?"

Ivy's lips parted, but no words came out. She closed them, eyed the full width of the room around them, and sighed. "If it would spare her anger and fill her with peace, then yes. When a person stands guard over anger, they spread it. How's that serving the world?"

She did have a point. "How do you drop anger though? If the person hurt you or someone you love, how do you condone the act and end on a hug?"

"See, that's the thing." Ivy tapped her knuckle against the counter. "Forgiving isn't condoning. I acted ugly toward my friend. She acted ugly toward me. We were ugly and wrong for it. So what are we better off doing: Gripping that ugliness for the sake of righteousness or letting it go for the sake of peace by admitting that sometimes things go haywire? Sometimes we say the wrong thing. Sometimes people are asshats and hurt you. Are we to cling to the bitterness and remain victims to it?"

"Forgiving her would send the wrong message if you were right and she was wrong. Doesn't that bother you?"

"I don't forgive her as a gift for her. I forgive her as a gift to me. It's not about her. She has nothing to do with it. It's about my peace."

"That's not how the world works."

"That's exactly how the world works, Harper." Ivy swayed and folded her hands in front of her. "I chose to forgive her. That's empowered me. I want to help people, and I can't do that if I cling to a past that angers me. I'm tired of being a victim to that bitterness. I deserve to be happy, and I can't do that from a place of bitterness toward her or myself."

"Well now you've got me curious. What happened?"

"I kicked her and my five year-old godson out of the apartment you'll be living in. I lost it one day. My patience with her vanity and lack of respect for my time got the best of me and I pitched a tantrum and sent her packing."

Ivy dueling it out with someone? It'd be easier to imagine a minister committing an armed robbery. "You sent her packing?"

"I did. I carried that grudge around like a suit of armor. It justified my bitterness. I'd go to sleep at night and allow this grudge to suffocate me. I'd wake in the morning and further allow it to accompany me through the day and diminish my spirit. To sum up this span of time – I wasted many months of my life."

"Months? That long, huh?" Harper asked, sarcastically.

"Well, how long has it been for you?"

Harper pointed at her. "Oh no you don't. I see what you did there. I share, you share? Oh no." She laughed.

Ivy tucked a piece of her hair behind her ear and peered at Harper with innocent eyes. "If you don't like sharing, how will you survive my workshop?"

"Well I've never been a good student. And I can't promise that my new work here at Oasis won't get in the way. I take a lot of pride in my work."

"We're not going to keep you that busy. We'll let you breathe from time to time."

The way her lips curved caused Harper's heart to sputter. "Breathing is good."

Ivy closed more of the gap between them. "Harper, to live in peace requires a certain trust in the universe. I'm starting to learn that." She moved in, so much more that her breath tickled Harper's cheek.

Harper closed her eyes, relaxing into her breeziness.

"Embrace the whisper brushing against your heart. It's telling you to let go, restore the flow, and release from the burden of self-induced captivity."

When Harper found her balance again, she opened her eyes. A seriousness sat between them, one that grew heavier with each tick of the clock. She needed to lighten the emotional load. "That was incredibly eloquent."

Ivy shifted her eyes back down to the lemon and stared at it, like it could provide her with shareable insights. "I don't know anything about your circumstance or where you're coming from with the forgiveness factor. I do know that the heart always wants balance. It wants to rest at the end of the day and not carry the burden of resentment and hate in it."

The woman was spot on. Could she read the inside of her brain? Had she shrunken down to a miniature-sized version of herself to ride around on a molecule, analyzing all the wiring, neurons, synapses, and electrical impulses in her mind?

"That was insightful. And helpful." Harper gazed deeper into her eyes. "You have nothing to worry about with that silly imposter syndrome stuff. You're not an imposter at all. You're living proof that you can learn from life and then share it. That's real and raw, and your 'Uprooting' listeners are in for a treat."

"Does this mean you'll be a good student?"

"Again, look at the size of this place." Harper glanced around the kitchen. "I'll be lucky if I have time to eat at the end of the day."

"We'll feed you." Ivy tapped the tip of Harper's nose.

"Any other magical powers you want to tell me about before we continue our tour? Like you're the world's best peanut butter and jelly sandwich maker, by chance?"

"I do consider myself a green witch, so there's that." Ivy swayed again.

Harper drew in a large amount of air. "I've no idea what a green witch is, but it sounds sexy as hell."

Ivy's beautiful blue eyes widened, then she tossed her a wink. "A *sexy* green witch. I like that."

11

PROPER PERSPECTIVE

IVY

After showing Harper around the entire center, guest houses, and gardens, Ivy met a few of the guests in the classroom to teach them some theory on intuitive plant medicine. She invited Harper to sit in on the class, and to her surprise she agreed.

Standing at the head of the classroom and sharing her passion for plants invigorated Ivy. The five guests who were gathered that evening, plus Harper, focused in on her. In that lesson, she taught them about how certain plants, specifically Hawthorn, helped create boundaries to help heal deep wounds and grant the heart the freedom to love again.

They spent an hour talking about the importance of setting boundaries as a first step to creating a life of purpose and connection.

At several points in her lecture, Ivy glanced at Harper. She wrote copious notes.

Harper struck her as someone who sported a tough exterior, protecting the vulnerable and delicate parts that could bruise if exposed. Ivy sensed her hurt and anger, too. She also sensed hope. A hope that one day soon she'd experience a lucky break like Ivy did. A break that would liberate her from the worries of annoying things like a rusted car door hanging off its hinges or the swelter of stress that refused to cool down.

As Ivy meandered around the classroom tables, she glanced at Harper's notepad. She had written musical notes. They strung along the paper like Christmas lights on a tree, magical and mysterious with their flickers of beauty.

Later on, as Harper volunteered to spend her first night around the campfire with the guests, Ivy met with her mother for their weekly management meeting to discuss plans for the following week's retreat guests.

"We have a family of fifteen coming next week," her mother said as she entered their shared living room. "They want to learn how to create flower essences." She raised her phone. "I've asked them to send in song requests."

"Song requests?"

"It'll be a nice test to see how engaging Harper will be with guests." Her mother bobbed her head proudly.

"Why are we testing her?" Ivy didn't like when her mother put on her boss hat. They didn't run a Fortune five-hundred company. They didn't conduct their weekly meetings at a twelve-seater mahogany conference table. Hell, they didn't even outsource a bookkeeper to manage their books. They were lucky to have Harper join them. She was a much better choice than the playlist her mother loaded onto her iPad and hooked up to the speakers by the fire pit.

"Because we've made poor choices in the past. You know, with Lila," she arched her eyebrows, "And that temp cleaning lady this past week. A spring breeze could've blown her over."

"People can request songs, but it's not a test. Barry and Nancy already vouched for her. She's staying."

Her mother scrolled through her phone, her reading glasses balancing on the bridge of her pudgy nose. "Someone's defensive today."

Ivy laid her head against Lil Boy. "I like her. She's grateful. She's talented. And she's motivated."

"You sound just like your father. He used to defend everyone and everything. One time he climbed a twenty-foot ladder to save a squirrel who caught his little leg in a vine."

Ivy's father passed away when she was a toddler. She didn't remember him. She grew to love him through old photos from his Navy days and from the few pictures captured during their wedding at city hall. She loved hearing tidbits like that.

"Harper isn't a squirrel stuck in a vine, Mom."

Her mother dropped her phone on the couch. "No, she isn't. But she is an investment, and that always requires a risk on our part."

"Mom, we invest in a whole team of staff members. Why is this any different?"

"They are part-timers. It's very different. A full-timer who is a live-in is much more of an investment. And, I guess I'm still gun shy to invest in someone so permanent, seeing how invested we become in them."

Her mother referred to Cris, their former cleaning lady of five years who got married and moved to New Mexico. And then of course, Lila. "If we can't invest ourselves in someone, what's the point?"

She pet Lil Boy's big head. "You're right. To tell you the truth, I'm looking forward to campfire sing-along nights. The guests will love it too, especially if we let them request songs." She looked up at Ivy. "It's not a test. Okay? It's good customer service is all."

OVER THE NEXT SEVERAL WEEKS, Harper acclimated herself to the center. She spent some time working with Ivy's mother in the gardens and around the grounds of the guest homes.

She worked diligently during the day and treated the guests to her magical musical abilities at night. Ivy worried that she and her mother were keeping her too busy, though. Her father had cancer, after all. Didn't she want to spend time with him? Ivy offered her time off to be with her father if she wanted it, but Harper brushed off the gesture by working even more.

Then one day, Harper offered to videotape Ivy's intro for her workshop. Harper directed Ivy on all the same moves she shared in the meditation room. Ivy wore a flowy skirt with a willowy top, and it blew in the breeze as Harper had said it should. She had pulled her hair up at the sides and pinned it in the back center. Harper directed her to tiptoe through the garden, stopping to delicately touch each leaf as she passed it by. Then Ivy did as Harper requested. She planted a peaceful gaze on the camera.

Harper offered to produce the video, and the result amazed Ivy. Harper's brilliant jingle brought it to life, and Ivy was excited to use it in her first "Uprooting" video.

So, Ivy got to work on massaging the ideas for her workshop.

One night, as she sipped tea and jotted a few thoughts down in her journal, her debacle with Lila creeped into her mind. Lila had yet to reply to her congratulatory message. That saddened her.

She couldn't control Lila's response, but she could control her own. She'd leave it alone. Lila's silence told her that she had to move on and do something more with her life than dream up a dismal future getting old by a campfire with her mother. She needed to focus even more on creating content that would help people.

She glanced over at Lil Boy. He snored, blissfully. His wrinkles vibrated with each inhale and exhale.

An image of Lil Boy licking Harper on her first day caused Ivy to break into a series of chuckles.

That Harper sure did massage the strings on her guitar. Each night, Ivy would sneak over to the gardens to admire the way she entertained the guests. That woman poured her soul into each song, and it stirred sensual and earthy pleasures in Ivy.

She laid her head back and thought about Harper's arm slung over the edge of her orange sunburst guitar, hair in a messy ponytail, eyes at half-mast as she dug into the rich melodies of her heart.

The woman was sexy, and Ivy craved to get to know her better.

As she lay there imagining Harper singing a soulful song to her, her skin flushed. She closed her eyes and traveled her fingers up and down her torso, craving to relive her orgasmic experience. A warm, tingly sensation spun. A delightful buzz numbed her mind as she imagined Harper's lips finding their way to hers in a mesmerizing dance of desire. She wanted to kiss her, to feel her full, wet, warm lips on hers.

Her chest rose and fell in visible successions. Every nerve ending pinged to life, charging Ivy with an insatiable urge to explore Harper Ray in her fantasies again.

As Ivy's fingers traveled to the places she imagined Harper's would, her heart pounded. Her desires turned intimate as she pictured Harper staring deeply into her eyes, like she was someone beautiful and worthy of love.

No one had ever looked at Ivy like that before. Not even her ex, for whom she moved to Pittsburgh.

Tears welled in Ivy's eyes.

In all her thirty-two years, she never pictured a woman tending to her heart the way Harper Ray just did in her mind.

Imagine if it were real.

Ivy pulled her blankets up under her chin and rolled over, sealing herself into the emotions. She drifted off into a relaxing sleep, and when she woke, she walked over to her desk.

Her restful slumber opened up her creativity. Ideas for her future workshop topics flowed into her mind.

How to have better conversations.

How to achieve what you want in life.

What would you say to your younger self?

Ivy sat tall and picked up a pen from her bedside table. She tapped the pen to her lower lip, mulling over her ideas. She loved that last one and decided to jot down some thoughts on it.

If you could have a chat with your younger self and offer a piece of life advice that would change the destiny of your future journey for the better, what would that be? What would that conversation sound like? Would you ever dare talk to her in a negative voice? With distaste that she isn't more like her friends? Of course you wouldn't. You would treat her with the kind of wise love you learned to cherish through the years.

Ivy dotted the last sentiment with a firm tap to the notepad. Satisfied with its start, she stood and glanced proudly at herself in the mirror. "That'll be great workshop material." She looked down at Lil Boy who woke from his nap and waited on something yummy. "Harper might enjoy that one. Am I right?"

He smacked his lips together.

She laughed, plucked a treat from the little bag on her dresser, and tossed it at him. He moved around like an elderly man in slippers most times, but toss a treat in the air, and he turned into a toddler, nimble and unbreakable.

"Come on, Lil Boy. Let's walk through the garden."

A few minutes later, she ventured toward the back garden to gather some herbs for dinner.

She spotted Harper standing in the middle of the garden oasis, cellphone pressed to her ear, other arm flailing about. She paced, speaking in rushed, guttural interjections.

Ivy snuck behind a trellis of grapes, latching onto Lil Boy's collar. She pushed his rump down, hoping he didn't notice Harper or Moonwalk who was curled up in a little ball on a patch of grass near the Azalea bush.

Stepping inside another person's conversation was like entering a pool of quicksand. You sank deeper with each attempt to escape the awkward and demanding pull on your curiosity.

Harper had no patience for niceties and small talk, with the way she manically paced the small, tense space.

"Absolutely not, Barry. If Tess wants to help, then she can do that. She's a grown adult. But to make me out as some sort of asshole for not chipping in money. Come on, now," she said firmly.

Ivy wished she could get away unseen.

"No, but... wait... Are you kidding?" She exhaled like a mad bull ready to charge. "Tess said that?"

Pause.

Deep breath.

Head angled up to the blue sky.

"Okay. Fine."

Pause.

Head bowed.

"I'm sorry, Barry. Tess gets me going. I'm sorry she's pulling you and Nancy into this."

She pressed her palm against her other ear.

Pause.

"Barry, it's too late. Some things can't be erased." Harper balled up her fist and hit her thigh. Hard. Her forehead creased. "I'll call her myself and tell her. She never should've stuck you in the middle of this."

Pause.

"I love you, too. Please hug Nancy for me."

She hung up and bent over.

Ivy pushed her heels against the dirt, but Lil Boy couldn't contain himself a moment longer. He whined and shifted, wagging his butt in joy to get close to her and Moonwalk.

Harper looked up and locked her watery eyes on Ivy.

Moonwalk and Lil Boy did a little dance around each other, bowing and barking before landing on a couple of excited stomps.

"Everything okay?" Ivy asked, coming out into the open.

Harper ran her hands through her hair. "I'm sorry. I didn't mean to be so loud." She glanced around the garden for affected guests.

"No worries. The guests are hiking right now."

"I should get back inside to clean the pool." She tapped the fire pit with the tip of her water shoe.

Ivy moved in. "Harper you can take a break if you need to."

"I'm fine."

"Remember that the amenities are available to you. If you need to duck into a deprivation tank for a few minutes, go ahead. It helps clear the mind and reveal answers to those tough questions in life."

"What you overheard is typical family drama. Nothing more. Nothing less."

"I get it. Family can be tough, and it's expected. My mother drives me crazy. You should hear us duke it out sometimes. Especially when she starts in on my love life. She has a Tinder account for research for a novel that has my picture on it."

Harper blew out a gush of pent up stress. "At least she's there for you."

Ivy resisted pushing. She let Harper's large boulder of a statement sit between them. She had a blessed life with a mother who was more her best friend than, well, her best friend.

Harper pushed her sunglasses up on her head. Her dark eyes, even though somber from her phone call, were warm and mesmerizing.

"I'm here for you, if you need to talk about anything," Ivy said.

"Thanks, but I'm fine."

"Are you sure?"

"I'm positive."

"I'm a good listener."

"I'm irritated, Ivy. I don't want to be psychoanalyzed," Harper said on a snap. "I just need to be alone."

"Okay." Ivy stepped back.

Harper glanced at the space between them as if it were an invading algae species coming in to attack her.

ONCE HARPER WALKED AWAY, Ivy headed inside.

"Why the long face," her mother asked when she entered the kitchen.

"It's Harper. I'm concerned about her," Ivy said. "She was upset, and I tried to help. She ended up snapping at me."

"Not everyone wants to talk things out, Ivy."

"If she'd let me in, I could help her."

"Don't meddle." She pointed her finger at Ivy. "Understand? Otherwise we're going to be right back where we were before we hired her, scrambling to hire someone else."

"I can't sit still and not help when someone is broken."

Her mother exhaled sharply and picked up her garden gloves from the counter. "Give her space and she may open up to you."

"If she doesn't?"

"Then she doesn't."

Her mother moved to her side. "Harper strikes me as someone who doesn't show her weakness to anyone. She wants everyone to see that she's strong and capable. So be her friend and let her be."

"Would a friend do that? Just let up?"

"Oh Ivy," she said, staring at her with her comforting motherly love. "My sweet Ivy. If you're frustrated and want a way to help, use your new workshop. Maybe she'll listen in when she needs it most. You can't force your help onto someone."

Ivy considered her mother's wise advice. "I suppose."

"You're great at giving advice." She tapped the tip of her nose. "You're terrible at executing it yourself."

"I can't argue."

"Trust yourself that you can do what you advise others to do."

Ivy laughed. "That's the problem. I see things clear as day for others. But for me, it's like the universe decided to toss a cloth over everything in my reality to see what kind of messes I can end up in."

"You love a good mess, and you can't deny that."

"I do."

"Messes are like a drug to you. You feed off them like a drug addict feeds off opioids." She shook her head. "Ease up. Don't be so anxious to get in. She'll put up locks you'll never be able to open."

Ivy placed her hand on top of her mother's. "Thank God for you. You know how to put everything into proper perspective."

Her mother waved her away. "All this mushiness is going to cause my mascara to smear. So onward we go. I'm going to the greenhouse to check on my tomatoes."

12

PEACE IT IS

HARPER

Harper really did need space. She trudged toward the greenhouse, pissed at the world and not wanting to deal with anyone or anything for a good long time.

She needed to focus on something other than her fucked-up father. Tess started a freaking crowdfunding page for him? People supported good hearts, not those who destroyed lives. Contribute and share the page on social media? Fuck that.

Maybe Harper should start her own crowdfunding campaign.

Argh.

The only thing Harper would support in that moment was Oasis. She'd dig into a project for them that she'd been considering since her first day a few weeks back: a way to rid the greenhouse of gnats.

Harper was about fifteen minutes into her gnat-reducer project when Annie entered to check on her tomatoes.

"Everything okay?" Annie asked.

Harper liked Annie. They had spent some time together in those first few weeks and formed an instant bond. She was a straight-shooter. A smart-ass. A woman who meant well.

"I'm not in a great mood right now. I should just work."

"Work is good for piss-ass moods. When I'm annoyed, I prune the bushes. And if it's winter, I sweep or shovel the driveway depending on the precipitation."

Harper slung a dish towel on the counter. "I'll pick up this mess. A few of the planters have gnats living in them. They're everywhere. It's disgusting. I'm trying to get rid of them for you." She swung around and showed her a pipe that she drilled holes in. "I have an idea. You're going to have to trust me with it. Either that or hand guests fly swatters along with their fancy towels."

"Do what you have to do."

Harper eyed her pipe gadget. "This will work fine." She placed it on the counter, picked up the cleaning spray, and swiped away her mess. Meanwhile, Annie continued to rake her over with concerned eyes.

"I'll be fine," Harper said. "Really."

"Ivy means well."

"You overheard us?"

"She told me you were upset. She only wanted to help, not make you more upset."

Harper gazed at Annie. Kindness sat along her pale, weathered skin. "I don't like to air out my problems, that's all."

Annie crossed her arms over her chest. "I get it. But you have to agree that they become stagnant when not aired."

Harper's temples pulsed. Her earlier conversation with Barry raced back into her mind. Tess expecting her to fork over money she didn't have for her father. Tess putting Barry in the middle. Barry actually calling up Harper to tell her that. Anger whipped around her mind, cutting off better judgment.

"You think airing my problems is the right thing to do?"

"In the right company, yes."

"The right company?"

Annie nodded.

"Okay, you want to hear the truth about how my life has been fucked up and mangled? About how my father emotionally abused us, and at times physically. That my mother's car accident, one that I caused, plummeted her into the sufferings of chronic pain? That then she needed to rely on opioids? That when she ran out of them, she moved onto heroin? That my father sobered up for two years after my mother's death and then got angry when he couldn't afford house payments and we had to move into a trailer with one bedroom? And because of that, he went back to drinking and killed someone with his car? And that now Tess struggles with depression and dependency issues because I chose to leave her when she needed me most? In what world would I want to give air to such things?"

Annie licked her lips one too many times. "I'm sorry. That's a lot of heavy shit. That must have been rough."

Harper trembled. "Oh, you don't know the half of it. I only let you in on parts of it."

"Have you had help?"

"I've handled it."

"Yeah, I can see that."

Harper fiddled with her gadget. "Do you see why I'd rather talk about music, even plants at this point?"

"Music and plants are easy subjects."

"Do you see why I want to keep this stuff away from this place? Oasis is magic to the soul. With all due respect to you and Ivy, I prefer keeping it that way."

"I get it." Annie wrapped her hand around Harper's arm. "I really do."

Her wise eyes comforted Harper, bringing her heartbeat back down to normal.

"Ivy's a fixer by nature. Her heart is always in the right place. If you need a friend, she's the best. She can help you churn through things without judgement."

"Some things are too hard to churn."

Annie looked upon her with compassion. "I can't begin to imagine what you've been through. I don't have any wise words other than what has worked for me. When I'm feeling like shit about things, I turn my attention to things I love. So turn your attention to things you love, Harper, whether that's a plant, tree, person, or a weird gadget with uneven holes in it."

Harper turned her attention to her gadget. "That's sage advice." She dug the pipe into a planter, picked up a water pitcher, and fed the water into it. "Gnats love moisture. Most of these houseplants only need the moisture at the roots. They don't need water pooling at the surface. So put the water where it's needed."

Annie laughed, releasing them both from the tension of moments ago. "That's quite innovative. Though, the gnats are attracted to more than the water, dear."

Harper stared at the planter and gnats swarmed around the surface. "Little fuckers. What gives?"

"What soil did you use for the potting soil?"

Harper pointed to the compost pile outside the side door. "Naturally, the good stuff."

"Exactly. Gnats aren't dumb like us humans. They know the good stuff when they see it." On that, she glided away. When she got to the side door, she craned her neck over her shoulder. "Anger is just like a gnat, if you keep feeding it, it'll come back for seconds, thirds, and fourths."

SHORTLY AFTER HER meltdown with Annie in the greenhouse, Harper sat by the fire pit. Ivy talked with a guest by the patio, animated as always.

Then Annie approached and handed Harper a glass of iced tea. "You look better. Do you feel better?"

"I do, thanks." Harper took a long sip of the lemony tea.

Annie looked over at Ivy. "She's got a big heart."

"She does. She smiles a lot." Harper chugged her drink. "That's good. Smiling is good. We need more happy people in the world."

"Amen to that." Annie sat on one of the chairs by the fire pit. "Why are you chugging your tea? Is everything going to always be this intense?"

Annie had a sarcastic grit to her that Harper liked. "It's the only way I know how to be."

"Intense like Ivy. Great. Now I've got two of you to deal with."
Annie looked back at Ivy. "She's becoming happier, thankfully."

"What do you mean?"

"She's been a little lost the past year. So you handed her a gift by
planting the 'Uprooting' workshop in her heart. Since she posted her
first few episodes, I've seen her light back up again."

"I don't deserve that credit. My brother Andrew and his wife
Catalina planted that seed. I just called it something catchy." Harper
sipped, proud of her creative naming. "Was it the best friend thing
that made her unhappy?"

"The earth-shattering blowout with Lila. Yep. If she lets it, that
blowout is going to ruin her life."

Ivy's gestures were light and fanciful as she spoke with the guest.
"She's smiling and always bouncing on her feet. Nothing's ruining
her."

"She covers well. I guess being in the public eye with her videos,
she's used to showcasing a winning attitude. She's got so many
insights to share. She's impacted people's lives, saving some from a
lifetime of misery. And she let one person ruin that for so many
others for over a year. It's a shame. But I'm hopeful she's starting to
heal from that. I'm a little protective of her. It's because I adore that
daughter of mine. Anyway, I wanted to thank you for boosting her
confidence, even if it was just in the naming."

Ivy glanced at Harper, tucked a piece of her pretty hair behind
her ear, and smiled at her. Their eyes locked, and Harper's chest
tightened in the trickle of discreet sadness that marked the stare.

"I'm glad her confidence is boosted again. It would be a shame for
her to give up because of a fight with a friend."

"Lila is a tough one. She's headstrong, selfish, and, in my eyes,
took advantage of Ivy's kindness. She could've learned a lot from Ivy,
had she played her cards correctly. Then when the blowout
happened, which inevitably it had to, Ivy shut down. So then no one
got to learn from her for thirteen months. She had lost her self-help
mojo. So she cleaned."

Harper understood how to shut down better than anyone else. "Cleaning is good self-therapy."

"We could all use some of that around here. Yes, even you." Annie rose and headed back to the other guests who gathered around pub tables and sipped iced tea.

Ivy

Ivy headed over to Harper after dealing with the guest.

Harper fidgeted with the towel, squeezing it tighter. Her forehead still creased with her stress from earlier.

Ivy resisted asking about the phone call again. "How's everything?"

Harper considered her question like one might ponder the meaning of life. "I could use some fun right about now. So you know what I want?"

Ivy cocked her head. "To float in a deprivation tank?"

Harper laughed and tossed her towel on a chair. "S'mores and a good game of checkers."

"S'mores and checkers?"

"Yes. Graham crackers. Marshmallows. Chocolate. The whole bit. And a competitive game of checkers."

Ivy beamed. "Grab your guitar and checkers. I'll get the s'mores fixings and we'll meet back here in twenty minutes."

Harper turned and headed out of the garden hearth and toward her apartment. Moonwalk trotted beside her. She glanced over her shoulder. "See you in twenty."

Within fifteen minutes, Ivy managed to gather everything and get back to the fire pit, light it, and even brown the first side of a marshmallow by the time Harper returned with her guitar and checkers.

The two spent the next thirty minutes eating three s'mores a piece. Then Harper fiddled around with guitar chords, stringing them together into a gorgeous chime. "That sound, right there." Ivy pointed to the guitar. "Do that again."

The smile on Harper's face grew wider as she played and replayed the melody.

Ivy hit the record button on her phone's camera. "We're not forgetting this melody. This is going to be your big breakout song one day. I can feel it. I'm pretty darn intuitive."

"Yes, I'm still reeling over your intuitive hit from Bella's. If it weren't for that, I might be strumming to a crowd on Light Street in Baltimore hoping they're generous enough to toss a few coins in my case." Harper fingered her strings and filled the hearth area with musical beauty instead of the anger from earlier.

After another round of s'mores, Harper pulled out her checkerboard. "This always used to relax me when I was a kid. We'd light a fire in the fireplace, roast marshmallows, and play checkers."

"I used to eat popcorn and play Pac-Man," Ivy said as she lay her checkers out on the board.

They played two rounds, and Harper won both.

As the log finished burning, Ivy eased back against the chair. She bent her head back to admire the pink and blue clouds painted across the horizon by the setting sun. "Okay, so, I've eaten a lifetime supply of s'mores and lost two rounds of checkers to you. Now you have to do something for me."

"What's that?"

Ivy couldn't not help. She wouldn't push as much as she'd show Harper she cared. If Harper waved her off again, she'd drop it for good. "Why were you so upset earlier?"

Harper eased back against her chair too, and stared at the last of the burning log in the pit. "My father is stuck in bed attempting to recover after getting a piece of his liver cut out a few weeks ago, and I'm roasting s'mores here with you."

They sat in silence for a few long moments. "Why are you here with me, Harper?"

"Because you bring me peace, and right now, I want to savor that peace instead of fear it." Her lips twitched as she met Ivy's eye.

Her sincerity caught Ivy off guard. A chance to connect further dangled between them. They shared a long gaze. In that gaze, Ivy spotted a scared woman teetering on the edge of a life-defining moment that could end up haunting her for eternity.

"Then peace it is."

Harper

The next day, Harper woke up and received an alert that Ivy had posted a new "Uprooting" episode.

Next time you're down on yourself, remember that we all have problems in life, some much bigger than others. That's life. No rhyme or reason to it. It's part of the fabric of being a human. We're all going to experience frustration, disappointment, tragedy, death, and sickness. We've heard it before, none of us are getting out of this alive. It sure would be nice that, while we're here, we have some peace. We deserve it. It's ours to claim.

All we have is this moment right now. The past is done and the future isn't certain. So how do we want this moment right now to play out?

It's a choice.

At any moment, you can, if only for this singular moment, drop any problem. Try it. Right now. Think of a problem you're experiencing. Allow it to weigh on your shoulders. Let it dig in. Absorb its weight, the strain it puts on your neck, the tension it creates in your head. Now, for just this moment, because that is all we have, right now, toss the problem to the ground and stand on it. Feel it beneath you. Breathe in the freedom. In this single moment, you're free, weightless, existing in the here and now with no problems weighing you down. The problem is there for another time.

Harper replayed the video and attempted her exercise. After several times, the tension disappeared. She'd follow Ivy's wise counsel and leave the problem for another day.

HARPER MET Annie out in the garden, and together they embarked on the fine art of weed pulling.

Kneel. Yank. Toss. Repeat.

"Mind if I leave you to the rest of the weeding?" Annie asked. "I've got to clean up and greet our new lineup of guests. A group of breast cancer survivors gathering to celebrate life."

"Go for it. I've got this."

Annie cupped her chin. "Be sure to stand and stretch in between weeding or you'll end up like me with a bum hip flexor."

Harper dug her hands in the dirt, enjoying the coolness beneath her nails. "Will do."

A few minutes later, Ivy arrived and kneeled beside her. "I love playing in dirt, even if with just one hand for now. If you ask me, kids don't do it enough these days. That's why so many of them end up sick. The beneficial microorganisms never get introduced into their gut to fight off the harmful little buggers that do get access."

"When I was a kid, my sister Tess and I used to make mud pies. I pretended to eat them so that she would."

"Did she?"

"Let's say that she probably has a healthier microbiome than me."

Ivy tossed dirt at her fingers. "I'm glad I wasn't your sister."

Harper tossed dirt right back at her, and before long, the dirt-tossing erupted into a full-out dirt fight. It flew everywhere: in Ivy's flowy waves, down her T-shirt, against her wrapped wrist, in her face. Ivy scored a few points by getting it in Harper's eyes, ears, and down her shirt.

By the time they finished, dirt smeared across both their faces. They resembled a couple of athletes fresh off the race path of one of those Warrior Dash races.

"You're mighty good at slinging dirt. Almost as good as you are with that guitar." Ivy sat back on her heels and tilted her head up to the sun. The rays cast a shimmery glow across her dirt-speckled cheeks.

"If dirt tossing were a career choice, I could become famous," Harper said.

"You're probably already a famous musician and too humble to reveal that."

Harper laughed. "Famous. That's why I'm cleaning your pools and guest houses."

"Well, you should be famous. You're that good. Is it hard to get gigs?"

"Not if you're my ex, Kate. She's got that magical touch when it comes to marketing herself and getting top pay."

"Is she talented?"

"She puts on a hell of a show. I became her video person, recording her performances and snapping pictures. She ran in big circles, performing every night. It exhausted me. Completely exhausted me. I would've much preferred performing instead."

"What does it take to reach that level of success?"

"Being in the right place at the right time. Kate got her big break one night when performing the opening act for a popular local band. The owner of a large nightclub was there, heard her, and asked her to be their front-running show on the weekends. That's where it started, and more opportunities poured in from there."

"Well, we need to get you some attention."

"Maybe one of your campfire guests will be the manager for a major record label." Harper tossed a handful of dirt in the air and swiped her hands. "Until then, I'll keep myself entertained with digging in the dirt here in the land of stillness." Harper swept her gaze across the view. A windmill dotted the horizon where tall grass swayed in the gentle Western Maryland breeze. "Someday."

"Yes, someday you'll get your deserved break. Until then, you get to enjoy the peace."

"I'll enjoy it while I can because, like I said, the life of a musician can be pretty demanding and chaotic." She shrugged. "As long as I'm performing, I'd get used to it."

"I'm the opposite. I run from chaos."

Ivy's porcelain, delicate nose beckoned for some chaos.

"Smart." Harper tapped her nose with her dirt-glazed finger, leaving a cute little dot on the top of it. "Very smart."

Ivy gazed at her for a few long seconds. "I'm curious about something."

"What's that?"

"Why did you not go see your father?"

"I told you already. I enjoyed your peace last night."

Ivy pulled in her lower lip, considering the answer. "Did he hurt you?"

Harper released a wry laugh. "He hurt a lot of people." She pushed around some pebbles at her knees, deciding how much more to say. Ivy's empathetic side did comfort her. "Now that he's dying, I'm supposed to forgive him. Just like that. Forget it all and let him go in peace."

Ivy wrapped her hand around Harper's wrist and gently squeezed. "It must be hard."

Harper glanced at the easy-going woman beside her. She was refreshing rain on a hot and miserable humid day. "It's no picnic in the park."

"Does your music help?"

Harper regarded her with a sidelong sweep before turning back toward the windmill. It mesmerized her with its sleek beauty and gentle grace. "It's my great love. My first love. My go-to support system."

"Is that your dream? To become a famous musician one day who can spend her life playing music on the road?"

"And not scrub toilets?" Harper cupped her hand over Ivy's, which remained on her wrist.

Ivy glanced down at her hand and back up at her. "Well, don't look at me to take your place. I'm not scrubbing toilets and swimming pools again."

Harper took her hand back and ran her fingers through her tangled hair. "I enjoy the cleaning. But if a promising gig ever landed in my lap, I wouldn't refuse it. I don't expect grand-scale fame or anything, but a local gig that allows me to enjoy music and pays me well would be nice."

"You need to be on the radio."

"Says me and a million other Indie musicians."

They sat in comfortable silence, staring out at the openness.

"A more realistic dream is to open a café with tabletops that are checkerboards, and have bookshelves full of great literary works and board games. A place where I get to play music without begging for a chance. I'd serve coffee, teas, fruit juices, but not alcohol. This would be a place for people who prefer the company of the sober conversationalists. That's my backup dream. Moonwalk would prefer that one. No sticking him in an empty room while I'm off entertaining large audiences."

"Sounds like paradise."

Harper glanced up at the canopy of gorgeous trees. "No, this is paradise." She picked up a stone and tossed it into the fish pond. "I am grateful to be here. In fact, all I want to do for the next few months is cut grass, walk the dogs, clean, pick a little guitar, and spend time outside clearing my mind for a while."

"Most people chase fame relentlessly as they run from other aspects of life like peace and family."

"I do tend to run."

"Hence your move to Rhode Island?"

"You guessed it, lovely lady." Harper put up her fist in a friendly gesture.

Ivy, pink cheeked, fist-bumped her back. "Why did you run there? Your tough father?"

"My tough father, among other reasons. Let's leave it there for now."

Ivy cocked her head. "Deal."

More comfortable silence enveloped them in a shared moment of tranquility. It reminded Harper of the times in her life when she parked her butt on a comfy leather couch and escaped into no worry, no Kate. Just peace.

Peace was a gift that Harper rarely had access to. One couldn't buy it. One had to seek it out and mindfully engage with it. Hard to do when survival, or as of late, impending death, curled up at her ankles like a venomous snake threatening to cut off her circulation from everything blissful.

"I'm planning a new episode for 'Uprooting' on success," Ivy said, breaking the silence. "What does success mean to you?"

Harper didn't need time to muddle over that. She'd shuffled

through the concept of success all her life. She concluded long ago that the more one chased it, the more it eluded them. "It needs to be achievable."

"What's achievable?"

"Have I shared a smile today?"

Ivy broke out into a wide smile.

"See, how easy it is to be successful."

Ivy continued her gaze. "I like you."

Harper needed to tread carefully. Although smitten, she wasn't in a rightful place to get comfy with it. Harper chuckled away her statement and rose. "Come on. Let's go back to our respective showers, clean up, and then build a campfire and sing some songs for your guests."

Ivy's eyes teased her. "First, make me a promise."

Harper raised her chin. "I'm not good at making promises."

"Well, how about a fair try?"

"I can do a fair try, depending on what it is."

"I know what it's like to live with deep regret. It's why I spent the past year cleaning toilets. So, promise me you'll do what you can to avoid ending up with regrets with your father."

"Are you asking me to forgive him?"

"At least consider it," she whispered. "You're angry with him now. But ten years from now, you might not be, and it might be too late."

Harper understood Ivy's reasoning. "That's a big ask."

"Most important things in life are. Can you promise you'll consider it?"

She could do that much. "Yes, I promise to consider it."

Her face lit up. "Yeah?"

"Yes." Harper couldn't resist brushing her hand against Ivy's as they paced forward together, carrying a burden she didn't want Ivy to see.

13

THE DANCE WITH HARMONY

IVY

Many guests came to the retreat center in search of answers to complicated questions on things like the meaning and challenges of life. Guests craved clarity and space, and Oasis gave them that. It was a place that Ivy always craved for herself, even as a little girl. Her mother and aunt understood that because they were on the same wavelength. So when they all inherited the estate, they agreed to create the oasis they wanted for themselves and others.

Sunshine Valley was a quaint town nestled in a valley of lush trees and rivers. The town attracted mostly hikers from the nearby Appalachian Trail. Their annual county fair festival brought locals and tourists together to compete in pig races, bow and arrow competitions, and their famous blueberry pie bakeoff.

Her grandfather had planned to turn his property into a more robust wilderness retreat than it was. He dreamed of a retreat center complete with a main building for recreational things like an open hearth fireplace, cocoa and coffee stations, and oversized couches for reading the vast library of books he had collected since his youth. Of course being a fisherman, he also planned to carve out guided hiking trails along the river where large-mouth bass, tiger muskie, and bluegills were plentiful.

Then Ivy's grandmother got sick and the plans fell to the wayside. Caring for her became the most important priority.

After their deaths, Ivy, her mother, and her aunt arrived and got to work on a version of his dream mixed with their own.

Ivy remembered the excitement the first time she drove along the hilly, winding roads edged with a dense, rich display of tall and mighty trees. They had passed vegetable stands where local farmers wore sunhats and overalls as they piled bright red tomatoes and over-sized cantaloupe into wooden bushels adorned with handwritten signs touting "Freshly Harvested" and "Organic." The air had a fresh cucumber and watermelon scent to it, reminding Ivy of summer days spent running back and forth under the refreshing streams of a sprinkler in the front yard of her childhood home.

On their first visit out to his property after his death, her aunt Kathy had turned down the bumpy road. They all wore smiles. The road was lined with a broken wooden fence and overgrown fields where Ivy remembered goats used to pasture. Eventually, the road opened up to a large pond on the left where a family of Canada Geese lazily floated and flapped their wings, leading to their new home surrounded by trees and gardens.

The gardens. Oh, the gardens had always been a sight with their colorful, healthy flowers and vegetables. They became the genesis to the retreat center. Throughout the center, plants played a major role in setting the caliber of peace everyone so desperately sought.

Since learning to live in harmony with plants and admiring their unique healing powers, Ivy turned into a new person. Far less preoccupied with her former codependent inclinations, she no longer operated according to how others interpreted her.

Shortly after opening up Oasis and training under her aunt Kathy, Ivy learned to focus on helping others. That purpose drove her. She wanted to help others connect to nature's healing qualities. Back then, she learned to be balanced, connected, and rooted to something greater than herself.

Harper Ray struck her as a woman who needed such grounding, too. The stress of life stretched clear across her face in the fine lines around her dark eyes and in the deeper grooves along her forehead.

The woman needed a refresh, and Ivy had a great idea on where to start.

She gathered basil and mint along with a few essentials like baking soda, jojoba oil, kosher salt, Epsom salt, and lavender essential oil. With the ingredients, she would create a flower-powered sea salt to help root and ground Harper in prosperity and personal power.

Ivy glanced at Harper through her apothecary window. She mopped the patio over by where they had their heart-to-heart and dirt fight the day before.

She blended the dry ingredients in a large bowl and dripped the oil in it, imagining it empowering Harper. While stirring, Ivy noted Harper's precise sweeps. She admired her tenacity and respect for her and her mother's business and clients' satisfaction. Had fear pushed her to perform with such determined focus? Did she fear losing something she needed – a way to earn her way through life mopping someone else's floors?

A little while later, Ivy went out to greet her.

Harper sprayed water on new grass seed she planted where Moonwalk had dug up a hole. "I'm sorry about him digging this hole. I'll keep a better eye on him."

"No worries. There's plenty of yard to go around for everyone to have their fun in the dirt." Ivy stood before her, hands folded behind her back. "I made something for you."

"You've done enough by letting me stay and work here. A gift isn't necessary."

"It's something I enjoyed making for you. So by accepting, you offer me the opportunity to feed my spirit. When you remove that opportunity, you're essentially stealing a bit of my soul."

Harper tightened her grip around the nozzle of the hose. Little beads of sweat formed on her forehead. "You're very dramatic, pretty lady."

Ivy warmed at the compliment. "I prefer authentic."

"Fine. Authentic, then."

"So are you curious?"

Harper waved her free hand at her. "Okay, let's see it."

"It's not a chore to accept," Ivy laughed. "I could give it to someone who might want it."

Harper turned and pointed the nozzle at her, opening the stream to a gentle mist. Ivy jumped backward. "Harper Ray! Turn it off!"

Harper opened her mouth to talk, but no words came out. She succumbed to laughter followed by guttural words, "I can't even..." More laughter. "Your face..." *Cackle. Snort.*

Ivy circled around the grass and Harper followed her with the hose, leaving a trail of giggles behind them.

When Ivy reached the front porch, soggy and drippy, Harper turned off the nozzle. She stood gripping the hose and cackling some more.

"Why?" Ivy swiped the water from her clingy T-shirt and jean shorts. "Look at me. I'm a drowned rat. Figures, I planned to go live on my video channel. In ten minutes!"

Harper shaded the sun from her eyes. "You're welcome."

"What?"

"You're the authentic voice. Nothing screams authentic like the drowned rat that you are right now."

"I was being kind to you." She kept the gift hidden behind her back.

"Wrong." She misted her with more water again and Ivy ducked behind an Adirondack chair. "You were ready to give it to someone else."

Ivy stood and faced Harper's watering. "Because you were being rude."

Harper turned the hose off again. "I was having fun with you. I didn't mean any harm."

"Wrong," Ivy said matter-of-factly. "You drowned me with cold water from a hose."

Harper dropped the hose and raised her hands in surrender. "I'm sorry." She approached her. "Would it help if I tell you I am curious about the gift?"

"Maybe." She lowered her arms from her tight grip behind her back. Thankfully she had removed her wrist bandage; she no longer needed it. "I made you an herbal bath salt to place in your bath water tonight. To help empower you and bring you prosperity."

Harper wrestled with more laughter.

"You think it's ridiculous, but it works."

Harper opened her hand. "I love it. Thank you."

"You're welcome." She stood her ground. "It works. I soaked in a month's worth of prosperity baths when we first went before the zoning board. And they approved our plans. They weren't going to, rumor had it. So we bathed, prayed, and practiced some spells, and well," Ivy waved her hand. "Here we are today." She waved toward Harper. "And here you are. So if that's not proof that the universe works in wonderful ways, then I don't know what to say."

Harper smiled at her. "You're very strange."

Ivy opened her mouth to protest.

"And very beautiful when you defend a good thing." Harper sealed her eyes closed for a long blink. "It's admirable. I'd be honored to soak in an herbal bath with your salts. Can't say I'll know what to do with the salts other than sit, soak, and reflect. It doesn't require any special chanting, prayers, or sexy green witch stuff to work does it?"

Ivy pinched Harper's cheek. "Gosh your innocence is adorable. Now, I've got a live video to record." She curtsied.

Ivy turned and exited their space through the main retreat center's glass doors, leaving Harper to her hose and whatever else she'd get herself into.

Harper

With her emotions in check, Harper called Tess to talk with her about leaving Barry and Nancy out of their father's issues.

"It's great to hear from you, Harper. I was about to call you and ask you about something."

"Oh? Everything okay?"

Long pause.

Harper waited on a breath, hoping all was okay.

"I want to have a dinner party."

Dinner party meant her father. Would everyone expect her to sing happy folk songs around the tight space in their trailer home?

Tess cleared her throat. "I want you to come, Harper. I'm making lasagna. Andrew's making his signature garlic bread. Maybe you could bring a dessert? We'll have it Saturday at 6 o'clock."

Harper gripped her cellphone. "Why are you doing this, Tess?"

"Dad asked me to."

Harper clicked her tongue. "Did he?"

"This is our last chance, Harper. He's out of the hospital and resting here. He's tired. He's barely eating. He's depressed. I don't want him to die this way. Everyone deserves to go out with dignity. He's our father after all. He begged me."

"Did he also beg you to set up a crowdfunding page and ask to put Barry and Nancy in the middle?"

"He needs help, Harper. Where's your heart?"

"Why do you care so much, Tess? He was a terrible father. He spent his money on alcohol and drugs instead of us. He forced us to sleep in the streets and beg for money with him. He beat me when I didn't bring home enough for him to get his next fix. How do you expect me to sit in his trailer home and eat lasagna?"

"He was all of those things. Was, Harper. He's not that person anymore. He's sober. He's sorry. He's sad. I can't bury him with so much hate coming from you. Do this for me. Please. As an addict myself, we need this opportunity to move forward."

Harper could glide into a graceful act at that point. An act that someone like Ivy would admire. Ivy would do that for someone. She'd line the death path with roses if given the opportunity. But she wasn't Ivy.

"He doesn't deserve any such opportunity."

"Screw you, Harper. You always did assume you were so much better than me and Dad. I'm not going to beg. Keep sitting there on your high perch in that paradise casting your judgments. We don't need you." She hung up.

Harper stared at the phone, her temples pulsing an angry beat. "No. Screw you, Tess, and your fucking martyr attitude. Go ahead and be the good daughter. I'm fine with being the asshole," she muttered through gritted teeth at a dead phone.

THAT NIGHT, Harper had to entertain a group of fifteen chatty women sitting around the fire pit and requesting country songs from Brad Paisley and Garth Brooks. Ivy served them red wine and fancy cheeses and crackers.

When she passed by with the bottle, Harper motioned for her to fill her glass.

Ivy twisted her mouth and poured a little.

Harper pointed to the large empty space at the top of her glass. "Fill her up."

"This is powerful wine. Are you sure?"

Harper nodded and fingered the melody to "Whiskey Lullaby." "Helps me get into the creative zone."

"Why don't you play your song?"

"'Anxiety'?"

"Yes. You should play it."

Harper wanted to get as far removed from anxiety as she could. "This isn't the right time for that. These women want to hear country." Harper winked, sending Ivy along her merry little way with her wine bottle and tray of cheese and crackers.

Harper stopped strumming and sipped. After many more sips, her head swirled along with the wine in her glass. Finally, the honeyed buzz settled into her restless brain, washing away all traces of her troubles.

Did Tess rely on that numbing, settling buzz when she drank

whiskey? Who was Harper to deprive her little sister of that? Who was Ivy to be eyeing her from across the garden space, wary and judgmental over a stupid glass of wine?

If she wanted to drink a glass of wine, she could. She deserved it. She needed it. She relaxed better in its company.

As the hours slipped by, she couldn't break free of Tess's hurtful words. They twisted her like a vice grip, leaving her mangled. She wanted to be angry with Tess and with her father.

She searched for the anger, but it wouldn't grip. She cared too much for Tess for it to take root.

As far as her father, sadness seeped in where anger should've been. That sadness threatened the one thing that kept her going all those years: her bitterness toward him.

She couldn't find it in that moment. No matter how many memories she turned over in her mind, she couldn't find any fitting ones to keep the sadness away. Instead, memories of his former niceties steamrolled over the insults, blamings, dirty looks, and dinnerless nights. She wanted to be angry. She needed to be angry.

She guzzled more wine after she completed another song, biting back the bitter after-burn of it in the back of her throat.

"Fuck him and his life," she muttered.

Instead of empowering her, those words caused her throat to buckle and tears to roll.

So she grabbed the bottle of wine beside an older woman's chair. "Can I have a little?"

The woman nodded.

A little more wine ought to water-down the last of her stupid emotions.

The next afternoon, Harper woke to a not-so-surprising headache from hell. She put on her sunglasses, swished some mouthwash and spit it out, and eventually bit into a plain piece of toast.

Harper would never drink again.

Never.

She ventured out to the garden. First task of the afternoon: weeding.

Ivy had already parked herself in front of the area to tackle. "I have extra time on my hands." Ivy cupped her hand over her eyes to shade the bright sun. "Figured you could use some company?"

Harper kneeled. "You're the boss." The words banged around her skull. She closed her eyes and steadied against the wave of nausea.

"Are you okay?"

"I'm perfectly fine."

"Have you done the bath salt soak, yet?"

Harper dug her glove-covered hands into the rich dirt. "Haven't had the time."

Ivy placed her hands on her hips. "Take the time, Harper. It'll help."

"Sure." Harper avoided her concerned eyes.

She and Ivy dug into their weeding project in silence at first. Then, in typical Ivy fashion, she jumped into coaching mode and dug for something she could nurture. She asked question after question about the situation with her father. *How is he feeling? Is he still in the hospital? Will you keep your promise to me?*

Harper had enough of it. "I don't want to talk about him."

"I'm sorry. I'm concerned. You don't strike me as the drinking kind and you were sort of wasted on that wine last night. Around the guests. So I wanted to check in and make sure you're okay."

"Sorry about that." Harper yanked a patch of weeds, avoiding Ivy's gaze. "Please don't cook this up into more than it is. The wine was strong. I discovered that too late." She sighed, upset at herself for doing something as stupid as getting drunk in front of Ivy, Ms. Empath and Life Coach Connoisseur. Now that she reopened her life coaching business, did she plan on trying out new techniques on Harper?

Fuck that shit.

The only thing Harper wanted dug up were the weeds so she could get on with her next task. Show up. Stay in flight. Do the work. Get in. Get out.

Harper pulled hard on a stubborn vine.

Fuck.

Harper continued to work despite Ivy's consistent worried glances.

Ivy eased up to where she kneeled. "So everything is definitely okay, then?"

She tore off her gardening gloves and tossed them to the ground, digging into the cool dirt bare-handed. "I just want to pull up this patch of weeds and leave well enough alone."

Ivy placed her hand over her heart. Shock settled into every cell on her pink face. "I'm so sorry. I'll leave you be." She braced her hands against her knees.

Remorse buckled Harper over. She hurt her. Charming and lovely Ivy with the big heart in the right place.

"I'm sorry. I'm being insensitive. You're only trying to help. It's what you do." Harper wrapped her dirty hand around her arm. "Please don't leave." She brushed the dirt from Ivy's skin, but only managed to smear it. "Oh geez. I've made a mess."

"It's only dirt." Ivy helped her brush it.

"I didn't mean the dirt." Harper lifted Ivy's chin with her finger, creating more of a dirty mess. "Geez, at the rate I'm going, you'll need me to hose you down again by the time I stop apologizing."

A tiny hint of laughter leaked from Ivy's lips. "You don't have to apologize. If we can't be honest with ourselves and those we care about, what good is anything? The beauty and comfort of any friendship is knowing you're safe in the space of each other."

Ivy considered her a friend. Harper didn't have many of those. "That's sweet."

They shared a long gaze before resuming their weed pulling.

"Do you want to make some tomato sandwiches after we weed and before I entertain the guests with some folk music?" Harper asked. "I've got some mayo and bread."

Ivy sat back on her heels. Specks of dirt had spread on her cheeks. "You have no idea how much I'd rather do that than what I'm about to do tonight."

"You've piqued my curiosity. What are you about to do tonight?"

"I accepted a date through one of those online dating apps. I'm meeting someone named Mark for dinner in Frederick." She wrinkled her cute little nose.

"Mark, huh?" The male name pricked at Harper. Ivy had mentioned having an ex-boyfriend. Was she only into guys? Had Harper read her signals wrong? Did she treat everyone to her flirty vibe?

Ivy bit her lip. "I hate dating."

"Why?"

"The small talk."

Harper laughed. "You're a genius at it."

Ivy brushed her off. "It's the expectation, the judgment, the fear of rejection. Will he have someone call him to relieve him of his dating duty? Will he say he has to pee and leave me sitting alone with the bill? Those kinds of things."

"Then why do you bother?"

"Well, it's not like a ton of single people book getaway weekends here at Oasis. I spend most of my time here. So if I ever want to meet someone, I need to venture out I suppose. I guess I don't want to miss my chance at meeting the one."

"Do you believe in that?"

"I want to. Call me a romantic at heart. I want to believe there's someone out there and the timing isn't right yet. Then another part of me argues that most of the decent men are already taken."

Harper took her in with a side glance. "Maybe you need to widen your search beyond your current filter."

A playful glimmer shone in Ivy's eyes. "You mean women?"

Harper sat back and draped her arm over her knee. "We can be quite charming."

They shared a long gaze, and giddiness flooded Harper's body.

A peaceful glow shimmered across Ivy's face as she fiddled with a leaf that fell on her lap. An eternity flowed by, and then she whispered, "What about you? Do you use online dating apps?"

Harper's heart skipped at the flirty undercurrent in her soft voice. "I've taken a break from dating life."

Ivy shifted closer. "Why?"

"It always feels forced. When I fall in love, I want it to happen naturally. I want to be surprised by it, you know? Like when I'm least expecting a beautiful woman to waltz into a room and look at me with playful eyes, ones that dare me to look away, only I can't."

Ivy stared at her with eyes at a seductive half-mast position. "You haven't experienced that yet?" she asked on a whisper.

They shared a long gaze, one that rocked the ground beneath Harper. "Oh, I didn't say that."

Ivy studied her with teasing eyes. "No, you didn't."

"I most certainly didn't."

Ivy

Ivy's lips numbed. Floating on the succulence of Harper's playful words, she swayed to an inner lullaby. She sat taller, rolling her shoulders back, and Harper continued to massage her with seductive eyes.

Ivy's face burned. What should she do with such a look? She could muster a playful volley in her fantasy. But there, in real life, with Harper inches from her, Ivy's entire body sizzled.

She gathered her watered-down sweet tea and stared off into the flowery aisle of the west side of the garden. Her hand brushed up against Harper's. "Can I ask you a personal question?"

Harper stretched her neck. "If I say no?"

"You won't." Ivy's voice carried a flirt to it.

"Then you may as well ask it."

They shared another long gaze.

"What's it like to kiss a woman?"

Harper's eyes settled into a tease. "I can show you."

Ivy tilted her head, swallowing hard. Her heart thundered in her chest. Her knees grew slack. Her temples pulsed. Her breaths shallowed. "One day I'll take you up on that." She rose. "I should go and shower."

"You should. You wouldn't want to be late for destiny." Harper winked, and Ivy's cheeks blushed.

Dizzy and wobbly, she braced for balance. "Right."

She turned and began to strut away.

"Wait. I have a question," Harper said.

Ivy turned back to her.

Harper rose and met up with her. "How about right now, before you go and meet a potential Mr. Wonderful?"

"A kiss?"

Harper leaned in closer, and Ivy's knees buckled. Harper traced her finger down her cheek and gazed down to her lips. "A simple kiss."

"A kiss of this nature is never simple." Ivy couldn't feel her toes.

"It's a kiss, not a vow for life. A simple, seductive, sensual momentary connection between two women intrigued by each other."

Ivy's face grew steamy. Harper Ray was intrigued by her. She marinated on that fact as Harper inched even closer and they shared a pocket of air in the space between them. Then the world stilled when Harper closed that space and feathered her lips against Ivy's. Her delicate caress intensified Ivy's desire for more.

Harper placed her hands on Ivy's hips and pulled her in even closer.

The air rushed out of Ivy when Harper's hips met hers. Her sway caused an electric pulse to surge between them. Ivy floated, finding her grace in the capable arms of a woman well in tune with how to light up another's desire.

Ivy pulled back slightly to take her in. Harper's eyes twinkled naughtily as they fell upon hers. "See? A simple kiss."

"I don't know where you got your definition for simple."

"Now you can go on your date with this Mark guy and not fret over the curiosity of what it's like to kiss a woman. You're now out of the dark."

Harper's hands remained on Ivy's hips.

"That was pretty fucking amazing," Ivy said.

Harper brushed Ivy's bottom lip with her finger. "Ivy Homestead, Ms. Flower Essences, dropped the f-bomb. That is fucking sexy as hell."

Gentle wind blew around them. The bright blue sky glistened. A bird chirped merrily. Nothing around Ivy had changed from a moment before, yet everything felt different. Ivy felt beautiful and floaty.

The door to the main house opened on a creak. Startled, Ivy stepped backward and folded her hands neatly in front of her. Her mother hung her head out the door. Her mouth hung open, an amused grin sprouted. "Sorry to interrupt. I was looking to see if Lil Boy was out here."

Ivy darted her eyes around the space, birdlike. Peck. Peck. Peck. "Nope. I don't see him."

Suddenly, Lil Boy stuck his big, goofy head out the door.

"Oh, there you are," her mother said. She waved at them. "Carry on." Then she closed the door.

Harper touched Ivy's cheek. "I'll let you go and get ready. Wouldn't want you to be late for your date."

"My date. Yeah." Ivy sucked air through her lips, lips that Harper Ray had so delicately brushed with her own.

Caressing her cheek with a soft touch, Harper held her gaze as if deciding on the fate of the world. "Can I ask you something else?"

Ivy inhaled her sweet breath. "Sure. Anything."

She hesitated on an inhale. "How would you like to go to a dinner at my sister's with me?"

"Tonight?"

"No," she laughed, and dropped her hand from her cheek. "Saturday. Six o'clock in Baltimore."

Ivy cocked her head, soaking up Harper's smile. She didn't have any classes planned with her retreat guests that weekend, so timing was good. "I'd love to."

"Great. It's a date."

"Yes. Saturday it is, then." Ivy turned and crossed the patio bricks. She felt Harper's eyes following each one of her steps as she floated on the lightness of her newfound self.

14

LESSONS

HARPER

Harper called Tess. "Can we call a truce?"

"Yes, thank goodness. I hate fighting with you."

Harper hated it, too. As much as she dreaded what she was about to say, she needed to say it for the sake of long-term peace and sanity. Ivy was right, she wouldn't want to have any regrets. "I'll come to dinner."

"Really?! You're coming?"

Harper smiled at the happy ring in Tess's voice. "Yes." She paused and then launched her question. "Would it be all right if I bring someone?"

"A girlfriend?" She asked with tease.

"A friend. Ivy from Oasis." Ivy would reduce the chance of Harper saying something that she might really regret later on down the road. Having her there would fill the air with a good energy and take the focus off the tension between her and her father sitting down to eat dinner together.

"Oh!" Tess's voice curled into an audible exclamation point. "Catalina told me about Ivy and how she uses flower essences and spells to help bring good energy and respite to people who are suffering. Dad and I both could use some of that good energy. We'd love for you to bring her along."

She hoped Ivy could help Tess in whatever capacity she needed. Her father was too far gone for help at that point. "Great. So Saturday at six?"

"Yes." Her voice came out as an excited jig. "Sorry for the short notice on dinner. He's not doing great, so I wanted to do it sooner than later."

"So the surgery didn't go as planned?"

"The cancer spread. So no, it didn't go as planned."

Ivy

After Ivy got some lemon water in the kitchen, she walked past the living room on her way to shower. Lil Boy and her mother were lounging on floor pillows. Her mother's eyes were closed while Lil Boy watched her tiptoe past them.

Ivy headed down the hallway to her end of the house.

As she tore off her dirty clothes, her tummy flipped. Harper kissed her and it was every bit as sensual as Ivy had dreamed. She enjoyed the buzz that trickled down the length of her, swirling and teasing her body into a series of pirouettes.

She chuckled and headed over to the bathroom. Before she could close the door, her cell pinged an alert.

She strolled over to where she had left it on her dresser earlier.

Her heart zapped and popped when she spotted Lila's voice message alert.

Lila had finally responded.

"I'm throwing a party for Tommy's sixth birthday on Saturday afternoon at four o'clock at the Pizzarama in Baltimore. Can you come? We'll be having pizza and cake. Text me to let me know."

Four o'clock in Baltimore. That could seriously mess with dinner at Harper's sister's house.

Ivy's desire to be loved and forgiven filled her with an unrealistic amount of optimism. She could make it work, even if she showed up to his party for fifteen minutes. Enough time to hand him a gift and get a hug from both of them. That would afford her plenty of time to drive back and get Harper to get back to Baltimore for their six o'clock dinner date with her family.

She went to call her back and stopped.

On one hand, she wanted to call her right that second and hear her voice to confirm their friendship would survive and that she could finally erase all the guilt and self-doubt she suffered over the past year.

On the other hand, her heart galloped like an out-of-control wild horse on the loose, rounding dangerous curves that could toss her off balance and kill her spirit all over again.

She spoke in her message as if they'd shared peanut butter sandwiches by the pool with Tommy splashing and tossing balls the day before.

A year of buffer had offered Ivy a healthy perspective along with a thick coating of humility. Act too quickly and she might crush the opportunity to rekindle their friendship. Wait too long and Lila might reconsider.

Not unlike herself, Lila also tended to fret about even the simplest things in life like what color lipstick to wear and where to get her manicures and pedicures. She probably hung up the phone and now paced and pecked the floor, skittishly trying to resolve what dress she'd wear to their reunion.

Ivy needed her mother's guidance. She wrapped herself in a bathrobe and headed back out to her. Her feet couldn't carry her fast enough, so she resorted to blurting out her arrival.

"Mom," she yelled out as she marched into the living room. Lil boy popped his head up and his tiny ears folded over. "You'll never guess who called."

Her mother sprang into a seated position, and her hair stuck up everywhere. "Oh, I must have dozed off." She petted Lil Boy's head, and he laid back down, already done with the excitement. "I haven't seen your face that bright since, well... since I caught you and Harper gazing at each other a few minutes ago."

"We'll talk about that after. Right now, I'm sort of in shock over a phone call. Lila left me a message and invited me to Tommy's birthday party this weekend."

Her mother's eyebrows furrowed. "Really?"

"Mom, my chest is tightening already. Should I go? Will it be awkward? We should have coffee first, right? Air out the hurt before we're trapped in a room full of screaming kids, wearing our awkwardness like scarlet letters."

"You're complicating this more than need be."

"Or is it better to start off in a room full of cheerful kids?"

"This could be great practice grounds for you," her mother said.

"I hate this." One moment Ivy's heart soared with Harper, the next it plummeted toward the potential impending disaster.

"You've worked so hard over the past year on your new boundary spells. Now you can put them into play and learn how you need to tweak them."

"I'd rather suffer through one of her and Tommy's explosive fights every night than have to muddle through this stupid awkwardness. I hate fighting. I hate conflict. I want everyone to be happy."

"Call her back. Accept the invite. Tell her you're bringing dear old mom along."

"Really? Would you?" Relief poured through Ivy, releasing the constraint around her chest.

"No. I was kidding. Testing really. Testing to see if all that boundary work panned out. Have more faith in yourself. Call her back and accept the invite. It's a birthday party, not a death march."

"I'll wait until I get back from my date with the Mark guy. I don't want her to assume I've been sitting around waiting on her return call."

Her mother lifted her chin and stated, "You're afraid."

Ivy ran her hand over her cell. "No, I'm not."

"What did your aunt Kathy always say about fear?"

"Run from it only if it's a tiger chasing me down."

She glanced around the room. "I don't see a tiger." She pat Lil Boy's head. "Do you see a tiger?"

He sat stoic, statuesque.

"Fine. I'm showering first. I can't take myself seriously with this dirt on my face. For such a monumental call, I need to be at my best."

"The dirt on your face didn't get in the way of your hanging out with Harper in the garden."

Ivy flushed. "Because she's Harper."

Her mother jutted out her chin. "Exactly. You know, sweetheart, you're at your best more when you're real and authentic. Like you are when you're with Harper." She pointed to her face. "Like this. Dirty and smiley."

Ivy's face burned now.

"You wear that red nicely on your cheeks." She laughed and laid back down, nuzzling her face up against Lil Boy's back. "Go on now. You've got people waiting on you."

IVY SAT at the bar waiting on her date and texted Lila back. "Thanks for the invite. It made me happy. I'll be there." She sent it, then added, "I miss you."

She slipped her phone back into her pocketbook and sipped a Martini. The chaos of bar life unfolded before her. The bartenders took orders from customers as they glided and bumped into each other in the small space behind the counter. The frenetic energy twisted her into a tense ball.

She should've canceled. But with only an hour buffer between her kiss with Harper and the drive to Frederick, that would've been rude. Mark might've missed her message and sat waiting on her.

Why had she agreed to venture all the way to the busyness of Patrick Street in downtown Frederick? She hated the traffic, the crowds, and the high stakes of being in a densely populated city where people didn't follow rules and tension brewed like a bad spell.

She went along for rides because she couldn't say the word "no."

That's how she always landed in the swamp of dread and regret. That's how she got herself into the mess with Lila and Tommy. Where the word "no" fit, the word "yes" shoved it out of the way and claimed the spot.

Ivy sat a victim to "yes."

Yes, I'll do that. Yes, I'll be there. Yes, I'll toss my whole life to the side so you can climb all over it and smother me with your problems. Yes, sure. Come on in and trample over me. I'm a fixer. I'm a doer. You need someone to lift you to higher ground by standing on her shoulders and burying her in the muck? I'm your girl!

She would work on that part of herself more.

She drummed her fingertips on the bar. God, how she hated dating and the anxiety it created. She wished she could be smelling the comfy scent of wood burning and listening to Harper's soothing songs instead.

She considered Harper's invite. She could always invite Harper along to Tommy's party to save her from spending too much time driving back and forth. But that might be weird. A date at a kid's party?

Or Harper could shop at the mall next door while Ivy spent more time at the party. That way she wouldn't have to drive around like an idiot up and down Interstate 70.

As she volleyed those options around her erratic mind, her date Mark arrived at the bar. Twenty minutes late.

"I'm sorry. I ran late with a client."

He couldn't text her?

Mark was tall with dark hair and wore a casual blue sports coat and a white T-shirt underneath. He used words like "please" and "thank you" a bit too much for Ivy's taste. Lately, she enjoyed a snarkier approach to dialogue.

Like Harper's style.

About half an hour into their date, laughter curled up around her and Mark from a group of women. Ivy studied two of them huddled together for a selfie. The red head planted her lips on the cheek of a shorter brunette who smiled with her eyes. They snapped a few rounds. Then they began to make out right there in the middle of a fancy steakhouse bar.

The other women cheered them on. That's when Mark's interest piqued and he turned over his shoulder to witness the flirty play.

"Vanity," he said on a light chuckle. "It'll make people do silly things."

Ivy sensed tension from Mark. The same kind of tension Ivy tried to avoid ever since kicking Lila and Tommy out on the streets. The kind of tension that leaked from a person like poison, creating a toxic film that staved off any chance at freshness. His jaw flinched. His eyes blinked a few too many times. Some of the Martini dribbled down his chin at his feeble attempt to be calm in a situation that caused his skin to itch and his blood pressure to rise.

"Do you want to go somewhere else?" Ivy asked, wanting him to be a bored jerk who wanted to abandon the stupid date. Then she could also go home and sit in a lounge chair under a blanket of stars. There she'd treat herself to the soothing tunes of Harper Ray as she strummed her guitar and sang in her soulful voice.

"We'll be up for our table pretty soon. Unless you want to?"

He shifted in his chair as if trying to get away from the women's circle of nonsense.

"Let's grab those seats at the other end of the bar," Ivy suggested.

His eyes lit up. "Absolutely." He leaped off the stool and grabbed Ivy's hand.

His cold hand sent a horrible chill down her spine.

"You grab the seats, I'll be in the little girl's room." Ivy stole her hand back and darted toward her escape.

She entered the empty bathroom and waited for the unease to pass.

Ivy went into the stall and sat, pulling out her phone.

"Sure," Lila had texted back.

Sure? Argh. So typical. Lila coveted the upper hand. Again. She likely derived great pleasure in knowing how batty she drove Ivy.

Ivy refused to respond. She'd see her at the party. She did her part. She took the higher road.

She scrolled through her Facebook feed to pass a few minutes. Lila had posted a poll asking people what kind of cake she should serve at Tommy's birthday party.

People she'd never met before chimed in like they were best friends. Lila had snapped a selfie and posted that in the comments. Her eyes glowed. Again she got on with her life without Ivy.

Perceived strength and desperation ran a tight race though. They tracked different on the surface. But when one went in deeply and examined the true source of it all, the two traveled similar paths. Lila had a tough life, one Ivy wouldn't want to live.

Ivy had an easy life, comparably speaking. She had no such demons to answer to except for the ones she caused Lila. Her other demons were self-imposed. Like her date for instance. Mark was a nice, polite man. He was educated. He was a lawyer. He'd be great father material, son material, friend material, even husband material for someone.

Just not Ivy.

Hell no.

She'd get through her steak dinner, wave to him, and bake up some excuse as to why a second date fell off the table as an option.

"Get it over with," she said aloud.

And so she did. She headed back out to their new seats at the other end of the bar and suffered through the dullness. Ivy sat and nursed her drink as Mark talked about his law practice the way one talked about their kids or dogs.

As he talked, she wished she could be sitting in her salt room, reflecting on her breath instead of the long strands of his eyebrow popping up with every inflection.

As Ivy prepared to massage the conversation with some tidbits of her own, Mark's cell rang. He picked it up and raised his eyebrow in dramatic flair that cued Ivy into his next words.

"There's been an emergency at work. I need to go."

Ivy couldn't have been happier.

~

THANK GOD for fake phone calls, Ivy thought as she sipped her second cup of tea back in the comfort of her bedroom.

Her mother pinged her from her bedroom on the opposite end of the house.

"Don't mind me," she said as she lowered into a downward dog pose. "I need to stretch. Too much sitting around by the campfire tonight." She groaned as she stretched deeper. "I'm glad we hired Harper. Barry and Nancy were right about her becoming a quick asset. In the past month, she's impacted Oasis greatly with her can-do attitude. The guests love her. God, can she clean. I've never seen the place so shiny and fresh."

Her mother continued to stretch, and her face tensed.

"You're not breathing," Ivy said.

Her mother stood and closed in on her iPad screen. "It hurts to breathe." She plucked up Harper's straggly dog. "Say hello to Moon-walk. He's got a little sniffle." She kissed the top of his head, and the dog sealed his eyes closed. "Harper let me borrow him so I can practice some Reiki on him."

"He's so cute. Does Lil Boy care that he has to share his bed with Moonwalk?"

Her mother hugged the dog against her cheek. "We switched. Lil Boy happily followed Harper back to the apartment when he spotted Moonwalk in my arms."

"That is so adorable." Ivy hugged herself.

"You're glowing. Tell me why."

"You're nosy." Ivy wrinkled her nose. "I'd prefer chatting about such things over a tall glass of ice cold lemonade on our front porch than through technology."

Her mother pulled her iPad closer and spoke directly at her. "I'll prepare myself to drink several glasses, then. We could invite Harper to join us? Or will you be bringing up her name so that might be awkward?"

Ivy laughed. "I love you, Mom. Get back to your downward dog. We'll sip our lemonade soon."

Harper Ray stirred up new seedlings never before tilled. The energy from uprooting the dormant soil created a hot flicker deep within. It opened Ivy up to a brand new set of emotions that dizzied her.

~

THE NEXT MORNING, Ivy woke and stretched her arms above her head, drinking in the bountiful sunshine.

A moment later, she sat at her desk and opened up her aunt's journal. She'd spent the last five years working her scripts around her aunt's writing, and craved to bring the same level of authenticity and insights to another "Uprooting" episode. Today, she'd tackle the topic of taking the high road in order to embrace oneself and provide the self-love necessary to heal from hurt.

She had finally landed in the proper place to talk about such things.

She closed her eyes and imagined the violet heart with its roots from her first float in the deprivation tank.

After balancing her chakras, she applied some light lipstick, blush, and powder. Then she went into her studio to record a live session.

TAKING *the high road is about creating a foundation for ourselves that's strong and flexible, and one that allows us to connect with a deeper part of ourselves. It's a journey that goes unnoticed by others. It's a choice we make for ourselves. Here's the reality: We can't control the hurtful actions of others, but we can control our reaction to them.*

When people wrong us, we want to tell them that they can't get away with treating us with disrespect. Ultimately, confronting in such a hostile way will cause ugliness in the overall landscape of our life. It'll leave us bitter and sorry in the end—sorry that we lost our self-control and allowed them to push our buttons.

In the long run, taking the high road allows us to move forward without causing further harm to a potentially volatile situation. It also creates increased confidence that allows us to make better choices.

As living beings, we're powerful beyond our recognition. With that power comes the gift of grace or the evil of hurt. We choose our direction.

When we place ourselves in the pivotal energy of grace, we grant ourselves a world-class view of what friendship and love offer, which is a symbiotic fluidity of dignity, integrity, and respect.

Here's the thing about taking the high road: You're building your repu-tation to be one that is fair, trustworthy, and in the best interest of others. No one can steal that from you. Your actions speak volumes. It's critical to stay in control and act according to how you want the world to know you. In the end, no one will be able to destroy you to anyone worthy of your friendship because a worthy friend will see past the lies and hurt and embrace the bright light you shine on the world.

IVY ENDED the live session and noticed twenty people had tuned into it. She scanned the attendees, wishing like a fool that one would've been Lila.

They had both been evil monsters to each other back on that dreadful day when Ivy kicked her out. Ivy had succumbed to the lure of a tantrum instead of the mature choice to think before she acted out. Sure Lila took advantage of her generosity, but she also had sweet parts to her soul that outshined the selfish parts. Whenever she went shopping, she always brought Ivy something home. She often baked Ivy and her mother cookies and left them as a surprise on their kitchen counter. When the wind whipped, she gathered all of Ivy's favorite deck plants and brought them inside for safety. She may have had selfish tendencies, but she had a good heart.

A pool of dread lapped at her ankles. She couldn't wait to get to the party on Saturday.

Saturday was a long ways away.

She peeked out the window at the gorgeous day ahead. It was the perfect day for blueberry pancakes. So blueberry picking it would be.

She tied her hair back in a ponytail and went into the bathroom. She brushed her teeth and remembered the lingering, provocative gazes and delicate kisses. Ivy's stomach tumbled.

A good tumble.

A few minutes later, Ivy entered her backyard paradise. She held her blueberry collecting basket and reveled in the beauty of her lilac bush. It radiated and filled her with a sense of peace. It created a space where beauty graced more than just the surface. It grew deeper than that. It pulsed beneath the ground.

The corners of her mouth turned upward. She loved how Harper had brushed dirt on her knee and under her chin.

Ivy moved on toward the blueberry bushes near the far end of the house.

The summer morning sky was painted in shades of pinks, yellows, and blues. The watercolor clouds broke up as the sun filtered through them and brought out the greens of the garden. Time for Ivy to rid the cobwebs of her melodramatic mind and climb back into the woman she had become over the past year. A stronger, more resilient, balanced woman who didn't spend her time worrying about past mistakes and not doing anything about them.

Ivy was a woman who could rise to the occasion and take that high road.

She finally slid back into her transformative life-coaching groove, and loved it.

A breeze came to life on her skin. Ivy's thin T-shirt didn't shelter her from the chill, and that was a good thing. Ivy was alive. For that, nothing else mattered. Today was a brand new day with a fresh, clean slate. Anything was possible. She opened her arms up and stretched again. The day was full of possibilities, and she couldn't wait to see which ones would tickle her soul.

Her fingers grazed the wrought-iron fence of where her rose-bushes grew. The backyard was eloquent, full of life. They kept it as close as they could to how her grandfather had left it, even down to the gazebo with its arched bridge over the pond.

Maybe she'd eat her blueberry pancakes in the gazebo that morning.

She landed before the blueberry bushes and plucked some, dropping them into a bowl. She spied the wooden shutters and the large windows of Harper's apartment. They sparkled thanks to Harper. Before she moved in, they had needed a serious cleaning because they were full of smudges. Ivy hated cleaning windows. The smudges were likely from Tommy's hands and mouth. He was an odd kid, always smearing his lips across tables, walls, and apparently windows.

A branch tickled the side of her cheek as she reached for a set of ripened blueberries.

She glanced back at the oversized window and noticed a crack running from the top to the bottom. She'd need to get that fixed. The windows were old and didn't open with any great ease. To keep it open, Harper had apparently propped it with a book.

Ivy traveled her gaze from the thick book to inside the window, to the white Jacuzzi tub and the vase with wilted flowers on its edge.

Her eyes swept from one end of the tub to the other, and she caught a flash of movement. Harper swept across the room and toward the tub. She was naked, stretching, and standing before it like a goddess ready to descend into a pool of herbs to cleanse herself. Ivy's eyes traveled from her breasts, to her hips, down to her...

Then Harper caught her eye.

They stood staring at one another in shock.

Harper stood before her, nipples erect, boobs perked, hair gorgeously wet and dripping droplets of water down past her breasts and onto her toned abs. She wore a teasing smile that dared Ivy to look away if she could.

As long as Harper didn't flinch, why should she?

So what that Ivy stood in a blueberry bush outside her bathroom window?

So what that Harper stood before her window, bare assed, perky, and not the least bit rattled that Ivy gawked up at her like a weird peeper. She could've yelled to Ivy to stop gawking if she didn't like it.

That led Ivy to draw a remarkably interesting theory. Harper Ray enjoyed the spontaneous disruption to her morning. It told Ivy to remain planted by the blueberry bush collecting ripened, succulent berries until her fingers turned blue.

Ivy, not wanting to appear as a giddy, hormonal, horny woman, went right on picking blueberries. So what that a naked woman stood before her with not an ounce of modesty? So what that Harper's playful smile caused her legs to wobble and her clit to tremble, and hot desire to pool between her legs?

Pluck.

Pluck.

Pluck.

She added a friendly smile, as if that would lessen the obvious blush spreading across her tender face.

"Are you hungry?" Ivy said loud enough so she'd hear her through the screen. She charmingly cocked her head and revealed a pile of blueberries in the palm of her hand.

Harper matched her charming head tilt. She removed a fluffy white towel from the titanium railing and let it dangle from her fingertip. "I'm starved. Can I help you?"

"I've collected what I need."

A tease played out on her face. She gripped the towel and swung it around her backside. Then she slowly clasped it into a rough knot at her chest. "I'll meet you in the kitchen."

"Feel free to carry on with your bath first." Ivy poured her handful of blueberries into the small basket.

"I'll do that." She crossed her arms over her chest, staring at her.

"Oh, don't mind me. I'll be on my way. I didn't mean to interrupt."

"I'm sure it's not the first time you've come across a naked woman staring out of your window."

"I assure you it most certainly is."

"Good." She turned and headed away from the window.

Ivy backed away, saddling into her giddiness as if mounting a beautiful Gypsy horse and galloping away into the sunset.

Harper

Harper lingered in her bathrobe for a few minutes. She lay on her bed and stared up at the ceiling as little giggles released. Moonwalk, who had slipped back into her apartment after his night with Annie, busied himself by staring out the large window.

Harper relaxed under the wind of the ceiling fan. She chuckled at the memory of Ivy trying to hide her shock at seeing her naked. How was Harper to know she'd be picking blueberries by the window? Why didn't the window have a shade?

Fuck it.

She didn't mind.

In fact, the manner in which Ivy scanned her breasts and torso before pulling in her bottom lip and plucking blueberries highly entertained her.

A part of Harper hoped her date with the guy named Mark sucked. She wanted more kisses, more opportunity to keep the door to potential slightly ajar.

Her appetite perked at the thought of blueberries tossed into a delicious batch of homemade pancakes. Tess always loved blueberries. Their mom used to bake them blueberry muffins every Sunday morning before they'd shop for groceries.

Tess.

Dinner with her father.

Inviting Ivy.

Too many variables to consider so early in the morning.

One moment at a time.

Moonwalk perked his ears at a rabbit hopping by the window. They were both lucky. Landing in that paradise until she could get her footing helped keep her spirits high.

She sat up and got dressed. While she did, she listened to an episode of Ivy's "Uprooting" workshop. She turned on her Bluetooth speaker and tuned into an episode on building inner strength.

YOUR INNER VOICE *can do some serious damage if you allow it to run wild. It'll tell you things that simply aren't true. It'll make things bigger and scarier than they are. That voice can stop you in your tracks and talk you into running in the other direction, the opposite direction to where you might need to go. Without intervention, it'll place doubt in your mind and cloud your vision.*

When you're strong in spirit, you're grounded, you're stable, and you're able to weather whatever life tosses at you. All that happens because you become an active participant in the evolution of whatever is about to unfold. And that's a great position to be in because you're no longer standing before life and all its curveballs as a victim, but as the leader of what's to come. Nothing is more powerful than having the ability to bend with the curves and come out on the other side of them wiser, more capable, and positively transformed.

You've got to feed your mind, body, and soul to be strong. Your body is a garden and you're the gardener. You have the power to decide what seeds you're going to plant, water, feed, and nurture. Only you have that power. No one else. Being strong is a choice. It is a choice between sitting down in the mess of the moment or climbing to your feet and declaring your presence as an active participant and a more than capable adversary in the journey of going from a place of perceived weakness to actualized, bountiful power and strength.

HARPER CONTINUED to digest the ten-minute episode as she slipped into a comfortable pair of yoga pants and tied her hair into a ponytail.

Ivy did have some great insights. Tess could use some of that guidance as she cared for their father. Harper understood that she needed to get on board and help support her during the difficult time ahead or live with regrets.

"Come on Moonwalk. Let's get some breakfast."

When she entered, Ivy placed a glass of lemon water down on the table. "That soak must've made you thirsty?"

"Indeed."

Ivy glanced around the counter nervously.

"So blueberries, huh?" Harper asked to break the awkwardness.

"I was craving them." Her smile doubled in size. "Could you get the orange juice from the fridge?"

She opened the fridge, pulled out the juice, and placed it down next to Ivy's bowl. She steadied for an awkward plunge. "I was thinking of what you said in one of your episodes."

"My what?" Ivy stopped stirring the pancake batter.

"Your episode," Harper said, focusing on the juice, "about building inner strength."

"You listened?" Her voice, in all its charming excitement, rang like a wind chime in the tall kitchen.

Harper bypassed her question. "Maybe sometimes a person might not have the ability to see their potential strength."

"Oh, come on. You're equipped with the stuff you need to be your own superhero."

"I'm not talking about me right now."

Ivy's forehead creased. "Okay. Fine. Let's not talk about you. Let's generalize it. Anyone can be their own superhero."

"How?"

"That's next week's lesson." Ivy closed her eyes playfully and released a cute giggle.

"I wrote the jingle. Surely that gets me some advance payout."

Ivy regarded her with a sidelong glance. "Well, it's not going to be easy. Seldom are great triumphs easy. If they were, they wouldn't be a powerful catalyst for better things. So firstly, I'd say to this person to accept that what is happening is really happening. They shouldn't resist the issue. They're going to have to deal with it to get ahead of it and gain the upper hand. They'll have to be strong. And everyone, including them, has strength. It may be buried at certain times, but with the right support and enough love it always comes to surface." Ivy continued to stir the batter again.

"You make it sound so possible."

"Everything is possible." She arched her eyebrow. "Can I be candid and forthright here?"

Harper tapped her fingers on the counter. "I ruined your blueberry picking by standing naked in front of the window. I guess I owe you a little candidness."

Ivy laughed, and it lightened the mood. "You're something else, Harper Ray."

"I kind of like it when you use my first and last name together." She winked.

"Those winks of yours are distracting me." She shook her head on a laugh. "I'll leave it at that. Now onto my candidness."

Harper enjoyed the rise in color on her cheeks. "On with it."

Ivy let go of the spoon and turned to face her. "For strength to resurface, it helps to forgive yourself."

Harper clenched her jaw. "I'm not talking about me here, remember."

Ivy put up her hand. "Fair enough. But the statement still holds true. We all tend to hang onto things and they consume our love. Everyone has things they've either said or done that wreak havoc on the present and future. The more you spend time reflecting and sinking into those memories, the less power you'll have to do the important work you're meant to do. So dig a hole and bury those thoughts once and for all. Let them go. The past is the past. Carry the lessons with you and leave the rest behind."

"That's much deeper than I expected."

Ivy trailed a finger along the edge of the bowl of sweet pancake batter. "I hope I didn't push the matter too much."

"It helped." She opened her mouth to say more, but wasn't sure how to ask Ivy what she wanted to ask her. So she closed it.

Ivy lingered on a gaze, then whispered, "What's on your mind, Harper?"

Harper cleared her throat. "I've seen the work you and your mother have done with the guests. Now, granted some if it's a little weird for my taste. I can't lie. Talking to flowers and chanting things in the wind. It's a little over my head. But I see how guests come in here and how they leave. You have a magical touch with them. Admittedly, you calm me, and that's a big deal. I don't do calm like you."

Ivy laughed.

Harper drew in a large amount of air.

"You look like you could use some lemon balm." Ivy tossed her a concerned gaze.

"I could use a lot of things. What I need is your magical touch to help my sister, Tess."

"Of course. Anything."

"She's taking on the full care of my father, and I want to keep her safe and strong. She's been in and out of rehab a few times and she suffers from depression. When we're at her dinner party, would you talk with her and offer her some coping tips to keep her balanced while my father is nearing the end?"

Ivy wrapped her hand around her wrist. "I'm happy to help. What about you? Will you allow me to work on a calming spell for you to help you stay balanced during the stress?"

Say no and risk insulting her life work. Say yes and make her happy. Harper decided on the no-brainer choice. "Sure. Will this entail more baths?"

"It doesn't have to. Unless you enjoy that?"

Harper had so many things she could say about Ivy and baths, but erred on the side of cautious professionalism. "You're the green witch. I put my full trust in you."

A smile the size of a hardy hibiscus bloomed on her face. "I'll get started on you and Tess."

"Tess will love this shit."

"Shit?"

"Sorry. I mean whatever it is you do. Magic plant stuff. Floating in dark Epsom tanks. Lounging in a salt room."

"If I weren't so thrilled you're letting me help you and your sister, I'd slap your hand for being mean."

"Whatever!" Harper laughed and picked up the spoon and licked it. She dragged her tongue over the wood and savored the indulgent twinkle in Ivy's eyes. "What? Never seen a woman lick something delicious before?"

Ivy turned bright red. Everything on her did. Her face. Her ears. Her chest. Even her fingers. "Whatever," she said on a playful note right back to her.

"So, how did the date go?"

"He got an emergency call early on, and had to leave." Ivy pressed her lips together. "Can't say that disappointed me."

Harper couldn't say it disappointed her to hear Ivy say that either. "Better to know these things early on, I suppose."

"I suppose so." Ivy clicked her tongue. "Speaking of knowing things early on. I have a dilemma for Saturday."

"Got an emergency, too?"

"More so an opportunity to right a wrong with that friend of mine, Lila."

"The one you kicked to the curb?"

Ivy sighed. "I didn't kick her. It was more like a nudge. Sort of." She flipped her long hair over her shoulders. "Anyway, she invited me to my godson's sixth birthday party at a pizza place in Baltimore at four on Saturday. To make it easier driving wise, do you want to tag along to Baltimore with me?"

"To the party?"

"No, not the party. Just Baltimore. There's a mall next door where you can shop for an hour while I go to the party. Then we can drive to Tess's after that. Unless you want to come to the party."

And miss the drama? Harper thought. "Will they have cake?"

Ivy laughed. "Lila polled people on Facebook, asking what kind of cake she should serve."

"Shopping in a mall, which I hate to do, or eat cake?" Harper leveled both hands in front of her. "I may be leaning closer to cake."

"Seems we're on the same wavelength." Ivy giggled and turned to the griddle. "Are you hungry or would you rather we toss this at each other like we did the dirt?"

Harper came up to her side and stuck her finger in the pancake batter. Gathering up a healthy dollop, she placed her finger on Ivy's lips. "Indulging in the taste is so much better. Don't you think?"

Ivy parted her lips and welcomed Harper's finger with her tongue. She left nothing behind, including her obvious comfort with revealing an intimate, playful side to a very interested Harper.

15

QUEST FOR PEACE

The next day, at Ivy's insistence, Harper invited Tess, Andrew, and Catalina to the retreat center for salt therapy.

Lil Boy greeted them with his big sloppy kisses.

Andrew laughed in between Lil Boy's tongue passes over his cheek. "Kiss Tess." He rose and Tess kneeled. Then Lil Boy embarked on his discovery over the new human he'd claim as his own. Meanwhile, Moonwalk danced around them, eager to get inside and get treats from his favorite human next to Harper, Ivy's mother Annie.

The woman carried treats in her pockets, and Moonwalk ensured he had full access to her generous ways.

After the initial greetings with the dogs, Ivy grabbed Tess's arm and motioned for all to follow her. "Come with me. I'm going to introduce you to the great world of Himalayan Sea Salt."

"Are we going to eat the salt?" Tess asked on a chuckle.

"We do that around here, too. But no. This is our dry salt therapy room. It uses micro particles of salt to promote better breathing, healthier skin, sounder sleep, improved physical fitness, endurance, and overall wellness."

"You've spun some great ad copy," Harper said.

"Yet we haven't convinced you to sit in there. Well, you're getting in there today."

"Come on, Sis. Let's do this," Tess said.

Because Tess asked, Harper joined her, Andrew, and Catalina in the salt room while Ivy instructed them how to get present.

Harper fidgeted as Ivy guided them on a series of rapid breathing exercises.

Andrew gulped air like a guppy fish. Catalina's jaw flexed. Tess gripped her chair like she might fall off it. And Ivy pointed her finger at Harper and scolded her with furrowed eyebrows for not breathing deeply enough.

Harper playfully blew out a few breaths with dramatic flair.

When they completed that, Ivy passed out a raisin to each of them. Andrew pet his like he'd pet Moonwalk. "It's not a dog, Andrew," Harper laughed.

Ivy dropped a raisin into Harper's palm and placed her hand over it. "Pay close attention. Can you do that?"

"Will I be punished if I don't?"

"Harper, you're not twelve trying to be the class clown here. Focus!" Andrew pointed his *I'm being serious* face her way.

"Sorry." Harper swallowed her craving to laugh and sat up tall.

Ivy dropped her hand and resumed her position at the front of the salt room.

"Okay, so everyone pay attention to the raisin in your hand."

"It's so wrinkly," Harper said.

"Good," Ivy said, cheering her on. "That's what I want you to do. Investigate its texture. Admire its nooks and crannies. Lavish over its complex shape and crevices. Explore it as you would a lover."

Harper perked her ears.

"Close your eyes for now."

Harper closed her eyes, sort of. She opened them slightly to keep an eye on Ivy. Ivy was smart. She pointed that long, elegant finger at her and waved it indicating she caught sight of Harper's naughty ways.

"Roll the raisin around with the tip of your other finger. Is it soft?

Squishy? Pliable? Does it tickle?" Ivy asked in a slow, seductive voice. "How does it smell? Is it sweet? Robust? Or Earthy?"

The raisin softened against Harper's skin, rolling back and forth with the guidance of her guitar-calloused finger.

Ivy curled up along Harper's backside and whispered into her ear. "Place it on your tongue."

Harper did as commanded.

"Do not chew it." Ivy's breath warmed her ear. "Play with it. Use your tongue to roll it around, back and forth from one side to another. Do you feel its grooves?"

Harper nodded. Oh yeah. Every single one of them, she thought.

"How about its succulent flavor? Do you taste it?"

"Yes," they all said in unison.

"What does it taste like, Harper?" Her breath heated even more.

"Sweet and tangy."

"Good. Now everyone go on and bite down a little."

Harper wanted to sink her teeth into the entire raisin and savor its juice.

"Patience and focus is the point of this journey," she continued to whisper to them.

Harper nibbled on it and savored the syrupy flavor.

Ivy continued to coax them into a relaxing experience with a single raisin for the next ten minutes. By the time Harper finished with that raisin, she had pulled from it every last drop of sweetness and had memorized every single nook and cranny of its skin with her tongue.

"Okay, you can swallow whatever's left and open your eyes." Her purring tone caused a wetness to form between Harper's warm and pulsating inner thighs.

Harper slowly opened her eyes and sat like a flustered mess next to her sister, brother, and his wife. "What a trip," she said and laughed awkwardly to remove any clue that she experienced a sexual experience with them all around.

"The point of focusing on it as a single object will help you become present to what is right here and now in front of you. You may have had many encounters with raisins in your life, but never took the time to notice them in this intimate way. By focusing on the raisin, and noticing everything about it, nothing else mattered. What you're eating for dinner tonight, the project you're currently working on, aches and pains, they were far removed, weren't they Tess?" Ivy cocked her head at Tess.

Tess rubbed her eyes. "That was amazing. I almost had an orgasm."

Harper barked out a laugh for no other reason than to squash any notion that she did, too.

No one else laughed though.

"That's natural and to be expected. It means you're connected and grounded in the moment. Great work."

Tess beamed.

"So this is an exercise you can do when you want to ground yourself, when you're stressed, or when life overwhelms you. You can use a raisin or anything else that is commonplace in your life. When you take notice of something you're used to, you see it differently. Your experience then becomes part of a new journey away from the stressors that plague you."

"I always overcomplicate things. This was so simple." Tess drew the first peaceful breath Harper had ever seen her draw. "My father could sure use your help. He's too weak to travel here. He'll be at the dinner party on Saturday. Could you share some of this with him? Maybe not as seductively. His heart wouldn't last."

"I'm happy to help in any way I can." Ivy smiled, and in the smile, Harper finally understood real beauty. It had nothing to do with makeup, hair color, or toned muscles and everything to do with a love for life.

THAT NIGHT, as Harper soaked in another bath with more salts Ivy created for her, she listened to another of Ivy's "Uprooting" episodes.

· · ·

I HAVE A QUESTION FOR YOU. What would you say to your younger self if you could go back and chat with her? I ask this because it's one powerful way to help you navigate the complexities of life. If something is troubling you, by having a chat with your younger self, you open up to new possibilities of understanding. You're less likely to self-sabotage with critical judgments or insults. You're more likely to have an honest conversation and uncover things not possible when viewed through the limitations of the adult lens. It distorts things. It causes us to bottle up and swallow life's sometimes terrible pills. When you view life through the lens of a child, and that's essentially what you're going to be doing when you're having this chat with yourself, you tend to be kinder, gentler, and more honest.

Here's what I'd say to my younger self. First I'd tell her to listen more to what the universe is saying. I'd also remind her that there's perfection in imperfection. That nobody has all the answers, and it's okay if she doesn't. That means she has more to discover.

Recently, I asked my younger self why she tends to push other people. What does she gain from trying to control others? What does she lose? The answers opened my self-awareness and helped prepare me to finally right a wrong.

Ivy

An hour before the party, Ivy stood before her reflection and a sense of dread sailed in. She hated parties and the social anxiety they brought on. When she entered a room full of strangers not seeking her help, she clammed shut. Thankfully, Harper had a way of easing people. At least around the campfire. Not a soul who sat mesmerized by her musical ability carried an ounce of stress.

What could be more stressful than a kid's restaurant full of screaming, whiney kids playing video games, slurping sugary drinks, and slopping up cheese as it slithers off the veil thin crust of pizza?

How would Lila treat her?

Sure, on the voice message she sounded fine.

Lila was never fine. She had a scrappy side to her that Ivy never wanted to engage with. She still spewed angry insults at Damian, her cousin, for not returning her call when she stood on the side of the road with a flat tire. That happened seventeen years earlier!

She didn't forgive easily. She acted innocent and clueless, but inside, she planned her approaches meticulously. She could strategize like a Harvard graduate, shifting things in her favor and leaving people shocked.

"All will go fine. You'll walk in, eat some pizza and cake, laugh about things, find out she's doing fantastic, and walk out of the party lighter," she said to her reflection. "Yes, lighter."

Ivy slipped into a jersey knit dress. Its relaxed arm openings and loose bodice fit her fine. She smoothed her hand over her belly, tucked it in, and exhaled her pent-up stress.

The peace didn't last for more than a blink. The dread of the party ahead of her settled back in the pit of her belly.

Ugh. Why go? Who would care?

Tommy wouldn't notice, and Lila would be busy playing it up with her mommy friends.

Why did Lila want her there? As a goodwill gesture? Or had she feared no one would show and she needed extra heads there so as not to appear unloved in the parent circle? Why couldn't she bake a cake in her oven and invite close friends and family to celebrate? Why did parents invite twenty kids and their parents? Birthday parties turned into extravagant events compared to when Ivy was a kid. She was lucky to get a cupcake, no less a pizza party that included renting out a portion of an indoor playing field of video games and jungle gyms.

At least that meant Lila had money again.

Ivy sighed.

A knock on her door brought her back to the present.

"Come in."

Her mother opened the door. "You look amazing." She moved in closer and whispered, "Harper does, too. I'm glad she's going with you."

"Me, too." Ivy smoothed her hair.

"Is it like a date?"

Ivy turned around to face her mother. "Sort of."

Her mother kissed her cheek. "We'll have that lemonade on the porch soon and you can fill me in further. Until then, don't be afraid to let loose and have a little fun. It's good for the soul." She walked toward the door and glanced back over her shoulder. "I guess my spell worked." She winked and left Ivy to imagine the contents of that spell, and what they meant for her future.

IVY ENTERED the party zone with Harper.

"Thanks again for tagging along."

"Tagging along works great for me. I like pizza and cake."

"I hate crowds. Did I mention that?" Ivy asked.

"You'd hate tagging along in life with a musician then."

Yeah, she would. That didn't bode well for them should her fantasies of taking their kiss to a higher level ever come true.

Ivy inched forward toward the tables full of kids wearing birthday hats.

The room pulsed with an electronic beat, and not one that energized Ivy. Imagine her listeners and clients finding out she suffered from social anxiety.

She wanted to settle her heart with Lila and Tommy, to know they were okay and not hurt by Ivy's swift escape from the jailhouse of responsibility Lila had thrown her into when she asked to move in.

Ivy didn't need Lila to open her arms and squeeze her in a welcoming, forgiving hug. She only wanted to be free from the grittiness of their last encounter. It would be nice to finally be able to face her and package up the past.

She wanted nothing more than to giggle with her like they used to do as kids.

Surely two people who spent their lives tangled up in giggles could get past a little misunderstanding and hurt.

Ivy spied Lila's bestie, Rhonda, piling on the critical glare to other moms wrapped up in the cuteness of their children. Rhonda always wanted to stick herself in between their friendship, and now she got the bestie title. Good for her.

She'd send Rhonda a good dose of love and hope it would relax the stressed-out wrinkles on her face a bit. Fatigue stretched across the high planes of her cheeks and weathered forehead, like she'd been through a hundred-mile journey across the hot desert sands of Arabia. What happened to her? The woman could use a cup of green tea and a big chocolate bar.

Those always did wonders for Ivy.

Okay, enough with the judging. Ivy packed it up and tossed it aside, leaving room only for good vibes to swirl. They could swirl with the stench of greasy pizza and Rhonda's overpowering perfume. Those good vibes might die an early death in the company of that perfume. What was Rhonda thinking? Had she poured a glassful on herself? And why on Earth would she wear that clingy orange top?

Now, Ivy was no fashionista, for sure, but she at least succeeded at covering up her growing curves with a tasteful wrap.

Good thing no one could read her mind.

Stop with the judging, she silently scolded herself.

Some people thrived on the cusp of stress. They rose to the occasion, serving others instead of themselves. Not Ivy. Nope. Stress brought out the judge in her.

Focus, she internally hissed to herself.

Suddenly, Tommy wrapped himself around her leg and squeezed. "Auntie Ivy, you came!"

A dappling of love warmed her soul and cooled the judging rapture playing out in her head. "Of course I did. I wouldn't miss it."

He continued to squeeze her leg harder. "My mommy said you wouldn't come."

Ivy caught the bitterness in her throat before it could launch itself into a set of words she'd regret. "She did?"

"Yup," he released his grip, pointing to his missing front tooth. "The Tooth Fairy came for my birthday. She gave me ten bucks!"

"Wow, that's incredible!"

He smiled and then darted off toward his friends.

Ivy turned over her shoulder. She spotted Lila talking with some of her cousins. They waved. Even Lila. Ivy's heart instantly relaxed.

A few moments later, Lila came up to her and hugged her. "I'm so happy you could make it."

"Thanks for inviting me. It meant a great deal."

Lila glanced at Harper, studying the full length of her from her well-fitted polo shirt accentuating her perfectly-sized boobs down to her sporty sandals. "Who do we have here?"

Ivy heated. "Oh, this is my friend, Harper. We're heading to Harper's sister's house after this, so she tagged along." Ivy's insides jumbled, so she added, "She loves pizza."

Harper stepped forward and extended her hand. "And cake. Hi, I'm Harper."

Lila shook her hand.

"Well, go on over and sit near Tommy," she said to Ivy. "He'd love it. He's been asking about you for a while now. Oh, and my father is here, too." She glanced around the neon decorated space. "There he is." She pointed toward the Pac-Man machine.

"He's doing well?"

"A little over two years without a drink. Third time's a charm." Her lips spread into a smile, but her eyes lied.

"Great. I'll keep sending over the healing vibes."

"Thanks for that. I've been keeping my eye on him. He's got extra space in his home, so Tommy, the baby, and I are there with him for now."

"Where's the baby?"

"With a babysitter. Too many germs, you know?"

Ivy nodded. She wanted to ask about the baby's father, but knew the answer already from the sadness lingering around Lila's eyes. "Are you okay?"

Their eyes locked for an extended beat. "I am. It's been tough. But, yes." She smiled weakly and walked away, leaving Ivy with a deep sense of sorrow. Lila could be hard, but she deserved a better chance at life.

The birthday party went smoothly in that first half hour. Everyone laughed and bid good cheer.

Everyone except Rhonda. She wore a strange neutral expression, strange because she normally greeted her with strained judgmental reserve. Like Ivy might cast a bad spell on her and turn her into a puff of smoke. There were times when Ivy wished she could have such power, like the time Rhonda berated her for feeding her daughter regular ice-cream instead of vegan ice cream when Ivy babysat her. Or the time when Ivy first offered her flower essences to help with her chronic fatigue syndrome and she backed away like Ivy was a devil ready to steal her soul.

Soon, the foil from the casseroles were removed and the pizzas arrived. Ivy glanced around for the bathroom as Tommy wasted no time digging into the cheesy mess.

"I'm going to wash my hands," Ivy said.

Harper glanced at her hands. "I should do the same."

They headed to the bathroom and into their respective stalls.

A moment later, a few toilets flushed. Then in rushed Rhonda's familiar scratchy voice. She laughed about Lila's grandmother wearing a potato sack of a dress.

"Is that woman with Ivy her girlfriend?" Rhonda asked.

"Beats me," Lila said. "She has no luck with men, so nothing would surprise me."

Ivy's blood boiled. She wanted to scream out her defense and remind her that she wasn't the one fishing for a fourth husband.

"Well, if you ask me," Rhonda said, "she's annoying. She struts around with her head higher than everyone else like she's important. Just because she has a YouTube channel doesn't mean she's famous." She laughed, and Lila chimed in.

"I'm the authentic voice," Lila imitated poorly.

Ivy would never say it like that.

"Breathe and life will be perfect." Rhonda took her stab.

That's not how she sounded. Not at all!

"When I lived with her, she judged every move. *Don't eat that, it's for the guests. Don't drink that, it's my mother's. Are you ready yet? You're not ready? You're disrespecting my time.* Blah. Blah. Blah. She drove me crazy. Ivy always thinks she's better than everyone, like she's got some superwoman insider secret connection to Mother Earth. It's a bit too much, I'll leave it at that."

"Why did you invite her?"

"Tommy asked me to. He said it was all he wanted for his birthday."

"Well, he'll wise up eventually and see her for the weirdo she is. Until then, let's eat pizza."

"Yes, pizza!"

They giggled and exited the bathroom.

Ivy's brain numbed. All the vibrant energy that she summoned after her sage cleansing ritual before her shower evaporated into the wake of Rhonda's stinky perfume. A low hum rumbled through her head as her eyes narrowed in on her shaky hands.

Past therapy sessions raced at her, screaming for her to stay calm before the angst and drama destroyed all that progress she had steadily gained. Her first attempt at self-preservation through swallowing a small cry had failed. The tears rolled.

Ivy stood frozen in her stall. Silence banged against her head until a toilet flushed. Then came the knock on her stall door.

"Go away."

"Do you want me to kick her ass?" Harper asked. "I will. I've kicked plenty of ass in my life. I don't mind kicking hers."

Ivy unlocked the door. "Tommy wouldn't approve."

Harper leaned against the stall door. "Just think, this is good material for your 'Uprooting' listeners. I can see the title of an episode now, *How to not let others rattle you when they're being total bitches.*"

Ivy struggled with the tears, despite the chuckle that released. "I'm so embarrassed."

"Embarrassed? I'd be less of that and more hurt, personally. Then again, that's how I've had to live my whole life."

Despite that shared personal tidbit, Ivy struggled against the pool of humiliation gathering in her chest. "I wish there was a back door."

"I say you go out there with your head high, much higher than you've ever carried it. Besides, what about Tommy? The little kid wants his pretty auntie here."

The compliment sailed right through the murkiness and released some of the pressure. "Tommy. Yeah, of course." Ivy tossed her hair over her shoulders.

They headed to the sinks and washed their hands.

"I suppose right about this time in my workshop, I'd recommend facing the situation with a humble heart."

"Humble my ass! She's a total bitch. You have every right to stand up to her. You should. You should pull her aside and tell her to go fuck off. Just don't do it in front of the birthday boy and you'll be well within your rights."

Ivy laughed. "You give the worst advice."

"Fuck, though, she has it coming. No?"

"She does. But," Ivy began.

"No 'but' here. She has it coming."

"Harper, if I fight her again, I'll unravel all the work I did on myself since I kicked her out."

"You're a nice person, Ivy, but way too accommodating. I get it. You don't want to churn up all that crap again."

"I don't."

"So you're going to have to chew on this one until you can spit it out and leave it to rot somewhere other than inside of you."

"You're full of raw wisdom."

Harper studied her. "I can't tell if you're serious or cynical right now."

"I don't have a cynical note in my body."

Harper looped her arm in Ivy's. "In that case, I should start my own YouTube channel."

"Well, that goes without saying, but it's best if you stick to music."

"There is a cynic in you!" Harper led her forward and gripped the door handle. "You're afraid of the competition."

"Touché."

They stood staring at the back of the door.

"So what's our plan?" Harper asked.

Ivy liked her use of the word *our*. It meant they were a team, and Ivy liked being on Harper's team.

"Well, I didn't come to this party to leave without a piece of cake," Ivy said. "So we'll get our slices, say goodbye to Tommy, and leave."

"And Lila? Can I kick her? Just a little kick?"

Ivy laughed, releasing another wave of pent up tension. "We'll table that kick for now. If you want to stick your tongue out at her without me seeing, that would be acceptable."

Harper high-fived the air. "Yes!"

Ivy giggled. "I'm glad you came with me."

Harper pulled open the door. "I'm a sucker for cake. What can I say?"

When they reentered the party, Ivy spotted Lila laughing hysterically with Rhonda and her cousin.

Harper took her hand. "Want to get out of here?"

"Faster than you can imagine."

Harper encouraged her forward with a gentle tug. "We'll stop by Bella's and get our own damned cake."

Ivy spotted Tommy and went up to him. "Auntie has to go early because my mother has a fever. So she needs me to take care of her. You understand, right?"

He nodded. "When will I see you again?"

"I hope soon." Ivy kissed the top of his head and hastened away.

When they exited and stood on the sidewalk, Harper reached for her hands.

They stared at each other under the bright sun of that summer day. Horns beeped. Kids laughed. Doors opened and closed from the shops nearby. The smell of greasy pizza wafted in the air, swirling with trepidation and marching like an out-of-tune drill team's drums on Ivy's heart.

A gentleness shimmered in Harper's eyes, the same as the first time Ivy met her at Bella's. She also recognized the same nervous twitch dancing along her right cheek. That twitch had balanced her nerves that afternoon, and it did in that moment as well.

Ivy glanced back into the window, back at Lila still talking with Rhonda and staring back at her. Lila always tended to succumb to peer pressure, especially when it came from Rhonda. Also, Rhonda built her up, and Lila needed that more than ever.

If Ivy ever wanted redemption, she couldn't do so under the cloudy veil of the hurt in her heart. She needed to speak her mind. "I'll be right back."

"Ivy, you don't want regrets. Let it go." Harper followed her through the door.

Ivy marched up to Lila who kept her eyes glued on her for the entire stretch of the restaurant.

She stood before her, fighting back the urge to defend herself. Oh the things she wanted to say.

Stress marked every single fine line around Lila's eyes. Had Ivy been responsible for some of those lines? Lila never did cope well with stress nor with people pushing her buttons. She lived her life similar to Ivy, clinging to the opinion of others and wanting more than anything to be accepted as someone worthy. Only Lila approached it much differently than Ivy.

Ivy might've internally judged others as a defense mechanism against those who hurt her growing up, but she stopped short of launching those judgments aloud. Except for that one time a year ago. Back to the day her sense of place in the world had collapsed.

She stood on top of the rubble of their fallout not as a hero, but as a bully. Lila had brought out the absolute worst in Ivy. She wouldn't allow her to again.

If anyone was going to fix things and reinstate the peace, it had to be Ivy.

Ivy opened her arms up wide and wrapped herself around Lila. "I love you even if you don't love me back, my sister," she whispered. "I always have and I always will. You will always have a special place in my heart no matter what happens." She squeezed her tighter, and Lila softened.

Lila buried her head against Ivy's shoulder and sobbed.

Ivy rocked her and patted her back. "I'm so sorry I ever hurt you. Let's have a heart-to-heart soon."

After several long moments, Ivy backed out of the embrace and blew her a kiss before turning back toward the door and leaving a probably shocked Harper in her tracks.

To get over her imposter syndrome, she needed to improve. She needed to be a more forgiving, peaceful, and loving friend to those who loved her and to those who didn't. Only then could she set herself free.

Gosh how she couldn't wait to get home and record a brand new live episode where she could finally stare into that camera and authentically declare *I'm uprooting, and I'm a better person for doing so.*

16

TRUTHS

HARPER

"How did you do that?" Harper asked.

Ivy started her car. "If I want us to move on from the terrible place we landed last year, then I had no choice. I'm tired of suffocating under the tension. I did that for me, much more so than for her."

"You freed yourself."

"I did. And you know what?" She glanced at Harper, her eyes a shimmery shade of pristine sky blue. "I'm happy."

Ivy's face relaxed under the glow of the sun's rays. She was beautiful inside and out. If Harper screwed up and inadvertently hurt her, Ivy would swoop in with gentle flight and have mercy on her actions. Because that's the kind of person she was. Humble and graceful, elegant and colorful, flirty and fun, like a butterfly, the butterfly she longed to be herself.

Harper placed her hand over Ivy's and squeezed it. "As you deserve to be."

Ivy placed her sunglasses on her face, ready to drive them to their second trying occasion of the day. "I'm sorry we didn't get cake."

"That's okay. Tess is making lasagna. It's one of her greatest talents."

"We could use someone with that kind of culinary talent at Oasis. My mother and I are not the greatest of cooks, nor is our part-time chef."

"Well, you do make an outstanding blueberry pancake when you're not asking to toss batter at me."

Ivy met Harper's gaze over the rim of her designer sunglasses. "It would've been fair. You toss water. I need something to toss, too."

"You can toss batter at me all day long."

"Well, you can't toss water at me all day long."

Ivy put her car in drive and maneuvered out of her spot.

A drive that should've taken them fifteen minutes stretched to forty-five, thanks to gridlock traffic. Ivy parked alongside the narrow, pothole-infested road of the trailer park community.

"Here we are. Home sweet home of dear old Dad," Harper said.

Before getting out of the car, Ivy turned to her. "Are you nervous?"

"Why? What kind of energy spell do you plan to cast on him?"

Ivy tapped her arm. "You know what I mean."

Harper opened her door and her stomach tumbled when her feet hit the ground. One step closer to facing her own version of stress. "I'm fine. Let's get it over with."

As they closed in on her father's trailer home, Harper's tongue swelled to an outrageous size. It stole all the room in her mouth. Ivy tapped her hand. "You're pale and trembling. We can do some chakra balancing before we knock."

Ivy's ridiculous innocence knocked Harper back on track. Even her tongue fit correctly again. "We'll save that lesson for my father."

The rusty door loomed in the near distance. Ten more steps and they'd arrive. Crazy how ten steps could steal the air from her lungs.

The next few minutes blurred. Tess answered the door wearing a loud orange and teal dress. Andrew and Catalina wore matching concerned gazes as they pulled Harper into overly cheerful hugs. Barry and Nancy kissed Ivy's cheek. And her father wore a plaid shirt and blue tie. His hair was combed, beard shaved, and he gripped a cane with his worn hands.

Show up. Stay in flight.

They said their hellos amidst the delicious tangy scent of lasagna and garlic. As they settled into the surprisingly large central living space, Tess turned to Ivy. "Thanks for the other day. I'm more relaxed and tension free now."

"It was my pleasure. It's something I enjoy."

Humble and graceful as always. Harper remained focused on her gentle energy, hoping some of it would rub off on her as she defended against the strange warm gaze of her father.

"I told my father about you. It's nice of you to offer to help. He's in some pain." Tess's chin folded.

"I can teach him a few breathing and centering exercises to help him work through the pain. I can show you, too, in case he needs your help."

"That'd be great. While dinner is baking, we can sit here and you can show him now while he's still alert. He dozes off easily these days."

"Absolutely."

Tess turned to her father to welcome him into their conversation. "Dad this is Ivy. She's the one I told you about. She's going to show you a few things to help you feel better."

Ivy broke the ice with her gentle energy. "Your daughter suggested we sit and I can show you and Tess a few techniques to help ease some of your pain."

Her father, feeble, but surprisingly well-groomed and alert for the occasion, agreed with a nod. He glanced over his shoulder at Harper as Tess ushered him over to the rust-colored couch. In that glance, he spoke in silence of sorrow and repentance.

He stopped short of the couch. "Can we talk first, Harper?"

Everyone turned their gaze to Harper.

There went her wishful hope for smooth sailing. Nothing ever sailed smoothly with her father.

Say "no" to the man and Ivy would see the monster he created inside of her.

Fuck.

Ivy backed away, pulling Tess along with her. "Let's give you two a little space. I'll help Tess in the kitchen. She turned to Andrew, Catalina, Barry, and Nancy. "You can all help us, too."

They all clucked their heads in unison like chickens at feeding time.

"Yep."

"Sounds good."

"Let's butter the bread."

"I'll pour us some cool drinks."

Everyone dispersed and left Harper facing her father as he clung painfully to his cane.

The room closed in on her. The air swelled with tension. Her tongue outgrew her mouth again. "I can't do this," she said to him.

"Please."

She eyed him cautiously. "I don't want to say anything I might regret. Please can we not have this conversation right here, right now?"

"I don't have much longer, Harper."

Was that her fault? She gritted her teeth and swallowed more than her fair share of bitterness.

He clung to his cane and grunted when his feet shifted.

"Please sit. You're making me nervous that you'll fall."

Her sentence came out sounding much more caring than intended. She simply didn't want to wrestle an old, sick man dying of cancer over to the couch and risk him falling on top of her.

He hobbled to the couch and lowered himself on a painfully slow descent.

She remained a safe distance, hugging her chest.

"Can you please sit next to me so I don't have to shout this?" He groaned and closed his eyes for a moment.

Harper sighed. "Fine." So she offered him her full attention from the far end of the couch.

"I'm sorry," he said.

It would take a hell of a lot more than that.

"I blamed you," he continued.

"Yes you did."

"I was angry. I needed to blame someone."

"Conveniently, you decided against blaming yourself."

"She was the love of my life, Harper. I died along with her. Your father, the one before the accident, before the pain pills, before the heroin, before her overdose, he died."

"He sure did."

"I wish I could bring him back. But he died."

"Well everyone must die, I suppose." Harper flicked a crumb off the couch.

"I don't blame you for wanting this terrible version of myself, the one who was always drunk and high, to die now, too."

Harper's heart beat wildly, pounding against her now hollow chest, creating a vacuum where the couch, plants, and pile of records disappeared and left a gray haze.

"It's too late to be forgiven."

"I couldn't have forgiven me either. I wanted the chance to say to you as a sober man again, not clouded by the demons of drugs or alcohol, that I don't blame you for what happened. I said those hurtful things to you to hide from the truth."

"And what truth is that?"

"I caused your mother to die because I wasn't strong enough to help her." His voice landed on a whimper. His eyes filled with tears. His hands trembled. "I'm sorry it took me so long to sober up and face the truth. I don't blame you, Harper. You did nothing wrong. You were laughing in the backseat, as a child should."

"I laughed too loudly. You crashed. Mom fell out of the car. And the rest is history."

"You're not to blame, Harper. I am. I wasn't paying attention to the road. I'm truly sorry that I hurt you."

He shriveled down to an elderly man's size, all sorry and swollen from tears. Harper pitied him. She didn't expect her father to be small, weak, reduced to an emotional wreck on the other end of the couch.

The mean, bolstering, bully of a man vanished. Like someone

shattered his macho armor, peeled it, and the wind blew its remaining dust away.

For twenty years she held onto that blame. She took it everywhere. And in a matter of twenty seconds, she dropped it. Just like that, it fell to the ground and blew away like a tumbleweed. Her father's apology freed her instantly, though she wouldn't let him onto that. He didn't deserve that ease after causing so much pain.

"Play a song, Harper," he said. "A good song. One that'll help clear the air and allow us to enjoy the lasagna Tess worked so hard to make."

Everyone's eyes fell upon her as they reentered the room, probably praying she'd drop the hate and allow everyone the peace to enjoy one last family dinner before he died.

She deserved peace, even if the man who first stole it didn't.

"I didn't bring my guitar."

He pointed at the wall. "It's waiting for you."

Harper stared at the beautiful Gibson that he never let her play. As she rose, her knees wobbled. She moved toward the guitar, humbled by its rich potential to bring calm to the room.

She wouldn't condone his past. But she could learn to at least settle on the memory of who he was before he turned their world upside down with his drug use.

Ivy placed her hand over her heart.

What would someone kind like Ivy do in her case? She'd hug the man and allow him to pass on peacefully. Harper couldn't hug him. But she could allow him the peace he sought. She was never the monster he tried to turn her into through his fear-induced insults. She was a butterfly, free to fly out of the darkness and into the light.

She picked up the guitar, and strummed a few chords. "It's in tune."

"Andrew tuned it before you arrived."

Harper turned to face her brother, and he regarded her with that brotherly love Harper had grown so dependent on through the years. It comforted her by reminding her that he'd always have her back even when things got rough.

Which in that moment, things had gotten emotionally rougher than Harper expected. She didn't expect to pity her father. She didn't expect to linger on his apology. She didn't expect the lump in her throat to form as he delivered the words she'd craved to hear since finding her mother dead in their hallway, *I don't blame you, Harper.*

To protect against the emotions, Harper tuned into the music, her salvation, her rock, her home.

Soon, everyone waited on Harper to guide them on a musical journey. She closed her eyes, taking up flight in the melody of a song that had brought her face-to-face with self-love, her song, "Anxiety."

She lingered on the opening chords until her heart settled enough for her to engage with the lyrics. She escaped into words that glued her heart back together again through their indelible truth.

Turn the light down so I can sleep.
   Always had a hold on me.
   You gripped too tight and I can't breathe.
   Oh, you live by your name, anxiety.
   Dual feelings that I have.
   I can't find the words to say.
   It courses through my veins.
   Dual words I try to write just to get you out of my mind.
   But you won't leave.
   Anxiety.
   Anxiety.
   Shut the door so I can't go.
   I don't need the world to know.
   When I'm scared, I tend to flee.
   Oh, damned you. Anxiety.
   Dual feelings that I have.
   I can't find the words to say.
   It courses through my veins.
   Dual words I try to write just to get you out of my mind.
   But you won't leave.

Anxiety.
Anxiety.
Put your hands upon the clock.
Take a breath and try again.
Oh, I've done it all.
It never ends.
Dual feelings that I have.
I can't find the words to say.
It courses through my veins.
Dual words I try to write just to get you out of my mind.
But you won't leave.
Anxiety.
Anxiety.
Breathe.

ANDREW CAUGHT Harper's eye and sent her an approving wink full of respectful admiration.

Thank God for Andrew. He understood those words better than anyone else.

ON THE HOUR-LONG drive home from Tess's, Ivy held Harper's hand as they sat in comfortable silence. She didn't push her with questions. She let the air settle in between them untouched, untarnished by analysis.

Harper appreciated that more than ever. Ivy's presence comforted her, and she eased into it the way she would a good long song. Resting in its soothing melody and tranquil rhythm.

LATER ON, when Harper sat on her couch with Moonwalk, she

listened again to Ivy's workshop episode about talking with your younger self.

What would she say to her if given the chance? Would she tell her the situation would mangle her life? That it would turn it into something unrecognizable? Would her words shift her innocence? Should she state the honest hard truth that life was cruel and unfair, even for good people? Because, hey, bad things happened to good people. Would she tell her that she'd likely spend the rest of her days questioning why? Would she warn her that she'd likely end up a little envious of anyone lucky enough to have escaped such a harsh reality?

There in her cozy living room, Harper was a young girl all over again, staring wide-eyed at her mother lying motionless and blue. Would she want that young girl to blame herself for not taking better care of her, for not being a good enough reason for her mother to hang onto her life, to not stick her arm with that needle of medicine and leave her permanently scarred by life's cruel twists?

Twenty years earlier, when she stood over her mother's lifeless body, trying to shake her to wake her up, no one comforted her or instructed how to navigate the situation in that exact moment. That loneliness left a set of markings on Harper, deep grooves that had never filled back in.

In her mind's eye, Harper lowered herself to meet the girl. She took her limp, trembling hands into her own. They stared at each other, kindred spirits connected by tragedy.

The young girl squeezed her hands. Terror flickered in her eyes. The same terror that riddled Harper back on that dreadful day long ago when the clouds swallowed up the sun after she discovered her mother had overdosed.

That innocent girl couldn't have stopped her mother from caving into her addiction, yet she'd blamed herself.

Harper's heart ached for her younger self.

She wished she could go back and talk to her, tell her something that would ease her suffering.

She wanted to whisper to her that she didn't cause the tragic event. She wanted to tell the girl her mother would be okay. That the rescue workers would fix her and that they'd celebrate things together like birthdays, Mother's Day, graduation day, weddings, anniversaries, and the birth of new family members.

Hopeful statements like that led to anxiety.

Nothing was guaranteed, except hope.

"Isn't that right, Moonwalk?"

He looked up at Harper with loving eyes.

"Thank God for you." She lowered herself and kissed his freshly-groomed face.

A feeling of hope filled her.

Hope offered a fuel to keep going. Life would go on, the dirty waters would recede, the crumbled remnants of despair would disintegrate over time, and life could still offer her celebratory remnants to share with others she came to love. That moment so long ago didn't have to define her entire life. She was strong, loving, and capable of turning the page and writing many new chapters.

If she could talk to her younger self, she'd tell her that the end didn't have to signal despair. The end would happen over and over again in life. So each end would offer a new beginning, one where she could open herself up to the idea that she was still worthy, still lovable, still a big part to the cycle of life.

She wished she could tell her that she had people rooting for her to rise and come back from the edge of confusion, sadness, and blame and into a life where she could be more than a survivor of bad circumstance. She was a thriver. One who saddled up to challenges and rode them into shore, wrestling with and triumphing over the tumultuous waves of unrelenting changes.

Twenty years later, Harper now had the words to comfort her younger self. Words that weren't fluff or empty, but complete truth. "No matter what," Harper whispered into Moonwalk's fur, "we have hope."

The hope swelling in her heart at that moment comforted her. It reminded her that life would go on, even in the wake of darkness.

17

ADVENTURE AWAITS

The next day went by quickly. Harper busied herself with polishing the main retreat center's geometric-styled floors while the guests were out hiking with Ivy.

Later on, she met up with Ivy in the backyard gazebo. They sipped tea and read books until the stars lit up the sky and the moths began their dance around the gazebo lights.

With tired eyes, Harper stood and braced herself against the gazebo railing, taking in the beauty of the moon and the light breeze. Ivy came up beside her, looping her arm in hers.

Harper always wondered what home felt like to those who didn't have to worry about things like double-locking their door at night or scurrying to the bus stop with their thumb pressed against the trigger of a bottle of pepper spray.

Oasis was home. Ivy was home. Harper turned and reached out for her hands.

"Thank you for being there last night. You helped keep it peaceful."

"I'm happy you invited me, Harper Ray."

Harper tilted her head back on a moan. "There you go with my two names again." She glanced back at Ivy. "You know how I like that."

Ivy wore her smile like a big, happy ribbon on a present. "I do."

The moon's light sparkled in Ivy's eyes. "So."

"So," Ivy said, tilting her head. "I guess we should get some sleep."

Harper trailed her eyes around Ivy's delicate features. "I suppose so."

"I'm leading a small group from my workshop on a nature walk to learn about and collect healing plants first thing in the morning. You should join us."

"I'd love to, but your mother's to-do list for me is a mile long for tomorrow."

"Get to it afterward."

"Very bold of you."

Ivy tipped her head. "Adventurous is more like it."

"Your mother is a tough cookie. She causes me to sweat and tremble when she hands me a broom or rag."

"She's harmless. She much prefers when people slam it right back at her. So what do you say? Get adventurous. Nature has so much to offer."

"Adventurous, you say?"

"Very adventurous," Ivy said, touching Harper's shoulder. "It can help ease these tense shoulders down a few notches."

Harper lowered them on her own.

"You carry all your stress right here," she said, massaging a tender spot on her shoulder.

Harper eased into her touch.

"Close your eyes," Ivy whispered.

Fluid and teasing, Ivy was nutrition. She fed her vital nutrients after a long run through the desert with no water. She reawakened her to the delicacy of renewed sensory titillation, to the epicenter of where life sparked back to something deeply aligned with pleasure.

Harper let a moan slip.

"See what happens when you let me coax out your adventurous side?" Ivy asked.

Ivy's heat intensified against Harper's sensitive skin. "You have not seen my adventurous side," Harper said.

"Well, show me."

"Show you?" Harper asked.

Ivy hit another sensitive spot.

Harper moaned again.

Ivy curled back around to her front side, leaving a mere finger width between them. "Yes. Show me."

Harper breathed in her airy freshness, staring at her with semi-focused eyes. "I really want to kiss you again," she whispered, caught between desire for a woman who nurtured her soul more than anyone else before and survival to protect her current situation.

Ivy took the lead, cupping her hands around Harper's face and pressing her lips firmly and decadently against hers. "Adventurous enough for you?" Ivy asked.

Ivy sidled her backward until Harper's back hit the gazebo railing. Harper caved into her surprising authority, resting in the comfort of her touch.

"I have a pretty high tolerance for adventure," Harper managed to say on a shallow breath.

An intoxicating rush of desire pooled in her belly as Ivy's tongue found hers and led her into a deeply arousing dance.

Harper's shoulders relaxed all right. They relaxed and caught wind of her heart's wicked beat as the two of them trekked to unknown territory and got lost in the pleasure of each other's passion.

Harper wanted to lift the edges of Ivy's cute halter top and stroke her tummy. Yet another moan erupted from deep within and an unstoppable spike in heat weakened her knees.

Ivy kissed like she strolled through the garden. With intimate, deliberate, slow strides. She lingered on the primal pulse of desire, appearing to revel in the sensual joy of the journey.

No woman had ever kissed Harper with such reverent care before. When her fingers stroked the side of Harper's cheek, ending their kiss, Harper remained close instead of backing away from the tender glance Ivy bestowed on her.

Ivy lowered her hands from Harper's hips, and the break in connection brought Harper back to the gazebo, to the stars and moon, and to the sprawling rancher that housed her pretty, new, packaged life.

"So," Harper said on a lazy smile.

Ivy moved in and closed the space between them even further, feathering her lips against Harper's again. "So." She lingered on the kiss. "I guess we should head inside."

Harper blinked. "Yeah. I guess we should."

Neither one of them moved from their spot.

Ivy bit her lower lip, seductively. "I could stand here all night with you under this big, beautiful sky."

Harper treaded carefully, afraid to stir the moment with anything that might dilute it. "We've got an early class tomorrow, pretty lady." She caressed Ivy's hair. "So let's get you inside and sleeping so you bring your sexy, green witch self to class and dazzle us all."

Ivy's eyes glazed over in a blissful haze as she leaned in and kissed Harper's cheek. "See you tomorrow."

Ivy

Ivy loved hanging out with nature. She connected with plants on an intimate level, drawing from leaves, flowers, weeds, and trees an energy that fed her hunger for belonging to a collective spirit greater than any one individual.

The first time plants revealed their spiritual healing power, Ivy stepped into a bad situation at school and needed a helping hand. She was twelve years old and bullies razzed on her frizzy hair.

Aunt Kathy caught wind and invited her to vacation with her at Ivy's grandfather's, trekking through his garden paradise to make flower essences. Her aunt showed her how to use flowers to connect to her inner power and resilience.

By the end of those two weeks, Ivy had fallen in love with

collecting flowers and concocting remedies to help calm and soothe. She'd later start her own collection of them, giving them away as presents on Christmas and birthdays.

"With flower essences, you can focus on building a strong, respectful relationship with nature," she said to her class. "You need to spend time reflecting with them. Honoring them. Asking them permission to harvest them."

Harper trailed behind her intuitive plant medicine class members with a cocky grin on her face. She showed up, and that supercharged Ivy's energy as she led that group of interested future flower essence healers into the maze of her luscious garden paradise.

"You want to select a flower that piques your interest. Then sit with it for a while and listen for a sign that you're connected. That could be the wind rustling the trees or the sun warming your face."

Ivy led the group to a wide opening where colorful flowers bloomed in bounty.

"Once you get their permission to harvest, you'll cut them directly into your water bowl. Then when we return to the retreat center, you'll set your water and blooms out in the direct sunlight for three to six hours. During that time, I'll encourage you to meditate in the salt room or swim in the pool."

Harper fiddled with her water bowl like a restless little kid.

"What else is involved," a white-haired, peaceful woman wearing two ponytails and a set of jean overalls asked.

"After their time in the sun, we'll siphon water from the bloom by pouring the water through an organic coffee filter into a new jar. Then we'll use that flower water to make our essences by combining fifty percent of it with fifty percent brandy or, if you're avoiding alcohol, apple cider vinegar."

"Is one better for you than the other?" The older man with the peaceful older woman asked.

"The brandy one will last indefinitely. The vinegar one will last up to six months refrigerated. That's the difference. Both offer equal benefits."

Ivy continued to lecture on the facts of flower essences, how to harvest, how to make the essences, how to store them and how best to use them. All the while, Harper wrestled with a smirk.

That smirk normally would've irritated her, but not after their passionate kisses.

Ivy worked one-on-one with each person, saving Harper for last.

When she came upon her, Harper stood before a patch of yellow wildflowers, touching them with her guitar-calloused fingers, still smirking.

"I have no clue what I'm supposed to say to this flower."

Harper's innocent ignorance was one of her best qualities. Ivy could do something about providing her with the knowledge to wipe away any confusion, and that fact sent euphoric jolts through her.

"When I first sat before a flower, I didn't ask her for anything. I admired her details." Ivy pointed to the tiny speckles. "Her features are so beautiful."

"She's delicate," Harper said meeting up with Ivy's fingers on the petal. "And velvety."

"What do you feel from her right now?"

"Terror."

"Terror?"

"Well, I'm about to kill her for my own benefit. We're all a bunch of murderers with our scissors and water bowls."

No one had ever put it that way before. Ivy needed to step into educator role, no matter how much she wanted to keep her fingers dancing with Harper's along the petal of that beautiful flower.

"Can I please have everyone's attention?" She called out to the six others.

They stood calmly, like the flowers had already cast their beautiful essences on them.

"Harvesting is the cycle of life. We're doing our part in a nurturing, loving manner. We keep the loop alive by planting, nurturing, and sharing sustenance with the bees and other pollinators. Then they continue the loop by spreading more life. The flowers reward us for planting them in the first place by allowing us permission to harvest and ingest them to keep their life source flowing in us. We can then fulfill the cycle by planting more flowers."

Harper regarded Ivy with an appreciative smile.

Ivy stood taller in the silent accolade.

"That makes perfect sense to me," Harper said. She opened and shut her scissors a few rapid times. "I feel less like a murderer now."

"Well, what do you know? There's hope for you after all."

Pride spread across Harper's face. "Can we resume our chat with our flowers?"

Ivy waved them off. "Chat away."

Harper kneeled down in front of the groupings of yellow wildflowers. "A good conversation is brewing."

Although Harper joked, Ivy sensed a small bit of truth to her cheery tone. That's all she wanted. For her to take a small step toward understanding nature's power of healing.

Harper

In the week following their dinner with her father, Harper and Ivy spent time together by the fire pit, playing checkers and talking with the guests to the backdrop of acoustic music.

When the hospice nurse sat with their father, Tess ventured to Oasis and worked with Annie on mindful activities, massage, Reiki, and tending to the gardens.

"It's nice to see her glow return," Harper said as she sat alone in the Great Room with Ivy.

They hung out together on the comfy couch in front of the crackling blaze in the fireplace.

Harper put down her guitar, and Ivy took her hand and boldly laid it on her thigh. "You're an amazingly talented woman."

"You're an amazingly beautiful one."

Ivy squeezed her hand and they stared at each other in comfortable silence.

Harper tangled her fingers in Ivy. "I sent out a few more demo tapes this week, and someone called me."

Ivy sat up taller. "That's great news."

"They offered me less than minimum wage. So, I turned it down."

Ivy bowed her head and looked down at their tangled fingers. "I know it's just a matter of time before someone worthy discovers you. I want that for you."

"Thank you. Of course know that I wouldn't leave you hanging without help. I'd find someone to replace me if it ever came down to it."

"No one will be as attentive as you."

"I hope to become more than an attentive cleaning lady to you soon."

The dim lights flickered in Ivy's eyes. "You're so much more than that to me."

Harper worked out the kinks in her neck. "I hope to one day move forward and cement a way to earn income that's not coming from someone like you."

"Someone like me?"

"Yeah. Someone like you." Harper lifted Ivy's fingers to her lips and kissed them. "Someone I wish I could do this to all day long." She continued to kiss her fingers.

Ivy caressed Harper's cheek with her wet fingers. "Then a more acceptable gig we'll find you."

The room was bathed in cottony light. Heat blanketed them from the fireplace and intensified Harper's flush.

"Tell me about your mother. What was she like?"

Harper stiffened. "Let's not cloud this night with any talk of the past. Not tonight. It's too perfect for such heaviness."

"When you're ready, then." Ivy brushed her hand over Harper's cheek.

Harper would never be ready for that.

Ivy

As they sat staring deeply into each other's eyes, Ivy's desire for Harper intensified.

All the guests had returned to their tiny guest houses, and her mother had gone to bed. Both dogs had followed her.

So only the two of them remained in that wide open space of the Great Room.

"I should head to bed," Harper said. "My boss is a stickler. She likes me up before the sun rises." Harper sat taller, staring at their entwined hands.

"Always in such a rush," Ivy whispered on a playful tone. She wanted to sit in the peace. In that room. With Harper. "This is my favorite time of day when it's quiet. It's the time when I like to sit right here in this spot and just be."

"It's peaceful. It's no wonder you wear tranquility like a summer dress."

"Peace of mind is one of the great gems in life."

"Apparently so." Harper danced the tango with her fingers.

Ivy loved when Harper relaxed enough for her face to brighten.

They spent the next half hour easing into gentle conversation about Ivy's mother, the wellness center, and eventually onto a more exciting chat about the sexiness of music.

"It leads me to different places. While I play one song, I'm in the heart of Latin America. When I play a different one, I'm floating on a cruise ship in the Bahamas. Then," she paused and glanced at Ivy's lips, "then when I play another, I'm in the company of a beautiful woman, completely smitten with the way she cradles my hand and centers her attention solely on me."

There was so much Ivy didn't know about Harper, and that mystery served to stir the air with desire. She wanted to understand her complexities and earn her trust as someone she could be comfortable sharing her most vulnerable parts with. For right then, she'd settle on kissing her, on connecting with her in the physical sense in hopes that would entice her to want to uncover a more intimate knowing.

As the sky turned dark and the lights dimmed, the sparkle in Harper's eyes played a melody on Ivy's heart. She wanted to move closer, to breathe her in, to touch her lips and feed her hunger.

Harper offered a sultry glance. "Being with you is so easy."

Ivy craved to kiss her. She moved in and did so, and Harper tasted delicious like vanilla.

Harper weaved her fingers through her hair, and they tangled in the untamed curls humidity always brought on. Harper nibbled on her bottom lip and sought out her tongue to sway lazily with hers. She moved in closer, and Ivy reveled in the intimacy of Harper's heartbeat against hers.

Ivy dropped her head back, moaning, and Harper trailed her neck with kisses. She swayed gently, brushing her fingertip over the curve of Ivy's breast.

"Harper." Ivy placed her nose against hers. "Show me what it's like to make love with a woman."

"Aw, my sexy green witch, once you go there, it's hard to come back from it," she said huskily.

Her body heated. "Make love to me, Harper Ray."

Harper's lips searched out her neck. "Is that what you want?"

"Yes," she whispered.

Harper's eyes glimmered in the low lights of the expansive room. "I would love to make love to you."

Ivy closed her eyes and marinated on Harper's beautiful words. A delightful flutter coursed through her body.

Harper pulled her closer, tickling her with warm breath. Her tongue stroked her, as if savoring the intimacy between them, and Ivy opened up to allow her in. She floated on the softness of her kiss, relishing her richness and the flow of tenderness that teased her to the core.

"Let's go to my room." Ivy responded with a lift from the chair, extending her hand like she'd led women to her bedroom all her life.

Harper took her hand, and Ivy lead the way, into the foyer, out of the front double doors of the retreat center, and through the grounds toward her rancher home to where her private bedroom lay in wait for them.

Ivy closed the door behind them, and Harper curled up around Ivy's back, kissing her neck again. Ivy's knees buckled at the heat of

Harper's breath on her naked shoulder. The dichotomy of that heat combined with the air conditioning caused her skin to prickle. Ivy turned to face Harper's sultry smile. The room behind them blurred as Harper tugged at her blouse and led her backward to the bed.

She fell into the sweet, loving grin Harper cast her way.

Harper lowered her lips onto Ivy's, not breaking her gaze. She kissed her softly, passionately, with something more than a desire for quick release. Ivy kissed her back, losing herself in the warmth of her.

Ivy buried her head in the crook of Harper's neck, and Harper pressed her hips firmly against hers.

They swayed together, caught up in a private dance that stirred pleasure deep into Ivy's core. Each rock of Harper's hips against hers filled Ivy with a desire she'd yet to experience before. Ivy didn't scrutinize her own moves like she always had with her ex. *Did she look sexy enough? Was her tummy too flabby? Did her makeup smear?* Those thoughts stayed far away from the beautiful moment, allowing space for the intimate pleasure that Harper delivered to her to expand. With each sweep of Harper's lips against her skin came a dull ache for more.

Ivy had never been more comfortable in her own skin. "Harper Ray, you make me feel so alive." Her words leaked out in a staccato whispery beat.

Harper cupped Ivy's face between her hands and pressed her lips against hers, opening Ivy up to a whole new world full of intoxicating wonder.

Harper

Everything was so pink. The pillow shams, the throw blankets, the lampshade, even the carpeting. Pink and delicate like a rose. Like Ivy.

Ivy was a rose to discover, to breathe in and admire. Petal soft, fragrant, and colorful. Ivy's refreshing breath tickled her as Ivy kissed her cheek and found her way to the side of her neck, to that spot, that sweet spot that turned Harper to mush.

"You have a way about you, Harper," Ivy whispered in her ear.

A smile grew on Harper's face that she couldn't control. It grew larger than any other smile. Her heart raced like a teenager's, discovering the intoxicating bliss of being so close to someone as special as Ivy Homestead. She ran her fingers through Ivy's messy waves, enjoying how they tangled.

Harper wanted that moment to be perfect and slow. That was Ivy's first time, and she wanted to fill it with pure pleasure and love.

Her tummy rolled in nervous delight as she gazed into Ivy's teasing eyes, flickering with desire.

Harper sought out her lips again, and Ivy moaned. When she lowered her mouth to her neck, and then her shoulder, Ivy relaxed in her arms.

"Harper," she murmured. "I'm falling in love with you."

"That makes two of us," Harper managed to say, continuing past her shoulder, unbuttoning Ivy's blouse and unclasping her bra as she traveled into the deep alluring mystery of her. She found her soft breast and when she kissed her nipple, Ivy's moans intensified.

She pushed Ivy's skirt to the floor, lowering to help her legs through it, and kissing the delicate skin of her inner thighs, her calves, and back up to her hips. She traveled to her navel and then to her naked breasts as Ivy tore off her unbuttoned blouse and unclasped bra and flung them across the room. Then Ivy helped Harper out of her clothes as well.

Harper slid her fingers across Ivy's torso. Rocking against her, she settled into another slow, passionate kiss. She proceeded to kiss her way down the length of her. Then she turned her around and traveled back up, lingering along her spine until she reached the middle of her shoulder blades. She traced her bare skin in delicate circles.

Harper nestled against her, soaking up her heat. She surrendered to the moment, turning Ivy back around and allowing herself to let go and enjoy her kiss, the thrill of her fingertips scraping against her bare back, the groan she delivered into her mouth when their tongues met. "Are you ready for me to show you?"

"Harper," she whispered. "Show me. Yes. Please."

Harper eased Ivy down on the cushy pink bedspread. She kissed her harder, nudging her leg in between Ivy's. She trembled beneath her.

"Are you sure?"

"Never been surer," Ivy managed.

Harper showered her in kisses, while sliding her hands down to that trembling sweet spot between her legs. Keeping a slow and easy rhythm, Harper reveled in the luxury of Ivy's passion. She lowered to Ivy's breast and wrapped her lips around her swollen nipple. Ivy arched her back, moving her body in time with hers, giving herself to Harper.

With a steady pulse, Harper brought Ivy over the edge and her clit clenched between Harper's fingers. Ivy's moans echoed softly in her ears. Her supple body tensed and then relaxed as the waves of pleasure overcame her until she collapsed under Harper, out of breath and gloriously damp with passion.

"Wow," she said, laboring for a breath. Ivy turned her sultry gaze to her. "I never knew it could be so amazing."

Harper propped herself up with her elbow, draping her arm over Ivy's bare skin. "You are so beautiful." She traced her finger along the delicate curve of her cheek.

Ivy brushed Harper's cheek with the back of her hand. "You were right about something."

She continued to stroke her cheek. "What's that?"

"It's going to be hard to ever come back from this place you took me."

Harper's heart opened even wider. "Then don't. Stay here with me."

"I'll stay as long as you'll have me."

Harper searched her eyes, discovered hope, and sank into the sweetness of her loving arms.

18

THE CALL

For the next two weeks, Ivy helped Harper pass out demo tapes to a few local pubs in the Hagerstown area. They all had talent lined up already, but would keep her in mind. "Maybe we should extend your net to the Baltimore area," Ivy said. "Hagerstown isn't exactly bustling with musical opportunity."

Baltimore would infringe on her job at Oasis. "Let's keep trying."

So they did.

When they weren't busy searching for Harper's place in a Hagerstown pub, they continued their work at the center. The summer was edging to a close, and soon Hagerstown would be buried in fallen leaves. She looked forward to playing in piles of the crisp, autumn-colored leaves with Moonwalk and Lil Boy.

Ivy gained new listeners to her "Uprooting" online workshop every day, bringing her students to well over two hundred. One of them was Lila.

"Are you sure it's her and not some other random woman named Lila?" Harper asked as she shoved the vacuum cleaner into its upright position in her apartment's hallway.

"It's her." Ivy beamed. "She signed up last night, and sent in a journal entry assignment. Which, by the way, is more than you've done." Ivy pressed her finger against Harper's chest.

Harper groaned. "I've been a terrible student."

Ivy tickled her side. "That's because you're already the teacher's pet."

Harper pulled her into her arms and nuzzled her nose against hers. "Can I have a break, pretty boss lady?"

Ivy dipped her head back, taking Harper in with all her sexiness. "What will you be doing on this break?"

Harper moved in and nibbled Ivy's lower lip. "Showing you my industrious side, of course."

"Tsk. Tsk. Always in working mode, even when taking a break."

"You love that side of me, and you know it," Harper bathed her in affectionate kisses.

"I love every side of you that you've revealed so far." Ivy giggled. "Show me more."

Harper led her to her bedroom. "With pleasure."

LONG AFTER HER break expired and she made love to Ivy, Harper's cell rang and woke her.

"Harper, it's Barry."

Harper sat up, pulling the blankets up over her naked chest. "What's wrong?"

Ivy rolled over and waited with wide eyes, placing her nurturing hand on her wrist.

"It's your father," Barry said.

Harper didn't need to hear the news. She could tell by Barry's low tone her father was near death.

"He's been admitted to Saint Agnes. It's time Harper."

She bowed her head, surprised by the gush of pain that rushed through her. "Where's Tess?"

"She drove herself. Andrew is on his way to her now. He asked me to call you."

"Okay."

"Do you need a ride?"

Harper swept over Ivy's concerned face. "No, that's not necessary. Do you want me to pick you up so we can go together?"

"That would be great, Harper."

"I guess I'll see you soon."

"Make it real soon," he said. "His pulse is extremely faint."

She hung up after bidding him goodbye. "It's my father. He's close. They admitted him."

Ivy sat up taller. "Let's go. I just need to put on some clothes." She climbed out of the bed, and Harper pulled her back down.

"You're willing to come with me?"

Ivy brushed Harper's hair back behind her ears. "Yes, of course. Why wouldn't I?"

Harper blinked back tears. Kate would've dove back under the blankets and wished her luck. "I love you, Ivy Homestead." She kneeled and cupped her face, kissing her, hoping Ivy's love would always be her home. "So much."

HARPER AND IVY picked up Barry and Nancy. "Tess is taking it hard," Barry said, clenching his fingers into the seat.

"Relax, Barry." Harper gripped the steering wheel. "Breaking your fingertips isn't going to save you from getting banged up if we crash."

"I'd prefer we not crash at all." He gritted his teeth. "I understand why you're tense, but please stop weaving in and out of the lanes."

Harper passed a slow driver riding his brakes. She glared at the driver in the Volvo. "He's on his phone. Idiot!" She yelled.

Barry slapped his legs. "That's it. Pull over. I'm driving."

From the backseat, Ivy cupped Harper's shoulder. It instantly calmed her.

She slowed down and pulled into the right lane. "I promise I'll get us there in one piece."

Beads of sweat broke out on his forehead.

Not long afterward, Harper turned into the parking lot of the hospital.

"There's Tess's car." Barry pointed to her beat-up Civic.

She parked it crooked and barely missed the fender of the car beside it. She must've been a wreck driving.

"How on Earth will the driver of that car be able to open their car door?" Nancy asked.

Tess sucked at driving. She wrecked five cars in one year once, and blamed each accident on the other car. Easy to do when she paid no mind and likely swerved in front of them or slammed her brakes.

"It's like she's drunk." Harper backed into a spot across from Tess.

"Let's pray not." Barry gripped the door handle and cracked open the door.

Harper locked his wrist. "Is she okay, Barry?"

Red blotches covered his face and neck.

Harper's throat scratched.

"Barry?"

He rubbed his chin. "Harper, she's fragile and is struggling with work again and now with your father dying."

"I knew it." Deep within, Harper understood her sister suffered from an illness. She also understood her father and mother did, too. How did she come out unscathed?

"It's not like she's doing this on purpose. She's an addict. We'll get her the help she needs. Let's get through this first."

"By this you mean my father's death?"

He shrugged. "I'm sorry that sounded callous. I didn't mean for it to."

A few minutes later, Barry and Nancy ventured to the gift shop to get some flowers. Harper and Ivy continued on to her father's room.

They entered, and only Tess was there. Her father was sleeping and tubes snaked around most every part of his face, neck, chest, and arms. His skin had turned yellow and saggy. He laid against the bed as a ninety year-old instead of a fifty-five year-old.

"Where are Andrew and Catalina?"

"Getting us coffee," Tess slurred. She staggered by the bed and over to her, clutching her arms across her bony chest. Her greasy, tangled hair matted to her head. Dark circles formed under her eyes. Her shirt had a coffee stain down the front. "He won't wake up."

"What did the doctor say?"

Her chin quivered. "That we should say our goodbyes."

Harper glanced down at him. The ignorant bastard should've known better. He should've taken better care of himself. He gave up when he should've stepped up. Tess planted her head on Harper's shoulder. She smelled of whiskey.

"Are you drunk?"

She lifted her head. She was a ten year-old girl backing away from a scolding. "It's been stressful, Harper. I'm trying to keep everything together with my new job at a diner and with Dad."

Harper steamrolled past her dramatic performance. "Did you drive here like this?"

Tess blinked back more tears. Even her bony cheekbones trembled. "Harper, Daddy's dying."

As if Harper needed that reminder.

The alcohol stung her nose.

"If you must know," Tess continued, slurring. "They wouldn't let me ride in the back of the ambulance."

"So you drove here drunk?" Some things needed to be said, and Harper tired of tiptoeing around her. She was cranky, hungry, and pissed off that her sister was drinking again.

She glanced over her shoulder at Ivy who stood silently against the beige wall.

Tess crumbled into the chair and wailed. Ivy inched forward, and Harper put up her arm to stop her advance.

"For crying out loud," Harper hissed, slinging insults around in her mind. "Keep it together, will you? Do you want Dad's last memory of you to be this?"

Someone knocked on the door gently.

"Come in," Harper barked.

The door opened and in came Barry and Nancy carrying an enormous bouquet of flowers. Andrew and Catalina followed in behind them.

"Is everything okay?" Nancy asked carefully, glancing at Tess and back at Harper.

"Not exactly." Harper didn't have to pretend to have it altogether around any of them. Well except for Ivy. There were still parts she didn't want to tarnish of herself to her.

They eyed her father who lay helpless like a waterlogged tree trunk floating in a swollen river.

Andrew pressed his hands together, signaling his motion to do something to help. He couldn't stand around and do nothing. Charity was hardwired into his system, tangling up in his veins and vital organs. He lived and thrived on stepping in and being the lifesaver that pulled victims to safety.

Andrew had seen his fair share of crap in his life and came out smiling on the other end. His birth parents sold him to friends for a hundred dollars, and those friends forgot him in their rundown, rat-infested apartment. If he hadn't wailed on for hours, the homeless man who knew the purchasers of baby Andrew never would've found him and delivered him to the fire station.

If it weren't for Andrew, Harper wouldn't believe in hope.

Catalina examined their father. "His breaths are so shallow."

"Because he's almost dead," Tess said, hugging herself.

Harper shrugged. "Yes, he is."

They draped Harper in compassionate glances, causing her skin to prickle.

"Wipe those looks off your faces," Harper said. "This is fully expected. The man's dying. He lived his life and now it's coming to an end. We're all going to get there, too. This isn't a big shock. No one should be sniffling. It's life." She sighed and headed over to the window. Their stares penetrated the back of her head. She focused in on a red cardinal perched on a tree branch in front of her.

Her father had fucked up his life in so many ways, and that's why the sadness that was clinging to her heart pissed her off. That sadness manipulated its way into her and sat in a prime position, taunting her. She shook it off and turned to meet up with everyone's concern.

Andrew swept his eyes toward Tess who rocked herself like a catatonic patient. "I'm sorry, Tess. I wish I could find the right words."

Tess locked her red, swollen eyes on Andrew. "Thanks for understanding." Then she glared at Harper as if to scold her for not being as compassionate. She lifted her chin and loosened her grip around herself before crawling her gaze to her father. She perked. "His eyes are open. He's awake." She leaped from the chair and dashed to his side. "Daddy, you're awake!"

Harper joined Tess at his side.

Her father sought out Andrew at the foot of his bed, grappling to find sight in the darkness of his entrapped being. His body was wrinkled and tired, like he aged thirty years in the past day, lying in that beige-walled hospital room. No one should have to end up like that. Not even him.

Harper's heart clenched as an image of him as her young, handsome father popped into her mind. He was strong, muscular, and in control. He loved abundantly and would balance both her and Tess on each of his knees, bouncing until they giggled so hard they toppled. He'd untie her shoes, tuck her into bed, and play songs on his beloved guitar until they fell sleep. She latched onto that memory instead of the one forming in front of her.

His eyes grew larger as they landed on Andrew. Their cloudy haze pleaded for Andrew to understand him before he drifted off to his permanent peace, wherever that might be.

"Daddy," Tess said on a cry, clasping his upper arm. "What is it?"

If anything could keep him alive, it would be the whiskey on her breath.

His eyes cradled a smile as he stared at Tess. He kept his gaze on her for a few extended moments. His eyes spoke of a father's love for his youngest daughter.

Then he sought out Harper. She instinctively placed her hand over his arm, and he dragged his eyes to meet hers. Time stretched as her father's eyes filled with tears. He didn't need to speak. Harper understood him for the first time since she was a little girl bouncing on his knee. His remorse and request for forgiveness poured out through his tears, desperate to mend all the hurt he had caused her.

Harper squeezed his arm to offer him that in his final moment. Then she bowed her head.

"I think he wants to say something to you, Andrew," Tess said, motioning him to the other side of his bed.

He and Catalina stepped up to the other side of the bed with kindness in the fine lines of their well-smiled faces.

Her father kept his eyes locked on Andrew's. They brightened, turning back into his signature baby blue eyes that always got him into too much trouble with the ladies. They twinkled, verging on the cusp of a playful remark.

They stared at each other, and in the omission of words grew the intensity of a silent, shared understanding. One man to another. One father to a young man he admired.

Andrew nodded and his eyes twinkled, too. Then he pulled in his lower lip and the tears sprang.

Andrew was always a sensitive one, and Harper loved that about him.

"I'll take care of them, Sir. You do not have to worry about that. They'll be okay. You have my word." He traced a shaky hand on her father's arm. "You have my word."

Her father squeezed his teary, twinkling eyes together. Then he reopened them as if to say thank you and closed them again for the last time.

19

HEALING AND LIGHT

IVY

I vy admired the strength of Harper's bond with Tess, Andrew, Catalina, Barry, and Nancy, and she was humbled to be brought into that inner circle.

The day after they had buried their father, Tess gathered all of them together and whispered, "I need an Alcoholics Anonymous meeting."

Her family surrounded her like the guardian geese in a flock. They swooped in and lent their support and love.

Catalina insisted Tess stay with them again while she healed.

Everyone did their part to make sure Tess understood she was loved and supported.

For the first month of her recovery from alcohol, Ivy and Harper visited her at Andrew and Catalina's a few times a week. They played cards, Harper strummed her guitar, and they sipped soothing teas.

"I'd love to work up some healing spells for you, if you're open to it?" Ivy asked Tess one night.

"I'd be honored."

So on their next scheduled visit, Ivy worked her magic in the Oasis kitchen, after thoroughly cleaning it physically and spiritually. She procured the ingredients to make a special tea potion, one that would deliver magical prowess. In her mortar and pestle, she added yarrow to strengthen boundaries, hawthorn and hibiscus to keep her heart open, and a rose quartz crystal for sweet love. After reflecting on the contents of her spell, Ivy added a pinch of mint for good luck.

As she blended the herbs, she imagined the tea surrounding Tess with the comfort and support that her family had so generously shown her. She lit a white candle to harness the purity of her intentions and then dripped in moon water that she had infused the previous month.

Satisfied that the potion was complete, she thanked her herbal allies, blew out the candle with gratitude in her heart, and strained the concoction into a travel mug to bring to Tess at Andrew and Catalina's.

Harper

Watching Ivy cast her magic mesmerized Harper, taking her sensual beauty to a whole new rawness. What originally struck her as hokey-pokey silliness, had turned into a serious appreciation for her talent and good-hearted virtue. Harper loved soaking in a tub of her carefully crafted bath salts. She always emerged more energized and clear-headed.

When they arrived at Andrew's, Tess was relaxing in their living room.

When Ivy handed the special tea to Tess, she examined it hesitantly. "I hope it wasn't too much trouble?"

"I love this stuff." Ivy beamed. "Any potion is as effective as the witch casting it, and I can assure you, I'm a good witch and put a lot of love into it. Remain open to it, and you'll attract the energies into your life."

Tess smiled and sipped it. "It's delicious."

That night, Catalina cooked up a pile of spaghetti and meatballs, Tess's favorite. She smothered it in parmesan cheese and marinara sauce, and Tess slurped up every last spaghetti strand and drop of tangy sauce and cheese.

She was happy. She was at peace. She was sober once again.

After they cleaned up, Tess headed off to bed.

The rest of them sat close to each other in the living room, whispering their gratitude and hopes for the future.

"Do you suppose Tess might want to spend some time at Oasis, helping to prep meals?" Ivy asked as she handed Andrew a napkin to wipe away a spill down his shirt.

"I can't imagine a better way to heal," he said.

"I'll ask her." Harper rose from the couch and kissed Ivy's forehead. "I'm going to say goodnight to her."

A moment later, Harper knocked on Tess's door.

"Come in," Tess said.

Harper slipped in and sat beside her on the edge of her bed. She placed her father's Gibson on the floor beside her. "Doing okay?"

"Yeah. So much better. I'm sorry that I've wrapped you up into all of this." Tess curled the blanket up to under her chin.

She resembled a little girl.

"Dependencies are tough, but not the end of everything. You're living proof of that."

"I owe many thanks to you and the rest of the gang for being my support. I don't know what I'd do without you and my sponsor."

"You'd still thrive because you have strength in you."

"As do you, Harper. You're so strong, and I admire that. I'm so glad you've never been dependent on anything."

"Well that's not true." She shrugged. "I do have a slightly aggressive form of dependency on Cadbury and Hershey chocolate."

Tess laughed, and for the first time in a long time, she radiated joy. "I know what to get you for your birthday, then."

"You have to couple them with graham crackers and marshmallows," Harper said.

"If you promise to sit around a campfire with me and roast marshmallows like we used to do with Dad and Mom."

"That'd be cool. I'd like that." Harper ran her fingers through Tess's hair like she used to when Tess was scared of a thunderstorm or when their father flipped out in the kitchen over the electric bill or some other inconvenience. "I want to continue to help you Tess. I'm not sure what more I can do, but I'm willing to learn."

Tess hugged herself. "Just don't lose faith in me or view me as someone who is weak and in need of constant attention. I know I've fallen, but I've gotten back up, Harper. I'm a strong person with an even stronger desire to move forward."

Harper messed Tess's hair. "You sure are strong. We're made of the same blood, and we're both strong."

"Yes, we are."

"You know," Harper said, tracing her finger along Tess's comforter. "Ivy and Annie invited you to Oasis again. You can use the sauna, hot tub, pool, salt room, floating tanks, Pilates, and fitness studio. I'd even do it all with you."

"You in a floating tank?" She laughed.

She'd be willing to sit in mud if that helped her stay sober and feel loved and safe. "I love you that much," Harper said melodramatically.

"That sounds amazing. But Hagerstown is so far, especially without a decent car."

Harper understood the car thing. She'd invest in a new one soon, after she paid for her father's funeral expenses. "Ivy and her mother want to offer you a job prepping meals for their guests. You impressed Ivy with your lasagna. You can stay at my place. I'm hardly there anymore."

Tess scooted up in her bed. "Oh really? Are you in love?"

Harper smiled. "I am."

"I'm happy for you. I hope someday that I can get to a point where I'm able to be someone special like you are for Ivy."

It took Harper a long time to get to that point. She imagined Tess's journey wouldn't be any less difficult. "Focus on you for now, Tess. The rest will fall into place."

"Can I be honest?" Tess's eyes filled with pain.

"Of course."

"I may be strong, but that doesn't mean I'm not fearful of messing up again."

"Tess, we all mess up and have moments when we need a lift. I promise to always be here to lift you should you need some encouragement. Just please don't ever give up the fight."

Her eyes brightened. "I promise to never give up the fight."

Harper steadied on a breath and took in the sight of her little sister full of desire to stay strong in the face of her struggle. That struggle would accompany her forever, always inches behind her, waiting to pounce at a vulnerable moment. And through her strength, she would triumph over that struggle one moment at a time.

"So what do you say about Oasis? Come stay for a while? Ivy's mother already found a church where they host A.A. meetings. It's right down the street."

"What's the catch?"

Harper messed her hair. "You and I are way too much alike. I asked the exact thing when they hired me. They like to help people."

"Good things do happen to good people."

"Yes they do."

"So there's no catch?"

"The only catch is you stay focused on healing yourself. If you're like me, the best way for that to happen is to let things go, even if for this moment."

"I'm getting to a point where I believe I can let things go, finally. I've gripped a lot of anger and resentment about the way our lives had gone in the past, and how unfair the challenges had been for us. I needed to blame someone, so it would make sense. So I blamed myself for many things and abused alcohol and drugs to ease the self-induced blows of that blame."

"You weren't to blame."

"You're right, and I know that now. It's not our fault our father wanted to be drunk rather than take care of us."

Tess's profound statement washed over Harper, clearing a new, pure path for air that her soul desperately craved. She clasped her hand over Tess's and they sat in healing silence for several long beats.

The truth in her statement comforted Harper, lifting her to a new confidence that everything was going to be okay.

With new lightness surrounding them, Harper squeezed her sister's hand. "What do you say we sing some songs?"

"God, yes." Tess sat up taller.

Tess reminded Harper so much of the innocent little sister she used to be, oblivious to their father's dependence on alcohol and drugs. Harper shielded her from a lot of the brunt of his often emotional outbursts about a crumb on the counter or dinner not cooked to his liking. In one ear, Tess would hear their father's rant. In the other, Harper chided with her about her pretty hair, hoping the niceties would neutralize the effect of their father's intensity.

"Can we play, 'This Land is Your Land'?" Tess asked, hugging her knees to her chest.

Their favorite.

"Absolutely." Harper swung around and grabbed her father's Gibson guitar. She slung its strap around her shoulder and finger-picked the melody.

Tess unwrapped her knees and braced taller, plumping her pillow behind her back. Her hair, freshly washed that morning, filled the room with a cleansing, refreshing scent.

Harper began to sing, and Tess fell into her groove with her amazing soulful tone. They made a good team.

They sang a few songs that night, and Tess folded the blanket back up to her chin and laid back. "I'm sleepy."

Harper instinctively tucked in her little sister, as she had for so many nights following their mother's death when they were younger and essentially on their own.

She kissed her forehead, silently promising to never leave her without ensuring her well-being ever again. Harper had the chance to right one of her wrongs. And she didn't take that second chance lightly. She'd do whatever she could to help her sister regain her footing.

"Tomorrow, come to Oasis. You can help me do some weeding in the gardens and then win Annie over with one of your delicious recipes."

She opened her eyes. "That would be amazing."

"Good." Harper turned to leave, and Tess grabbed her wrist. "Thank you."

Her earnest blink told Harper she meant it.

As the weeks passed, Tess healed dramatically. She enjoyed working with Ivy's mother on meal preps for guests and learning about the healing power of plants.

"My sister seems to be enjoying herself at Oasis. Are you and your mother happy with her work so far?" Harper asked Ivy on the afternoon of her thirty-third birthday as they hiked in Harpers Ferry, West Virginia.

"My mother loves her. She said her waist doesn't, though. She cooks like a gourmet chef."

"She's got culinary talent, for sure."

Ivy laced her fingers in Harper's as they climbed one last steep step up to a flat rock overlooking the quaint town of Harpers Ferry. From their view, the town reminded Harper of a toy train set. The tracks ran under the mountain where they stood. It stretched ahead, nestled behind the sharply pitched rooftops of old buildings stacked right up against each other.

"She's a strong person and that strength will serve her well on her journey," Ivy said.

"She said the meetings help her a lot. She told me that she's learned a lot from her sponsor. Seeing her succeed helps Tess to envision her own success."

"She's got a journey ahead of her." Ivy squeezed her fingers. "The fact that she's got such solid support will help her."

"She's told me that sometimes she desperately wants to cave. That the liquor calls out to her like an irresistible desire." Harper sucked in her breath. "But then she tells me that her sponsor and other friends she's met at her meetings help her cope in those moments of struggle by teaching her how to refocus on what truly matters."

"Knowing what matters is the key. It provides that direction when the world gets dark. She's a smart, determined woman."

"She really is. Honestly, I never saw her as strong before because I never understood the demons she fought daily. From our talks recently, I now have a better grasp on how much strength it takes to overcome the disease, and I'm blown away by her strength."

Ivy brought Harper's hand up to her lips and kissed it, bathing her in a loving glance. "I love how much you love her. You are a good woman, Harper Ray."

Harper basked in Ivy's words as they stood in silence after that. They stared out over the beautiful town below. Birds chirped. The sun cast a golden sheen on the weathered trees and the air smelled like fallen leaves.

Harper rested her chin on Ivy's shoulder. "I need to pee."

Ivy chuckled. "That's what you get for drinking almost all the water yourself." She pointed to a heavily wooded part of the path to their left. "It's secluded over there. I'll keep lookout."

Harper kissed her cheek and headed into the thick brush of a secluded stretch of the trail. As she squatted she spotted a lizard perched on a tree trunk. It stared at her as she peed. "Hey you. You look like a mini-dragon. You're not going to spit fire at me, are you?" Harper stood after she finished. She waved at the cool lizard. "Enjoy the sunrays."

Ivy would be proud of her for attempting to connect with nature.

When she returned to their spot, they sat for a while and admired the colorful late foliage atop the picturesque view of nineteenth century buildings and the key site of an abolitionist raid during the civil war.

"Andrew and Catalina invited us to a late Sunday lunch at their house tomorrow. Are you interested?"

Ivy beamed like Harper had asked her to marry her. "I'm honored. I'll bring some blueberry tarts for dessert."

Harper wrapped her arm around Ivy. "You and your blueberries."

Ivy elbowed her. "If it weren't for my obsession with blueberries—"

"You wouldn't have gotten to see me naked first."

Ivy kissed Harper's cheek. "Life is so perfect right now. I hope it always stays this way."

Harper cupped her hands around Ivy's face. "I love you, Ivy. Everything is perfect."

Ivy's eyes twinkled. "I love you, too."

They sat staring out over the lookout to the town below. The sun began its slow descent from the top of the sky and a mild breeze blew Ivy's hair.

"Thanks for making this a special birthday," Harper kissed her. It was the first birthday since before her mother died that her heart lightened. "It's been one of the best."

"What do you say we go back to Oasis and enjoy a campfire?"

"I'd say nothing could make my heart happier."

They descended the steep trails of Harpers Ferry and headed into the small town for hand-churned ice cream. "Now, I need to pee," Ivy said. "Can you get me strawberry in a waffle cone?"

Harper tickled her side. "A green witch afraid to squat in the woods. Good thing you're adorable and I don't mind standing in this long line without you." She kissed her forehead and nudged her away toward the bathrooms.

She pulled out her phone to pass the time, and checked her email, something she hadn't done in a week. She deleted ad after ad. Then her eyes landed on a message from someone named Larry Potter from Highland Entertainment. She recognized the company name. They owned a slew of upscale clubs.

Her heart skipped. She couldn't read through the email fast enough. *I run a network of upscale clubs in Southern New England and am hiring new talent. One of my associates sent me a video of you performing. I want to meet you. Any chance this week?*

When Ivy walked toward her in line, Harper still couldn't stop trembling.

Ivy rushed up to her. "What's wrong?"

"All those times you recorded me performing," she began, her voice a whisper from its normal range.

Ivy put her hand on her arm. "What about them?"

Harper struggled to swallow. "Did you send any of them to Larry Hopper at Highland Entertainment?"

"I have no idea who that is. So, no."

Harper opened her mouth to speak, but only a guttural moan followed. She handed her phone to her.

Ivy grabbed her phone and read the email. A huge smile spread across her face and when she looked back up at Harper, her eyes were filled with loving joy. "Wow, what a birthday gift!"

A whistle escaped Harper's mouth. She ran her hands through her hair, not sure up from down, back from front, left from right. The whole world tilted on its axis and disoriented her.

"Harper, do you understand what this could mean?" She grabbed a hold of Harper's shoulders and stared deeply into her eyes. "Your life is about to change." She released a small happy cry. "Big time."

As the seconds grew from her last word, recognition spilled into her delicate, loving face. Her smile straightened and her breaths shallowed in rhythm with Harper's.

Life was about to change big time, and neither one of them had a clue how to digest that news.

Ivy

With opportunity came choices. Difficult choices. On the other end of that phone call sat Harper's dream. She put Mr. Larry Hopper on speaker so they could both listen as they sat in the front seat of her car in the visitor parking lot of Harpers Ferry information center.

"We've opened five more clubs in the Southern New England region and need to hire the right performer to rotate between them as the opener to our headliner acts. A nephew of one of my associate's was at Bella's the day you performed at a charity event, and he's been trying to get me to sit still for a minute to watch his recording. As you can guess, I'm a bit overwhelmed, but not so much to pass up an opportunity to meet face to face. I can have my travel agent arrange the flight. How soon can you come?"

Harper sat tongue-tied. Ivy stared at her, pouring every ounce of love into her. That was her moment to shine, and Ivy wouldn't stand in the way.

Ivy tapped her to answer, waving at the phone.

"Um, let me check with my employer to make sure she's got coverage and I can let you know, if that's okay?"

Ivy shook her head frantically, mouthing, "Go. Go today!"

"Or if it's important that we meet soon, let's have your agent arrange it. I'm sure it'll be fine."

"I'll have her call you in a minute. We need an opening act for this weekend. The one I had booked canceled. The sooner we can get you here to talk logistics, the better."

Harper's fingers trembled so much, she couldn't even end the call. So, Ivy ended it for her.

"You're freaking out," Ivy said, placing her phone back in its holder. "Don't freak out. This is incredible."

Harper ran her fingers through her hair and bent forward on the steering wheel. "Then why do I feel like I'm about to throw up?"

Ivy patted her back, and put on her brightest smile to hide the sadness trickling into her heart. "Because, Harper Ray, that's what happens right before a dream is about to take off and launch you into outer space."

Harper

Not more than twenty-four hours after she learned of the life-changing news, Harper stood before Larry Hopper, proud owner of ten upscale nightclubs in the Southern New England region.

In the hour that followed, Harper learned the details of her lucky break. It consisted of everything she needed to thrive, a great salary where she'd be able to afford not just one, but two cars if she wanted and all the resources needed to live comfortably on the road.

On the road with Moonwalk.

Money.

Away from Ivy.

Resources.

Away from Tess and Andrew.

Potential fame.

All the perks she dreamed of and all the nightmares as well.

LATER THAT NIGHT, she arrived back in Maryland. Ivy greeted her at the airport with a toothpaste-commercial smile. She wanted Harper's happiness above her own, and that placed guilt on Harper's heart.

They hugged, and as they walked to the parking lot, Harper filled her in on all the details.

As they sat in her car, a heaviness hung in the air. One that foretold of their future should Harper sign the paperwork she brought back from Larry Hopper's office.

"What would our life look like if I took this, Ivy?"

Ivy's beautiful eyes glazed over. "A whole lot different I would suspect."

Harper ran her fingers through Ivy's hair. "Would you ever consider coming with me?"

Ivy hesitated on a sigh. "I might. One day."

"One day."

She cocked her head and regarded her. "I love my life at Oasis. Then there's my mother. Lil Boy. Guests. There's a lot to consider."

Harper blinked back the sting of tears. "Of course. In fact, I should never have placed the burden of that question on you. I can't expect you to drop everything for me."

"I can't expect you to drop everything for me either. You love music."

Harper released a breath. "I do. But I also love you and my life here."

"Harper, let's not kid ourselves. I can't imagine you love cleaning toilets by day and singing to twenty people at night. You're meant for so much more than this rest stop has offered you."

Harper didn't want to be her cleaning lady by day and lover by night. She wanted to live her dream, be self-sufficient, be strong and capable, and be with Ivy through it all.

"Besides," Ivy said. "Many couples have successful long-distance relationships."

"It scares me to do that to us."

"There's nothing to be scared of. We can take turns visiting each other."

"But you hate cities and large crowds."

"But I love you." Ivy grabbed Harper's hand. "Don't run away from it Harper. Embrace everything with love and you'll find your way. I don't ever want to be the person who held you back and makes you regret what you could've done with your life had I not been in it."

"I'd never regret you."

She leaned against her seat, a layer of concern blanketed her face. "You might. I mean, if I had listened to my adult self instead of my younger self back when I weighed my options on staying with my ex in Pittsburgh or starting Oasis with my mother and aunt, I'd still be searching for home. I found it when I stopped running from what was meant to be. Whether that's life on the road for you or not will be revealed when you let go and learn to trust yourself. That's when you'll feel most alive."

Harper leaned in. "I already feel alive when I'm here with you."

"You'll feel alive when you're living your dream on stage. Harper, this is your dream. Your chance to shine. You've got to try."

"What if I don't like it?"

"Then you come home." Ivy brushed Harper's cheek with the back of her hand. "If you do like it, then we cross that path when it appears."

"What do I do about Moonwalk?"

"He can stay with us while you're on the road. He likes it here. And Lil Boy's sprung back into being a pup again around him."

"What do I do about Tess?"

"Don't worry about her. She's a strong, independent woman. She loves it at Oasis, and she's a huge asset like you were."

Emotion choked her throat. "Were?"

"I didn't mean it like that." Ivy tapped her arm. "You said it yourself a while back, you don't want to be our cleaning lady. You stopped here temporarily to get your bearings until the world woke up to your amazing talents. It's woken up."

They sat in silence, drinking in the bitterness of their dilemma.

A tightness gripped Harper's chest. It increased in pressure as her future moved closer to her present, a future with so much potential in terms of joy and pain. Sure, they could make things work in the short-term. What about long-term? What about a life with kids, PTA meetings, camping, checkers, hot cocoa by the fire, and long walks through the garden?

"I'm torn," Harper said. "What should I do?"

Ivy caressed her hand. "A good life coach would tell you to stop running and seize the opportunity before you."

The stress stole air from Harper's lungs. "Which opportunity are we talking about?"

"Being the kind of objective life coach I crave to be, I'd tell you that's for you to discover. You have to surrender to the journey and be willing to uproot everything in order to find home within yourself."

Harper studied the cars tucked into their parking spaces in the airport garage. She centered her focus on the way they all fit together despite the challenge of being different sizes and colors. Maybe she needed to think like a car and park herself in a zone that allowed for such cooperation between her heart and mind.

Her heart and mind played at odds with each other. How could she be objective when viewing the dilemma through the lens of indecision?

"A wise life coach once told me in an 'Uprooting' episode to ask my younger self the tough questions to get the most authentic answers. I guess it's time I have another talk with her."

Ivy grinned with pride. "This life coach fully agrees. You deserve to live a life with great impact. You can do that through your music. You'll serve the world with that talent. You can't run from that."

A life of impact would bring closure to a past riddled with useless torment. It would offer a chance to do something significant that added value in place of tragedy. Harper wanted to create a life of impact. It's what her mother would've wanted for her.

A cry lodged in the back of Harper's throat. "Who am I to disagree with an amazing life coach like yourself?"

20
_____

WHAT MATTERS MOST

"I'm so nervous, I might throw up on stage." Harper paced her hotel room, gripping her cellphone and waiting on Ivy's soothing voice to settle her from across the miles.

"It's totally natural. I've already done a few success spells on you last night and today, so no worries."

Harper chuckled silently. Ivy and her spells. Maybe, just maybe, they did work like her bath salts did. In which case, she liked that Ivy cast them. She could use all the prosperity available. Tonight she'd perform on a stage in front of three hundred people at the trendy Fiona Club in New Jersey.

"I wish you were here," Harper whispered.

"Me, too."

Despite the sincerity in her tone, Harper didn't believe her. Such a crowded place would drive Ivy crazy.

"Now go enjoy yourself. You're living your dream, Harper. Make it count."

~

FIFTEEN MINUTES LATER, Harper climbed the side steps to the stage at the front of Fiona's.

Crowded pub-style tables filled the chaotic room. People talked amongst themselves and didn't notice Harper sitting before a mic on the center of the stage, slinging her father's Gibson strap over her tense shoulder.

That was her moment to shine. To prove to herself, to Larry Hopper, to the crowd gathered that she was worthy.

She inhaled and her chest squeezed. How would she hit her notes with that kind of pressure?

She hadn't expected nerves to slide in and take over. When she dreamed up that moment, she imagined she'd rock out the room and leave everyone breathless and wanting more. But her knees trembled beneath her elbow, and her breaths spilled out her nostrils like desperate beats out of tune.

Then bright stage lights cast a strong glow on her, and the crowd noticed. Their thunderous chatter settled to a low hum. A few throats cleared. Some glasses clanked. Then a bold silence stole the room.

Show up. Stay in flight.

She closed her eyes, inhaled deeply, and latched onto Ivy's last words, *you're living your dream, Harper. Make it count.*

Harper strummed the opening to "Desperado," and the energy of the room raised to an intoxicating level. She'd experienced that same exhilarating force when Kate took the stage. Like a swarm of bees, the crowd buzzed collaboratively in wait for what Harper would deliver.

By the time she sang the first lyrics, the eager audience fueled her with a foreign intensity that reduced her anxiety to ashes. She poured herself into that song, focusing on the beautiful words and the soothing tempo to carry her along the wind's swell of potential.

A potential that would change everything if given the freedom to take flight.

WITH EACH NEW PERFORMANCE, Harper's comfort level grew. The

butterflies that swarmed her stomach didn't flap as much anymore. She mounted the stage steps to each new club with a confidence born out of a growing familiarity.

By the third week, Ivy, Tess, Andrew, and Catalina were due to come out to a show. They were to arrive by three that afternoon so they could hang out, get an early dinner, and claim their prime seats at the Club Nouveau.

Harper arrived at the airport to pick them up. When she saw Ivy striding toward her, Harper lost it. The crowded airport blurred around her as she bolted toward her.

She pulled her into her arms and swung her, inhaling her freshly-shampooed hair. Nothing, not even a thunderous audience could intoxicate her like Ivy. "Now I'm living my dream," she whispered. "Oh, I missed you."

The five of them spent the afternoon catching up, giggling, and eating way too many sweets. By the time Harper hit the stage, she already began to worry how she'd miss Ivy when she went back to Oasis. Another three weeks would take forever to get there.

Ivy sat front and center next to a beaming Tess, Andrew, and Catalina. They sipped on sodas and poured their attention onto her as she performed. They sported proud smiles, lifting Harper to new heights, allowing her the freedom to embrace all that potential she feared on that first night she performed.

Maybe Ivy might discover she loved the city and the crowds.

Maybe she wouldn't mind living in hotels with Moonwalk as they embarked on the planned pub crawls of Larry Hopper's growing dynasty.

Maybe all that potential could work in their favor and not destroy the very thing Harper always wanted, a sense of home with the ones she loved.

As the crowd's energy increased, Ivy caved in on herself. She sat lower in the chair, hugged herself, and glanced around warily.

Later, when they mingled with some fans of the show, Ivy's discomfort stretched across her face. People walked by and bumped into her, and she twitched and hugged herself tighter.

"Are you okay?" Harper whispered.

She offered her signature toothpaste-commercial smile. "Of course. Yeah." She nodded, as if convincing herself that she could plant herself into the chaos of life on the road and be okay.

No amount of spells or sage were going to balance Ivy in that environment.

Ivy was miserable, and would lie to herself for Harper's sake. She'd sacrifice her own sense of peace and purpose in the world to keep Harper's dream alive. That's who she was, caring, amenable Ivy, afraid to hurt others through demanding her own needs.

"Let's go home," Harper whispered into her ear.

"You have fans waiting for you to talk with them."

"No, I mean home, home."

Ivy squeezed her hand in Harper's. "No."

"No?"

"I said no."

"What if I want to?"

"I demand that you don't." Ivy stared at her with a new confidence.

Harper didn't know what to do with that confidence. "Yes, ma'am."

"And don't be calling me ma'am."

Harper chuckled. "Very well."

"Harper Ray, you're amazing, and everyone knows it. This is home for now." She stared at her with stern love.

Harper nodded, and squeezed her hand back, wondering how she ever got so lucky.

Six Months Later

"Wave hi to your momma," Ivy said to the camera, picking up Moon-walk's paw and waving it up and down. Ivy blew Harper a kiss. "We miss you and hope your show goes great tonight. Oh, by the way, you'll never guess who finally got in the floating tank! Barry!" Ivy laughed, and her eyes twinkled in the light of the camera. "He came out and said he had a surreal insight that he'll share with us next time you're in town."

Harper clung to every second of her recorded video. She studied every fine line, every laugh, and every inflection.

Then Ivy's face turned solemn. "It's been too long since our last kiss, Harper. I'm sorry I missed the last visit. With the next rendition of the 'Uprooting' workshop, my schedule tightened. I'll be there on my next turn. I promise." She blinked heavily. "I miss you terribly. Bye, Harper Ray. Mwah."

Harper sat staring at the end slide of her video. She ached for her. For Moonwalk. For walks in the garden. For the scent of the campfire. For a competitive game of checkers. For everything to do with sweet Ivy Homestead.

A painful emptiness sat in her chest as she turned to look out the window and onto downtown New Haven, her next stop on the never-ending musical journey that engulfed her life.

No matter how much music she played, none of it could fill her emptiness.

In fact, lately whenever she hit the stage and the crowd cheered, she tuned them out as she played. With most performances, she went through the motions and performed well enough to get ovations. But the zest disappeared somewhere in the miles and time away from Ivy. She searched for the zest on the faces of her audience, waiting on one of their accolades to bring her to that nirvana she craved.

Playing music around the campfire at Oasis brought her to that nirvana. Ivy's loving eyes filled her with the joy she sought in that faceless, meaningless crowd. They were noise, distraction, and obstacles in the way instead of thrilling participants in the great songs of life.

She was living her fantasy, only it grayed and blurred. Where had the sunshine and rainbows from her earlier fantasies gone?

Not on stage under the limelight of local fame.

She pressed her forehead against the window.

She wanted Ivy.

She wanted Oasis.

Hell, she even wanted the floating tanks she'd yet to try.

Most importantly, she wanted home.

Ivy was her home.

Backing away from the window and the big city view with all its lights and glitter, she bent over and placed her hands on her knees.

She wanted her life back with Ivy at Oasis.

But Ivy would ask her not to dump that kind of potential regret in her lap.

She had to figure out a way to prove to Ivy that the regret lay in choosing Larry Hopper's big opportunity over her.

As she remained bent over at the knees, an idea popped into her mind on how she could prove it to her. It would require she shed her secrets and stand before her naked and vulnerable.

Harper was ready.

She hoped Ivy was, too.

She rose and called the only person other than Ivy who could help her to show up and stay in flight.

"Hello," Andrew said groggily.

"Did I wake you?"

"It's two in the morning."

"I'm sorry." She cleared her throat. "Actually, I'm not. I need to talk. Do you have some time?"

"Depends."

"On?"

"On if this conversation is going to cause me tears or not."

"Mr. Sensitive, always about you," Harper chuckled, loving that sentimental side of him. "You might cry."

"Ah, fuck."

"That's the spirit!"

21

WHAT LOVE LOOKS LIKE

IVY

I vy lingered in the garden, picking lemongrass for a tea she'd brew her guests that afternoon. It had been too long since she last met up with Harper, and the emptiness sat on her chest like a bag of rocks. She missed her self-assured comments and her challenging ways. She missed her music and the romantic innuendos that played on her heart.

Harper was living her dream, surrounded by fans who paid money to watch her entertain. She stepped into the infant stages of a demanding music career that would grow bigger and potentially widen their gaps between visits if Ivy didn't step up and deal with her discomforts.

Traveling back and forth from gigs to Oasis shredded Harper's energy and health. Her eyes always glazed over and her yawns outnumbered her laughing spurts.

Harper deserved more than tiredness. She deserved to live her big break with an open heart. Ivy wouldn't be the one to get in the way of that. She'd cast more spells to ease her discomfort with the crowds and cities. Plopping herself into those situations might be the best medicine for her, after all. She could view those times as practice grounds for setting energy boundaries with strangers.

Ivy spent the better part of that morning bent over her flowerbeds plucking weeds, mulling over those thoughts. The dirt cooled her hands. She uprooted that which didn't serve, allowing the flowering plants the dignity to thrive on their own without the clutter of weeds.

By the time the sun took its high perch in the sky, she convinced herself that things fell into place as they were meant to be. Harper caught her lucky break. She should be happy for her. That's all she ever wanted for her: to be happy and free. Harper was meant to shine on stage, not fade by a campfire light.

So she would show up more often and support her dream, even if it killed her inside. She'd return to Oasis after those trips and resettle her anxiety.

She loved Harper and was grateful for any amount of time she could spend with her. Many couples endured the challenges of a long-distance relationship.

They could, too.

Ivy's home was Oasis.

Harper's was on the road.

That reality didn't settle well into her heart. But it was their reality. Just as she needed Oasis to bring out her best, Harper needed music to bring out hers. For either one of them to block the other from their life source would be selfish and wrong.

If Ivy had convinced Harper to choose a life at Oasis instead, like one of those flowering plants, Ivy would've become a weed to her. A weed who sucked the life out of her instead of brought her to her full bounty. She let that marinate while she sat back on her heels and stared at the pile of weeds she'd pulled up. Some of them were pretty. The bees loved them. A few had circled around them, ducking in for a taste of what the uprooted weeds had to offer.

Ivy sat back and admired the stillness. She breathed it in and savored its pungent, earthy scent.

A few moments later, the crunching of pebbles from the graveled pathway startled her.

Ivy turned over her shoulder and met eyes with Harper's silly grin.

"If that hat was any wider, you might not fit through the front door with it."

Ivy's heart leaped at the sight of her grin. She tilted the hat to the right. "What are you doing here? It was my turn to visit you in a few weeks. Is everything okay?"

Harper extended her hand, and Ivy took it. "Always with the concern. Tsk. Tsk."

Ivy chuckled and rose, allowing Harper to lead her down the garden path. The scent of earth permeated the air and the hum of crickets filled in the space where an awkward silence could've stolen the moment had Ivy not been so mesmerized by it.

They strolled without words, Harper lacing her fingers in Ivy's as they neared the edge of the garden, over to the wrought-iron bench where Harper used to sing to her.

They sat.

Harper hung onto her hand, clasping it with her other, still staring pensively ahead.

"It's taken me a while, but I'm ready."

"Ready for what?"

"To share myself fully so you will grasp just how important a sense of home is to me."

"I don't understand."

"A little over twenty years ago on April nineteenth, I sat on the couch in my trailer home eating Cheerios with little chocolate chips and a splash of milk. That was my favorite breakfast and something I've never eaten since that day."

"Why not?"

"I was watching *The Smurfs* and wearing my favorite pajamas, flannels decorated with puppies. My mother stumbled by and stood in front of the television set, blocking me. I whined at her to get out of the way."

Harper's jaw flinched, then she continued. "She didn't budge. She placed her hands on her hips and blocked my view of Papa Smurf. She asked me if I wanted anything." Harper laughed uneasily. "Once my mother started drugs, she never asked me such questions. She shoved me out of her way instead."

She exhaled sharply. "I tried so hard not to be in her way. I slithered around, afraid to stand out. I tried not to speak too loudly, ask for too much cereal, or request new clothes for the start of a school year. Basic things."

She clicked her tongue, looking ready to confess murder.

"I noticed my mother clutching her tiny medicine pouch in one of her hands at her hips. That medicine always mellowed her. That day she kept tapping her hands against her hips and searching for something. I didn't want to anger her, so I told her I didn't need anything."

Harper strained for composure.

Ivy's heart clenched.

"Not long after she lumbered away, a thump echoed in the hallway. I thought she dropped something. So I continued watching *The Smurfs*, not wanting to get in her way. Sometimes she did housework when I failed to do my chores. Which wasn't often. Every once in a while I just wanted to chill out and enjoy *The Smurfs*, you know?" Harper's voice cracked.

Ivy clasped her other hand on top.

"A little while later I needed to pee. When I turned down the hallway, her body lay crooked across the floor. Her tiny medicine pouch had fallen and lay a few inches from her hand. Her eyes were open but she wasn't there." The tears erupted and Ivy pulled her into her arms. Harper laid her head on Ivy's shoulders and Ivy patted her back.

"My mother overdosed. I never got the chance to answer her question that day. I did need something. I needed her. Ever since then, I've questioned myself. If I had told her that I needed her, would've she stuck that needle in her arm and killed herself? Would she have taken pills after the initial car accident, knowing their potency?"

She choked on a sob.

"Would she ever forgive me for laughing too loudly and causing my dad to crash the car? If I hadn't laughed, she would've never been tossed out of the car and hurt her back. She never would've needed pills in the first place. Then maybe my father might not have died of cancer because he never would've been as stressed, drank so heavily, or smoked."

Ivy rocked her gently, kissing the top of her head, not saying anything, but rather letting the gravity of the moment set in.

"The reason I didn't want to open up to you about this is because I feared tarnishing the good we had. I didn't want to rehash the part of my life I've been trying to forget. I've spent my life running from those painful moments, ashamed of them. Ashamed of myself for not doing more. For not being enough. For not seeing my mom's pain and helping her through it. I sat there munching on Cheerios and chocolate, watching *The Smurfs* while she killed herself less than twenty yards away from me."

Ivy continued to hold her tightly.

"When I met you, I discovered something that I didn't want to spoil. I didn't want my ugly past to soil my hopeful future. In my attempt to preserve that, I fear I've destroyed it."

Harper succumbed to sobs.

"Hey," Ivy said, lifting Harper's chin with her finger. They stared at each other, and Ivy wiped her tears. "You know what they say about fear, right?"

Harper shook her head.

"You have to face it in order to move past it," Ivy said. "You showing up here and sharing this with me is you facing it."

"I still have a lot of fear in me, fear I've been too busy running from to settle. I need to face it. I know that now. I'm finally going to take Andrew's advice and go to an Adult Children of Alcoholics meeting. It's a safe place where people share their experiences of growing up with abuse, neglect, and trauma. I've also asked Andrew to recommend a therapist."

A peace settled around Harper's eyes.

Ivy wiped more tears from her cheek. "That's a great idea. And if you don't like any of his therapist recommendations, I can recommend the one I went to."

"You went to a therapist?"

"Of course. None of us get through life untroubled, Harper. We're all in need of a little help sometimes."

"That makes me feel better." She smiled. "Is that weird?"

Ivy chuckled. "Not at all." She wiped Harper's tears one by one with her fingers. "And just know that I'm here, too. Some say I'm a good listener."

"I appreciate that. I just don't want to rehash the dark places with you. I want our time to be filled with new memories and leave the rehashing and reworking through my past with a professional who can hopefully help me. I don't want to go backward anymore. I want to move forward. I want to trust myself that I can."

Ivy beamed. "You just proved that you can."

Harper exhaled relief. "Yeah, I did, didn't I? I always ran away to find home, and all along, home was here. Not on some lonely road. You are my home, Ivy."

"What about your dream?"

"I never dreamed of living on the road."

"What if I came with you?"

"You'd live on the road with me and leave this behind?" Harper whispered.

"I would. Yes. Harper Ray, I love you. I can't stand when I'm not with you. I got used to Pittsburgh many years ago. I'll get used to other cities, too."

Tears brimmed in Harper's warm eyes. "You're willing to sacrifice your peace for me?"

"I would sacrifice my life for you."

Harper kissed her, a deep, passionate, loving kiss. "You don't need to."

"But I want to."

"It's too late. I've already decided that neither one of us will sacrifice happiness anymore."

"I don't understand."

"I'm coming home to Oasis, to Moonwalk and Lil Boy, and to you."

"You can have your dream and me too, Harper."

She tipped her head. "My dream *is* you."

Ivy's heart fluttered. "How can you be sure this is the right decision?"

Harper twirled a piece of her hair, and stared into her eyes. "My favorite part about you is your beautiful peace. I crave that tranquility. I want to wake up every morning and see you there in our bed, in our home."

Tears stung the back of Ivy's eyes. "Our home. I like the sound of that."

"I'm home with you, here, in this place, tucked into this tranquility. I want a simple life."

"Simple, huh?"

"Yes. I want kids. I want dogs. I want lazy Sunday afternoon picnics on checkered blankets. Most importantly, I want you."

Her heart pounded. Harper Ray wanted her more than a chance at fame. "You can have all those things, and music."

"Don't worry. I'm not turning my back on music. There'll be plenty of music in our future."

She placed her hands on both sides of Harper's face and kissed the tip of her nose. "Then, if that's the case and you've already made up your mind, we'll work together to make sure the music never dies. We can record some new demos. I'll concoct a few spells and you can soak in the tub with prosperity salts. I'm here at your service. Willing and able!" She saluted Harper.

Harper knocked her hand down and grabbed it. "God, how I love you and your sexy green witch ways."

She beamed and then kissed her. Her tongue dove deep and landed in perfect rhythm with Harper's for a long delicious moment.

"You do your magical stuff," Harper said, "and I'll do my magical stuff, and together we'll pull off something magical."

"What magical stuff?" Ivy asked, cocking her head.

"Well, I experimented with something."

Ivy pulled away to catch a better glimpse at Harper's face. "Experimented with what?"

"I started a crowdfunding page while on the road, and I already have some patrons supporting me." Harper pulled out her phone. "See?"

"Some patrons?" Ivy glanced at the number of patrons supporting her. "Are you kidding me? *Some* patrons would be ten. But three thousand and forty-nine?"

"Is that good?"

Ivy punched her side, playfully. "Now is no time to be modest."

She bent her head back and laughed. "With the past two months' worth of patron pledges, I have enough to roll out my plan."

"Tell me your plan." Ivy squeezed her hand. "Tell me! Tell me! Tell me!" she squealed.

"Well, you know how I love checkers, cozy fires, and yummy teas?"

Ivy inched up closer. "Yes. I love those things, too."

"I'm going to work toward another dream I had. One where I don't have to compromise on any of the things I love most in life, which is time with you, Moonwalk, Lil Boy, your mother, Tess, and the rest of my extended family. And, of course, music."

"What is this dream that you speak of?"

"Let's walk some more and I'll tell you all about it."

22

ROOTED

18 MONTHS LATER - HARPER

Harper flipped the door sign from "Closed" to "Open" to officially kick off Rooted Café's one-year anniversary celebration.

Harper and Ivy, arm in arm, glanced around the bright café in the heart of downtown Hagerstown. The light, open space, highlighted in neutral shades, formed an airy and welcoming vibe. Whitewashed exposed brickwork lined the walls, creating the perfect companion for the forest green marbleized granite floor. A large square painting of a series of butterflies with the saying "Show up. Stay in flight," hung on the adjacent wall to the large windows at the front of the café.

Rooted Café was home for so many.

Checkerboard tables and shelves of board games filled the large space. A square stage in the center of the side wall of the café shone with its lights and mirrored etchings. That stage was the spot where Harper, along with musicians who deserved a chance like she always wanted, enjoyed their time in the spotlight, performing for those with a craving for folk-inspired music.

The stage at Rooted Café might not have been as impressive in size as the venues Harper gigged in during her short stint with Larry Hopper's clubs. But it sure did create more community impact.

She was proud of her café and the positive influence it offered the community: a place where sobriety came first. It was a safe haven for all, especially for recovering addicts, to enjoy a good time free of cravings and full of good music, food, and refreshing beverages. And board games. Lots of board games.

In the back of the café sat a meeting room draped in comfy corduroy chairs and cozy lights. Community clubs used it for meetings, as did Tess for a weekly Alcoholics Anonymous meeting she helped coordinate. In the constant struggle of her disease, Tess maintained her strength. She focused on what truly mattered to her, being a support to her newfound friends who were seeking their purpose in the journey of their sobriety as well.

Lila and Tommy arrived bearing a big fruit arrangement. "We're so happy for you. Really happy." Lila hugged Harper with her free arm.

"Thank you. It means a great deal that you came. Especially to Ivy."

Ivy and Lila hugged. "I wouldn't miss it," Lila said.

Ivy and Lila rekindled their friendship after sharing a good heart-to-heart with Annie and Andrew as moderators. Ivy shared that lesson of good practice with her listeners. Like any relationship worth saving, they still had work ahead of them. They enjoyed planting new seeds in the landscape of their friendship. Each time they did, something life-affirming revealed itself, strengthening their bond. They decided their friendship was worth more than the superficial power of their egos.

"Tommy, can you play us a song?" Harper asked.

"Sure!" his voice squealed. "I can't wait to show Mom how I learned the "This Land is Your Land" song. You love that song, right Mom?"

"You bet."

"Wait until she hears you play some Led Zeppelin," Harper said.

"Led who?"

Harper laughed. "Wait until you get deeper into your lessons. You'll know who. They're every guitarist's idol."

"I can't wait." He beamed.

Harper beamed, too.

Tess snuck up behind her and Ivy and nuzzled herself in between them. "Barry and Nancy made little chocolate cream pies just like on your opening day. I already ate four of them. It's a good thing I do Pilates."

Although struggle remained one step behind Tess, she didn't cave into it. Through her strength and determination, she was a success story. Being a newly certified Pilates instructor for Oasis, she was celebrating close to two years of sobriety. Her confidence and love for life beamed off her like the sun on a shiny red Corvette. She sparkled and radiated core strength and remarkable beauty. "Can you put five aside for me?" Harper asked.

Ivy pinched her side. "Harper Ray. Five?"

"I'm feeding for two of us. The baby's craving them, too. So I should say ten." She turned to Tess. "But five will do."

Ivy rubbed a nurturing hand over Harper's belly. "This child is going to come out demanding chocolate and sugar from day one."

"She'll fit right in, then." Harper kissed her wife's forehead. "Where's Andrew? Did he lock himself in the bathroom by accident again?"

"He and Annie are right behind me," Catalina said coming in from the back. "We just returned from walking the doggies."

A few minutes later, before the customers poured in, Annie raised a glass. "It's all who we surround ourselves with. I, for one, am surrounded by a tribe of people who lift and inspire me daily. Thank goodness for all of you. I no longer stick out like a sore thumb because you're all as wacky as I am."

"Amen to that," Ivy said.

"Amen to that," Tess seconded.

As customers eventually arrived and the café filled with the cheerful echoes of laughter and conversation, Harper climbed onto her stage with her father's Gibson, to that place where she came alive.

She played several songs and people sang along with her—even to some of her originals. She strummed and sang deep from her soul, songs affirming the celebration of life with all its twists and turns.

Life had worked out after all. It took some time and risk, but didn't anything worthwhile?

Everyone who wanted to catch a lift out of the ordinary had to take a risk or two, and thankfully that finally panned out for Harper and those she loved. She freed herself to help those around her find their lift in the world as well.

She showed up.

She stayed in flight.

She grew her set of butterfly wings.

Harper glanced around at her beautiful tribe and enjoyed the lift of freedom.

By uprooting from her past, Harper gained access to her dream, finally landing in the field of sunshine and rainbows.

ALSO BY SUZIE CARR:

The Fiche Room

Two Feet off The Ground

Tangerine Twist

Inner Secrets

A New Leash on Life

The Muse

Staying True

Snowflakes

The Journey Somewhere

Sandcastles

The Dance

Beneath Everything

The Curvy Side of Life

The Pet Boutique

Keep up on Suzie's latest news and projects

Grab a free gift: www.curveswelcome.com

Follow Suzie on Twitter & Instagram: @girl_novelist

23

NOTE FROM SUZIE CARR

As with all of my books, I enjoy giving a portion of proceeds back to the community by donating to Hearts United for Animals www.hua.org. Thank you for being a part of this special contribution.

24

A SPECIAL REQUEST

Word-of-mouth is crucial for any author to succeed. If you enjoyed *Uprooting*, I'd be so grateful for your honest review of it on Amazon, Goodreads, or your review site of choice. Even if it's just a sentence or two. It would make all the difference and I'd be so appreciative.

Also, if you could share your thoughts of this story on social media (especially in reader groups on Facebook!) that would be amazingly helpful. – Thanks! Love, Suzie

www.ingramcontent.com/pod-product-compliance
Lightning Source LLC
Chambersburg PA
CBHW031942240626
47153CB00003B/834